# "You arrived in your wedding clothes," he said softly.

"You have the uncanny ability to question me as if I'm on trial. Were you ever a lawyer, Mr. Draper?"

"I apologize for pressing you. It's none of my business. Although, I will say I understand the locals' frustration. You're beautiful, intelligent and talented. Any man with a scrap of sense would make a bid for your attention."

His praise emboldened her. "*You* haven't."

Adam's lips parted. His eyes thrummed with emotion quickly squelched. After clearing his throat, he said, "I'm not yet in that stage of my life. There are matters that take precedence over any desire to wed and produce heirs."

"What sort of matters? Your ranches?"

"My ranches…" His brows drew together. "Oh, yes. My business obligations are many."

"So you've never come close to falling in love?"

He fell silent. Deborah felt as though she were swimming in that endless brown gaze as the air between them thinned. Why had she asked such a foolish question?

\* \* \*

**Return to Cowboy Creek:
A bride train delivers the promise of new love
and family to a Kansas boomtown**

**Karen Kirst** was born and raised in east Tennessee near the Great Smoky Mountains. She's a lifelong lover of books, but it wasn't until after college that she had the grand idea to write one herself. Now she divides her time between being a wife, homeschooling mom and romance writer. Her favorite pastimes are reading, visiting tearooms and watching romantic comedies.

## Books by Karen Kirst

### Love Inspired Historical

#### *Return to Cowboy Creek*

*Romancing the Runaway Bride*

#### *Cowboy Creek*

*Bride by Arrangement*

#### *Smoky Mountain Matches*

Visit the Author Profile page at Harlequin.com for more titles.

# KAREN KIRST

## Romancing the Runaway Bride

**⊕HARLEQUIN® LOVE INSPIRED® HISTORICAL**

Special thanks and acknowledgment to Karen Kirst for her contribution to the Return to Cowboy Creek miniseries.

Recycling programs
for this product may
not exist in your area.

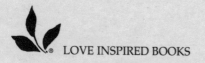

LOVE INSPIRED BOOKS

ISBN-13: 978-1-335-36970-3

Romancing the Runaway Bride

Copyright © 2018 by Harlequin Books S.A.

www.Harlequin.com

**Printed in U.S.A.**

31088101027801

A man's heart deviseth his way:
but the Lord directeth his steps.
—*Proverbs* 16:9

To my mom, Dorothy Kirst,
and my sister, Shelly Benson. I'm blessed
to have you both! Thanks for making my first
writing conference an experience I never want to
forget. Thanks for the laughs and fun memories.

## Acknowledgments

A huge thank-you to editor Elizabeth Mazer.
I've enjoyed working with you on this project.
And to the other Return to Cowboy Creek authors,
Cheryl St.John and Sherri Shackelford.
It's been a pleasure.

# Chapter One

Cowboy Creek, Kansas
June 1869

There was a blindfolded woman in the boardinghouse kitchen.

Adam Halloway's training kicked in. He reached for his gun out of habit, only to come up empty. His gun belt and Pinkerton detective badge were tucked away in his saddlebags, where they'd stay for the duration of this investigation.

He scanned the spacious room. It looked like an average kitchen with the usual equipment. Sunlight streamed through filmy lace curtains, painting the bulky working table and floorboards in innocent light. No evil villains lurked in the corners.

His narrowed gaze returned to the woman and made a quick assessment of her appearance. Short of stature, brunette, young. How young was impossible to say with part of her face hidden by a swath of black material. Her posture didn't scream distress.

He finally noticed the twin saucers of unfrosted cake on the table in front of her. Bowls of assorted sizes littered the far end, and baking tins crowded the hulking stove behind her. With one foot in the kitchen and one in the hallway, he watched as she lifted a bite to her mouth and chewed. A pleat furrowed her brow. She cocked her head to the right. Chewed some more.

What on earth was she doing?

The sense of urgency passed, and he did a more thorough inventory. Her hair was clean and shiny, parted in the middle and arranged in neat rolls. A perky purple and yellow flower was nestled above her left ear. The white apron she wore contrasted with her lavender cotton dress. Below the blousy sleeves, her arms were slender and pale, her hands fine-boned and smooth. Those hands spoke of a life of leisure. The delicate gold chain draped around her wrist and the tasteful diamond earrings winking at him couldn't be acquired on a cook's salary. Perhaps she had a wealthy husband who indulged his wife's desire to work? But there was no gold band to indicate she was married.

She was sampling the second cake when he spoke.

"Excuse me, I'm looking for the proprietress, Aunt Mae. Can you tell me where to find her?"

A garbled yelp escaped her. Fumbling to remove the blindfold, she got it off with an impatient tug, slightly mussing the neat strands of her hair. Wide, heavily lashed eyes the hue of polished golden topaz settled on him.

"You're new."

"I'm looking for the owner to ask about a room."

"I meant you're new to Cowboy Creek."

He eased farther into the kitchen. "How do you figure? A cattle town such as this one must see its fair share of folks passing through." A fact that made it easy for a criminal like the one he sought to blend in.

"A man as picture-perfect as you wouldn't have gone unnoticed." The second the words were out, she blushed to the roots of her hair. "I shouldn't have said that. Lucy wouldn't have given in to the urge."

"Lucy?"

"My younger sister. She is the definition of proper."

"Ah." Adam couldn't help but be charmed. "I apologize for interrupting your..." He flicked his fingers in the direction of the cake. "Um, what exactly did I interrupt?"

Her hands fluttered, the limp blindfold flapping against her waist. "I was trying to decide whether or not to include ground cayenne pepper in my chocolate cake."

"Cayenne pepper? In a cake?"

She shrugged. "I like to experiment with different flavors."

"I'm Adam Draper, by the way." The false surname left his lips in smooth sincerity. Working for the National Pinkerton Detective Agency since the war's end four years ago, he'd assumed dozens of personas in his pursuit of criminals. This time, he wasn't doing it for the Pinkertons. He was here for personal reasons.

She placed her hand in his outstretched one and offered a bright smile. "I'm Deborah, a boarder here. Aunt Mae hired me to bake desserts. I do it in exchange for room and board."

For long moments, Adam became ensnared by her beauty. Her eyes, almond-shaped and almost too large for her face, sparkled with optimism not readily found in his line of work. She had sleek, dark brown eyebrows that punctuated the lightness of her irises. Her nose was straight, her mouth small and dainty, her teeth white and even. The slight cleft in her rounded chin called for his thumb to rest there.

*Her name is Deborah. With a* D. The scrap of a note he'd discovered in the last known residence of Zane Ogden, the very note that had led him to Kansas, had been written by someone whose signature began with a *D*. The rolling script belonged to a woman, he was certain. And this one had failed to offer her last name, an unusual omission.

He ended the handshake more abruptly than he'd intended. "Do you have a last name, Deborah?"

Her smile faltered. "Frazier."

"Pleased to make your acquaintance, Miss Frazier. Or is it Mrs.?"

She blanched. "I'm not married."

Why would an innocuous question net that reaction?

Clamping down on his rising apprehension, he smoothed his expression. "I've come to Cowboy Creek in search of land. I read about the three men who founded the town and how it's grown by leaps and bounds. Have you been here since the beginning?"

Her gaze slid away. "Not quite. I arrived a couple of months ago." Picking up the saucers, she held them close to his nose. "Do you like cake? I could use an objective opinion."

Adam allowed the attempt at diversion. "Which one has the pepper in it?"

"I can't tell you. That would alter the outcome."

"This all sounds suspiciously scientific."

She laughed. "It's just cake."

He moved closer and bent to sniff the first slice. Pinching off a corner, he popped it in his mouth. "It's good."

Deborah's brows lifted in a silent bid for more. He took a second, larger bite. "Very good. The chocolate flavor is there. Not too sweet." What else did she expect him to say?

"Try the other one."

Since he didn't detect even a hint of heat in the first sample, he reluctantly did as she instructed. Cayenne pepper in dessert. Who would've thought to put—

"Oh." The combination of rich chocolate melded with a layer of subtle spice to tease his taste buds. "That's interesting."

"Do you like it? Is it too much?" She put the plates down with a clink. "I was aiming for the perfect balance. This is my third attempt. Be glad you weren't around to try the first." Her nose scrunched. "I must've drunk four glasses of milk that night, trying to cool my tongue."

Adam was glad, too. "I like it. It's unexpected."

Her eyes sparkled, and she looked pleased. "The unexpected can be fun."

"Or painful."

"True, but success is rarely achieved on the first attempt."

Their gazes locked across the expanse of cooking utensils. A breeze wafted through the open windows on their right, scented with the blossoms crowding the painted wooden boxes affixed to the outside sills. In her pretty pastel dress, the bloom tucked against her hair, Deborah Frazier was like a nostalgic summer dream. Adam's thoughts started to drift from his task.

He couldn't recall the last time he'd met a woman who made him think about moonlit strolls and picnics by the water. At eighteen, he'd escaped his family's Missouri ranch—and the devastation wrought by Zane Ogden—to join the Union army. There'd been no chance to think about romance during those long, cruel years. And once he'd hung up his uniform, he'd accepted an offer to join Allan Pinkerton's detective agency. Rooting out criminals and dispensing justice had consumed him, mind, body and soul. He couldn't rest until he put the man who'd destroyed his family behind bars. That meant no distractions.

Deborah Frazier wasn't comfortable with his questions. Nor did she offer the slightest bit of extra information about herself. His instincts insisted she had secrets to hide. If she turned out to be the person aiding and abetting his quarry, Adam would personally see she got the punishment she deserved.

He scraped his hand along his jaw, startled when skin met skin. He'd decided to shave his substantial beard for this case. He'd also traded his usual attire for a formal three-piece suit, complete with bolo tie and a pair of bona fide cowboy boots. Adam Draper, Missouri cattleman, had pockets that were well-lined. And he wouldn't allow an opportunity to flirt with a beautiful woman pass him by.

He affixed a teasing smile on his face and, reaching across the table, brushed a stray crumb from the corner of her mouth. "If I were able to secure a room here, would I be required to sample more desserts?"

Surprise lit her eyes. She pressed trembling fingers to her cheek. "Well, I suppose I could use someone to assist me in that manner. If you wouldn't mind…"

Adam straightened. She wasn't accustomed to flirtation, then. Why the notion should please him, he couldn't say. *Steady, old boy. Remember, the best criminals are sometimes the most accomplished actors.*

The door in the far corner that led to the rear stoop opened and closed. A woman he guessed to be in her sixties bustled in. She took one glance at the pair of them and, plopping her sacks on the counter, jammed one fist against her ample hip.

"And who might you be?"

Deborah watched as the handsome stranger softened Aunt Mae's bristling attitude with a dazzling smile and earnest manner. He indicated that he was in town to scout out potential locations for his expansive ranching operation and would need a room indefinitely. The promise of steady income pleased the businesswoman, of course.

As the pair made to exit the kitchen, the look Adam Draper shot over his shoulder at Deborah remained seared in her mind the rest of the afternoon. There'd been a flicker of something so dark and forbidding, it struck fear in her heart and sent her thoughts scattering to St. Louis and the arranged marriage she'd escaped with hours to spare. Her father was still furious, according to her sister's telegrams, and still scouring the state for her. But Cowboy Creek was so new it wasn't on the map. Surely, he wouldn't think to look in Kansas.

By the time the evening meal had been placed on the table, she was convinced she'd misinterpreted things. Mr. Draper was the first of the guests to arrive. He entered the wide, airy dining room and greeted her with an easy grin. His deep brown eyes hadn't lost their intensity or intelligence, but they weren't locked on her in suspicion, either.

Her stomach dipped. Yep, still devastating. Her mind hadn't mistaken that fact. He was tall, tanned and in excellent physical condition. The pressed navy suit he wore fit his rip-cord-lean frame to perfection. His straight, nearly black hair was brushed off his face, the better to savor his sculpted features. He had an aristocratic nose, defined cheekbones and unyielding jaw. That stubborn set to his jaw made her question if his charm was just an act.

"Good evening, Miss Frazier." He strolled around the square-shaped room taking its measure, peering through the window glass at the street traffic, running his fingers along the fireplace mantel, admiring the landscape paintings on three of the four walls.

"Good evening, Mr. Draper." She shifted the salt and pepper containers closer to the ceramic candleholders and fiddled with the folded napkins. "Did you find your room agreeable?"

He took up position behind a nearby chair, his hands curled around the topmost wooden slat. There was no gold ring, nor a line to evidence he'd ever worn one.

"I did, indeed. Aunt Mae put me on the second floor. I've a corner room overlooking the main thoroughfare, which means I'll have a bird's-eye view of events." He winked.

He was in the room opposite hers, then. While Aunt

Mae preferred to keep the men and women in separate areas, the house wasn't large enough to do so. Deborah wasn't sure how she felt about his continued presence in what had become more than a temporary hideout. The memory of his thumb sweeping over the edges of her lips caused her skin to prickle with awareness. He'd already caught her in an unusual situation…how long he'd observed her unawares was anyone's guess. She didn't wish to imagine all the different ways she could embarrass herself in front of him.

He indicated the various platters boasting roasted beef and potatoes, sautéed cabbage and other assorted vegetables. "This looks tempting. Are there any unusual ingredients I need to be concerned about?"

"Aunt Mae does the majority of the cooking. I assist her sometimes, but mostly I'm responsible for the desserts."

She was thankful for the chance to earn her keep while doing something she enjoyed. That meant she could save the funds she brought with her for other necessities.

His eyes twinkled. "And are we having chocolate cake this evening?"

"Not tonight." She didn't serve a new dessert until the recipe was perfected. Following their strange exchange, she hadn't had the fortitude to experiment with icing.

The arrival of another boarder, Sadie Shriver, brought a sense of relief. Having the cattleman's intense focus directed at her amplified her self-consciousness. There was a reason she'd chosen to slip out of her father's grand parties and spend the evenings in the kitchens with the staff. She was prone to say or do the wrong thing and embarrass both herself and her father.

Adam Draper had the same effect on Sadie as he'd had on Aunt Mae. Except, the telegraph office clerk didn't need softening. She was a kind, sincere young woman, sensitive to others' feelings and always putting others' comfort above her own. She'd become a particular friend. They'd met on the infamous bride train. During the arduous journey, Sadie had noticed Deborah's disquiet and, believing it was associated with the prospect of potential grooms, had set out to distract her. While Deborah hadn't confessed her true reason for being on the train—that would have to remain a guarded secret—she had appreciated her efforts. It had been nice to have a friend, even if she couldn't be completely open about herself or her past.

"It's a pleasure to meet you, Mr. Draper," Sadie said when the gentleman introduced himself. "I see you've already made Deborah's acquaintance." Sadie shot her a significant glance. "She and I arrived on the bride train together. She's established quite a reputation for herself. Folks clamor for a taste of her baked creations."

His startled gaze shifted between them. "Bride train?"

Sadie chuckled. "It's exactly what it sounds like. Each of us came here in search of a fresh start, at the behest of the town officials. Cowboy Creek has an abundance of marriage-minded men and not enough ladies to choose from, so they advertised in other states and offered to pay our train fare."

Deborah clamped her lips together. She wasn't here to snare a groom. She was here to evade one!

"So neither of you have found your perfect match yet," Adam said.

Soft color brushed Sadie's apple cheeks. "On the contrary. I've entered a courtship with a wonderful man."

"Much to the local bachelors' dismay," Deborah inserted. "Walter Kerr is a professional photographer who was invited to visit by his friend Will Canfield."

"One of the original town founders, correct?" Adam supplied.

Deborah nodded. "And our current mayor, though he's set his sights on Washington. Sadie has become Walter's favorite subject. I've lost count how many times she's posed for him."

The buxom brunette's smile radiated happiness. "If only you would give some young man the time of day, Deborah, you too could have your share of romance." To Adam, she said, "She's refused no less than ten men's invitations. Two of them offered marriage proposals upon sight."

"Is that so?"

Adam's expression revealed nothing of his thoughts. Even so, Deborah felt the urge to bolt.

Leather soles whispering across the polished floor heralded another arrival. The waft of rose water meant it was none other than Hildie Vilhelm, yet another potential bride who rode in on the train. Resplendent in a periwinkle outfit that complemented her fair hair and skin, she came to stand beside Sadie, her big blue eyes fastened on their new boarder with unconcealed interest.

"Our baker's refusal to give any man a chance is a common cause for debate," she said. "Especially considering she rode the train in her wedding attire."

A headache blossomed behind Deborah's eyes. She edged toward the exit.

Hildie introduced herself. "Tell me, Mr. Draper, what's brought you to Cowboy Creek?"

"I'd be happy to." He turned his piercing focus to Deborah. "But first, I think it only fair to give Miss Frazier a chance to defend herself. What do you say? Will you solve the mystery once and for all?"

## Chapter Two

The baker was hiding something. Adam had to work harder than usual to project an air of mild curiosity and to mask the trepidation that swelled inside him. But then, the stakes were higher than usual. This woman could be the key to solving the puzzle of his father's disappearance nine years ago. She could very well lead him to the blackguard who'd swindled an entire town, laying waste to countless families, including his own.

Not long after Gilbert Halloway went missing, entrepreneur Zane Ogden produced evidence that Adam's father had acquired a high interest loan against the family's property. Adam had smelled a rat. Not for one second had he believed that his father would do business with a man like Ogden, especially after he'd advised their neighbors against it. Adam's brothers, Seth and Russell, hadn't shared his conviction. After all, how could they dispute Gilbert's signature? Big Bend's sheriff had witnessed the transaction. Their differences of opinion on the matter and Seth's insistence on paying back the "loan" had been the impetus for his hasty decision to leave the ranch and join the Union army.

Adam studied Deborah's reaction with a practiced eye. Anxiety shrouded her. The skin around her eyes had become pinched. The pale blue vein at her throat fluttered like a nervous bird. Her hand searched and found the gold brooch fixed to her bodice, fingers clinging to the odd-shaped jewelry. Her lips parted, but no sound came out.

Their hostess entered bearing a basket of butter-slathered yeast rolls. "Sorry to keep you waiting. These beauties took longer than usual to brown." With a smile that transformed her mannish features, Aunt Mae gestured for everyone to have a seat while she assumed her place at the head of the table.

Adam clenched his fists at his sides. Deborah's shoulders sagged with obvious relief. She'd been spared…this time.

The blonde named Hildie steered him to the empty chair beside her, with a view of the hallway entrance and the blue and white parlor beyond. Deborah and Sadie found places opposite them. Aunt Mae asked him to say grace, something he hadn't done aloud in many years. His voice sounded rusty to his ears. His life had become a solitary venture, his faith in God a private thing.

His childhood experiences had been different. Back then, he'd accompanied his parents and two older brothers to church services every week, and social outings were shared with their fellow congregants. Memories of his mother and brothers evoked a multitude of emotions, chiefly sadness and regret. He hadn't seen them since the day he stormed off the farm. They'd exchanged a handful of letters through the years. Lately, though, he'd yearned for a long overdue reunion. Maybe, once he'd captured Ogden, he'd travel to Missouri and surprise them.

Hildie drew him out of his ruminations and peppered him with questions. She was a persistent young woman. Unlike Deborah, the blonde's eagerness for a husband was unmistakable. He could've told her that men who sensed a woman's desperation would run in the other direction.

Deborah remained quiet throughout the meal, speaking only when spoken to and not once meeting his gaze. He'd have to get her alone somehow. As impatient as he was for answers, his instincts said he'd have to go slowly with this one. He would have to earn her trust, make her think they were friends.

His opportunity came sooner than expected. At the meal's conclusion, she offered to help Aunt Mae clean the dishes.

Aunt Mae patted her hand. "You've been in the kitchen all day. Hildie will help me, won't you, dear?"

Hildie hesitated. "I was about to invite Adam to join me in a game of checkers."

"Plenty of time for that tomorrow." The older woman dismissed her excuse and pushed a bowl into her hands. "Carry that in for me." To Adam, she said, "It's Deborah's habit to stroll about town every evening after supper. Perhaps you could join her."

Deborah worried her bottom lip. "I'm certain Mr. Draper is tired from his travels."

He smiled at her. "I'm never too tired to spend time with an intriguing lady. And please, call me Adam."

Consternation flitted over her features. "Sadie, would you like to come?"

"I've got letters to write," she demurred. "Maybe next time."

Deborah gestured limply to the door. "I suppose it's just the two of us, then."

Did her reluctance to be in his company stem from embarrassment? Or did she suspect he was more than what he claimed?

Deborah was certain her companion perceived her unease.

*God, please don't let him ask about the train again. Or why I was clad in a wedding dress.*

Was it fair to ask Him for help in this deception she'd created of her own volition? Probably not. If she'd fought her arranged marriage at the outset instead of meekly falling in with the plans, she wouldn't have had cause to flee her home. Her father's initial declaration—that he'd promised her to his oldest friend and business associate, Tobias Latham, a man thirty years her senior—had blindsided her. Gerard Frazier had intimated that this union was her last chance to redeem herself and make up for all the ways in which she'd disappointed him. Unable to refuse the rare opportunity to earn his approval, she'd buried her objections.

The newspapers had printed the official announcement. Friends, some dear and some not, had attended a grand engagement celebration in her and Tobias's honor. Gerard had hired an assistant to guide her in the ceremony planning. The weeks had sped by in a whirlwind of activity until the day arrived for her to pledge her life to a man she barely knew.

Like a coward, she'd bolted without telling a single soul. Not even Lucy, the one person who understood her better than anyone else. She'd waited until reaching Kansas before contacting her sister.

*Oh, Lucy, I wish you were here now.*

"Would you prefer to go alone, Miss Frazier?"

Adam's quiet voice pierced her cloud of introspection. Beside her on the shadowed front porch, he watched her with a subdued expression. Guilt pinched her. Here she was engrossed in her problems, without giving a single thought to how he might feel. She'd been in his position not long ago and remembered feeling overwhelmed by the vast, untamed prairie and a little lost amid a crowd of rowdy cowboys, busy shop owners and unwed females jostling for the best bachelors.

"Of course not. I'm happy to show you the town." Descending the shallow steps and traversing the footpath through the tidy yard, she passed through the gate opening and onto the boardwalk. "Which way shall we go? Left toward the stockyards or right toward the opera house?"

Hands deep in his pockets, he looked both ways and shrugged. "I'll leave it up to you."

Deborah led him in the direction of the opera house, drawing his attention to various points of interest. At this hour, wagon traffic was almost nonexistent and the shop windows were dark. Town wasn't entirely deserted, however. Cowboys were usually out and about, dining at various eateries or paying a visit to Mr. Lin's laundry services. If there was a show at the opera house, folks congregated in the vacant lots surrounding the building. With all the activity, she felt safe walking the streets alone. That was something she never would've been allowed to do in St. Louis. Deborah savored the sense of independence.

As they passed the saddle shop, she pointed out the Longhorn Feed and Grain. "You'll do a lot of trading there if you decide to settle here." Her curiosity got the better of her. "What's wrong with your current place?"

Her blunt query sparked amusement in his rich brown eyes. "Nothing's wrong with it."

"Why then would you leave your home and start afresh?"

"I've a soul prone to wander, I'm afraid. I like to tackle new challenges simply to ascertain whether or not I can succeed." His teeth gleamed white in the darkness. "I have several operations across the state of Missouri, but none in Kansas."

Alarm skittered along her spine. "Missouri, huh? What part?"

"Big Bend."

Not terribly close to St. Louis. "Do you consider any of those places home?"

"There is one that's special to me." His smile struck

her as sad. "Over two hundred acres of prime land. Fertile fields dotted with cattle stretching into the distance, with occasional tree groves to block the wind. Near the house, there's this section of the stream that's wide and shallow, and my brothers and I used to fish and swim there every summer."

"How many brothers do you have?"

His face shadowed. "Two. Both older."

Sensing his reticence, she squelched her questions. "It sounds like a wonderful place to live."

They passed the livery, which was usually humming with activity.

"Have you ever been to Missouri, Deborah?"

There was no lying about the fact. The other brides knew she'd boarded the train there. "I was born and raised in St. Louis." Before he could probe further, she directed his attention to the bakery on the next corner. "Can you believe Cowboy Creek has *two* bakeries? Impressive for a town this size, don't you think?" She darted over to the main window. Bare, boring tables and chairs occupied the dining area. "I've wondered why the owner, Mr. Lowell, doesn't take more pride in the shop's appearance. A shame, really. The other one is much better."

His shoulder brushed hers, his woodsy scent pleasant to her senses. His presence wasn't entirely unwelcome, she acknowledged. It was nice to have someone to talk to, for a change, as long the subject matter didn't wander into dangerous waters. Perhaps she'd confide in him about her little quest to solve the mystery of the Cowboy Creek thefts. Ever since the bride train had arrived two months ago, odd items had gone missing from various shops and residences, including a porcelain doll. There were rumors that two children had stowed away on the train, but those hadn't been substantiated.

"I meant to tell you how much I enjoyed your rhubarb

tarts tonight. You could've chosen to bake a standard pie and everyone would've been equally pleased. Do you always pour so much of your energy into your baking?"

"It's the thing I most enjoy doing in life. It's my version of a challenge. Instead of building a cattle empire, I create desserts."

He tapped the window of the bakery. "Your tarts would sell out in minutes here. Does Mr. Lowell offer anything similar?"

"I haven't seen anything beyond basic breads, cakes and pies." The quality of his products was questionable. In her opinion, the only reason he remained in business was because the cowboys who passed through town didn't have high standards.

"Your talent is being underutilized at the boardinghouse. Have you considered opening your own bakery?"

Wistfulness gripped her, only to be replaced by cold reality. Her sojourn in Cowboy Creek was supposed to be temporary. Staying in one place would make it easier for Gerard and Tobias to find her. But she hadn't yet been able to bring herself to leave.

She turned to face him. "This town doesn't need a third bakery."

His eyes were molten and unreadable in the shadows, but his unwavering focus still twisted her into knots. No other man had affected her this way. None of her acquaintances in St. Louis, and none of the locals who'd approached her in hopes of courting her. Most assuredly not her older groom.

She shuddered.

"Perhaps Mr. Lowell would be interested in retiring."

A nervous huff escaped her lips. "I wouldn't know the first thing about operating a business."

"You strike me as an enterprising woman. If you truly wished to, you'd find a way to make it happen."

Dumbfounded by this stranger's evaluation of her, she reached for the comforting reminder of home. He noticed and commented.

"That's an interesting piece of jewelry." His fingers gently nudged hers aside to trace the brooch's edges. "What is it?"

Deborah's heart thudded inside her chest. Adam was standing very close, his head lowered to get a better look. Light from a nearby lamp shone on his dark brown hair and, for a second, she entertained the thought of skimming her hand over the shiny locks.

*As if that wouldn't be inappropriate.*

"I, ah…" She forced herself to stand stock-still as his knuckles skimmed her collarbone. "It's a rolling pin. A gift from Lucy."

Lucy, the example of propriety, who'd commiserated with Deborah over the years and helped smooth their father's ire whenever she displeased him.

He released the brooch and lifted his head. His face was so close she could feel the soft puff of his breath on her skin.

"Lucy again. Why isn't she here with you? Did she not share your yearning for adventure?"

Deborah struggled to order her thoughts. Why must a random cattleman rattle her so? "Adventure?"

"You're a single woman who has left family and friends behind to start afresh in a new, unfamiliar place. You may not want to admit it, but you, Deborah Frazier, possess an adventurous streak."

She couldn't help it. She laughed in his face. Thirst for adventure had been the very last thing on her mind that final day in Missouri.

An argument between two cowboys rose in volume outside the laundry, a few paces farther down the side street. Adam grasped her elbow and guided her farther along the main street.

"You haven't run into any trouble alone out here, have you?" he said.

"Not once. Sometimes they whistle or toss out invitations, but I've never felt threatened."

"Let's hope you never do."

Touched by his chivalrous attitude, she didn't at first notice he'd stopped short and was staring at the law office window. Belatedly, she angled back, only to catch sight of a curious expression on his rugged features.

"Is something the matter?"

He looked stricken, as if someone had delivered the worst news of his life. His throat worked. "Do you know this man?"

"Russell Halloway? Sure, I've spoken with him on occasion. He's a good sort, for a lawyer. I've heard of his extensive work with war veterans, a commendable service if you ask me."

His gaze glued to the gold lettering, he said, "I used to know a man by that name. Is he young? Old?" A vein ticked in his temple. "Can you describe him?"

"He's young, in his twenties. Short, dark hair. I'm not sure what color his eyes are, though. He's distinguished looking, like you." His gaze jerked to her. There was no amusement this time. He didn't seem to recognize her or their surroundings. It was as if he were lost in another time and place.

Deborah dared to lay her hand on his arm. His forearm jerked. "Are you all right, Adam? Did the man you once knew hurt you in some way?"

"What? No." He blinked and shook his head. His eyes cleared. "I must've been mistaken. Gotten the name mixed up." Gesturing in the direction of the boardinghouse, he said, "I'm afraid my travels have caught up to me. How about we continue this tour tomorrow?"

He did look rather fatigued. "Of course."

They returned to Aunt Mae's in relative silence. In the yard beneath the overarching branches of the live oak, he stopped her. "Thank you for spending the evening with me, Deborah." He took her hand in his and brushed a kiss across her knuckles. His lips were soft and warm, his breath a heated caress over her skin. Her knees threatened to buckle. "Considering you're a recent newcomer, I trust you to give me an honest view of the town."

"I'll do my best to help."

His answering smile was fleeting. After bidding her good-night, he disappeared into the boardinghouse. She climbed the steps in a daze and sank onto the porch swing. Cowboy Creek had just acquired another mystery, it seemed, in the form of one Adam Draper, Missouri cattleman.

# Chapter Three

The sights and sounds of a busy morning in Cowboy Creek failed to register. Lost in bittersweet memories, Adam traced the gold letters. Russell Halloway. It had to be his brother. Becoming a lawyer was all Russ had talked about those last years before Adam left. But what would he be doing in Kansas? In the last letter he'd exchanged with his mother—granted, that had been at least a year ago—Evelyn hadn't said anything about it. Adam had assumed she and Seth remained in Missouri and Russ in Philadelphia.

*People don't stop living because you're not around.* He recalled the words of a fellow agent, bemoaning the ending of a courtship. *They grow and change without you.*

There were probably many things he'd missed out on because of his chosen profession. While he gained satisfaction from obtaining justice for innocent victims, he did wonder sometimes how long he could maintain this solitary existence. Roaming the nation like a wind-tossed tumbleweed, lonely days bleeding into even lonelier nights, staying in towns just long enough to work cases…he was starting to yearn for more. A place to set down roots. Maybe even start a family.

"Good morning, sir." A gentleman approached from

his right. "My office doesn't open for another quarter of an hour, but I'd be happy to make an exception if you're in a rush."

Perspiration dampened his collar, and not from the June sun beating on him. His chest felt hollow. Anticipation warred with uncertainty. How would his brother receive him—with a hearty handshake or cool disdain? After all, Adam was the one who'd left in a wake of angry recriminations and failed to return home. He was the reason a rift existed in the Halloway family.

"Sir? How can I be of service?"

Sucking in a bracing breath, he slowly pivoted and looked his brother full in the face. The changes were marked. In the place of the ruddy-cheeked boy he remembered was a full-grown man decked out in a tailored suit. Taller and leaner, his features more pronounced, his hazel eyes holding a wealth of wisdom.

"Hello, Russ."

The confusion on his brother's face crumbled into shock. Russell fell back a step. His disbelieving gaze raked Adam from head to toe and back again.

Adam lifted his arms to his sides. "Have I changed that much, big brother?"

"Adam?" His voice sounded a lot less upbeat than before. "It can't be."

"Well, I promise it is—"

Before Adam could get another word out, he was engulfed in a tight embrace. His throat clogged with pent-up emotion. He wasn't to be shunned, then. *Thank you, God. I don't deserve this welcome, but I'll take it.*

Adam returned the hug, aware that they were creating a spectacle right there on the boardwalk. For this moment, though, he wasn't an agent on the trail of justice. He was a man who'd missed his brother more than he'd realized.

Russell pulled away first and gripped Adam's shoulders. A grin spread from ear to ear. "I can't believe you're here. My baby brother, all grown up. And looking quite dapper, I must say."

Adam patted Russ's jaw. "Look at you. When did you grow a goatee?"

He laughed. "When potential clients mistook me for an assistant yet to earn my degree." A man and woman edged around them, their curiosity plain. He tipped his head toward the door. "We should probably take this inside."

Russ unlocked the door, perched on the desk edge and regarded Adam with lingering wonder. "Wait until Ma and Seth hear about this." He smoothed his hand over his short hair.

Adam pointed to Russ's hand. "You're *married*?"

"Newly married and expecting a baby."

He slumped into a chair. "What? Who is she?"

"Her name is Anna. I met her in Philadelphia while at law school." He grinned sheepishly. "I was actually engaged to her sister, Charlotte, once upon a time."

"You scoundrel!" Shifting forward, he rested his elbows on his knees. "Tell me everything."

Time slipped away as Russ regaled him with stories from his school days and his eventual introduction to the Darby family. Charlotte had fallen in love with another man, but hadn't had the heart to break off her engagement to Russ. Assuming responsibility for the breakup hadn't earned him any points with the young lady's family. He'd thought his association with the Darbys over until the day Anna arrived in his mail-order bride's stead, not to marry him, but to inform him that yet another fiancée—albeit, a mail-order one—preferred someone else. However, when widowed Anna discovered she was pregnant, Russell proposed a marriage of convenience.

"You fell in love with her," Adam surmised. He'd seen

it happen. He'd also seen relationships sour. He was glad Russ had found happiness.

"She's the love of my life," Russell confirmed, studying him. "What about you? Have you found someone you'd be willing to give up the Pinkertons for?"

Quite against his will, he pictured Deborah Frazier with her blindfold and her experimental cake. Ridiculous to think of her now. He pushed out of the chair and began to pace. "Not yet."

"That implies you're searching for the right woman."

"Not actively, no." He hesitated to dampen the mood, but he had no choice. "Russ, I'm here on a personal matter. In fact, I've got an alias. Adam Draper, a successful rancher from Missouri. No one can know we're related."

Russell folded his arms. "Is it Ogden?"

"Yes."

"I see." A sigh rattled his chest. "Do me a favor, will you? Don't mention him to Ma and Seth right off. Wait until they've had a chance to rejoice in your homecoming."

Adam stared at him. "What are you talking about? A trip to Big Bend? Today?"

"Not to Big Bend, little brother. Cowboy Creek is their home now."

As on his first day of battle when faced with the grimness of death on every side, he grappled with a feeling of unreality. Was this a dream?

"I don't understand."

Russell came over and clapped him on the back. "Let's fetch our horses, and I'll explain on the way. You've got a lot to catch up on." He smirked. "There are some surprises I won't spoil, however."

Before he was quite prepared, he was on his horse and riding south of town beside Russell, who a short time later brought his mount to a stop on what was, apparently, Seth and his mother's new home.

Adam did the same, observing a wooden sign. "It's called White Rock Ranch."

A dormered, two-story house with deep, welcoming porches anchored the vast prairie. A row of young elms separated the house from the barn and corrals. Hay-filled fields rolled gently to the distant horizon. Sun sparkled on the surface of a small pond.

His brother had chosen well. He prayed Ogden wouldn't sully what amounted to a fresh start.

He flexed his fingers. "The last time Seth and I were together, I accused him of being a coward."

As the eldest brother, Seth had made the decision to sell off some of the land holdings, and his mother some jewelry and furnishings, in order to pay off the alleged loan. Furious, Adam hadn't been able to stay and watch his father's legacy crumble. He'd been young and impulsive. He hadn't taken the time to consider his older brother's side of things.

"That was a long time ago," Russ murmured. "Trust me, he's put it behind him. The question is, have you?"

He met Russ's steady gaze. "I'm ready to be a family again."

"Then what are we waiting for?"

While Russell summoned the house's occupants, Adam dismounted and tied his horse to the hitching post. He was surprised to find his hands were shaking.

"Hey, everyone, come on outside," Russell called into the house. "Someone's waiting to see you." Wearing a goofy grin, he held the main door ajar.

The first one through the door was his ma. He soaked in the changes, the streaks of gray in her brown hair, the crow's-feet about her eyes.

He rounded the horse and approached the porch steps, his heartbeat thundering in his ears.

"Adam!" Her cry was strangled. She launched herself

at him, and he caught her in his arms, breathing deeply of her familiar perfume. "Oh, my darling boy."

She caressed his cheek, her reddened eyes seeming to take inventory of how he'd matured. The heavy thud of footsteps echoed on the wooden slats, and they both turned to see Seth striding toward them.

There were equal parts caution and joy in his eldest brother's eyes. His brown gaze gobbled up the sight of him. He halted at the base of the stairs.

Adam took a deep breath. "How are you, Seth?"

Evelyn wiped her eyes and looked anxiously between her oldest and youngest offspring.

"Good. Really good." The breeze ruffled Seth's light brown hair, pushing strands onto his forehead. "You look hale and hearty."

"I can't complain."

"We thought you'd come and see us once the fighting was over."

Adam winced at the subtle accusation. "I should have. I meant to." He scraped his hand over his jaw. Pride had prevented him. And worry that he'd damaged their relationship beyond repair. "I don't have any acceptable excuses."

A muscle twitched in Seth's cheek. "For four years, we worried you'd get hurt on the battlefield. Or worse. Admit it, you weren't a prolific writer. Months passed without word. And then, instead of coming home, you joined the Pinkertons and couldn't be bothered to drop in for a day or two. Do you care so little about your own flesh and blood?"

For the first time, Adam glimpsed the intense hurt beneath Seth's gruff exterior. Hurt he had caused. Regret flooded him.

"Please don't argue," Evelyn whispered, her handkerchief pressed to her mouth. "This is a joyous day. My sons together again at long last."

Standing at the top of the stairs, Russell no longer wore his lighthearted expression. He watched the exchange with somber wariness.

"We're not fighting, Ma. He has a right to air his grievances. All of you do." Adam squared his shoulders and met Seth's eyes. "Everything you've said is true. I'm sorry I was callous and selfish. I'm sorry I didn't write more often. I could have visited. Multiple times." Grimacing, he shook his head. "I was foolish to ever criticize you. Everything that happened in Big Bend... We each dealt with the aftermath of Ogden's perfidy in our own ways. I was too young and stupid to see that then. Will you forgive me?"

The quiet stretched between them, punctuated by cattle lowing in the fields and the rustle of tree limbs swaying.

The grimness in Seth's features faded. "You're not the only Halloway with a temper and a hard head."

The tightness in his chest easing, Adam extended his hand for a shake. Seth gripped it, hard, then yanked him close for a hug. Evelyn started crying again.

"Don't ever stay away that long again, you hear?" Seth said gruffly in his ear.

Adam nodded and smiled, embarrassed to find his own eyes wet. "You have my word."

A loud thump sounded inside the house. Adam glanced past Seth's shoulder and saw a curtain flutter in one of the windows. At the sight of a child's round, smudged face, he froze. A second one joined the first.

"Seth?" He took a hasty step back. "Are there *children* inside your house?"

Everyone around him burst into laughter. Seth's eyes started twinkling. He urged Adam up the steps. "There are some things I have to tell you, little brother."

"More like people he needs to introduce you to," Russell added as he followed them inside.

Evelyn's expression became positively sentimental.

"The only thing that could make me happier than having you home, my dear son, is seeing you wed and starting a family like your brothers."

Try as she might, Deborah couldn't oust Adam from her thoughts. When he didn't show for breakfast, she assumed he'd overslept. Who could say what his eating habits were? Some people preferred to wait until midmorning to break their fast. But when the noon meal rolled around and he still hadn't made an appearance, she'd had the terrible suspicion that he'd left. If not town, then the boardinghouse.

She'd stooped to asking Aunt Mae—as discreetly as she could manage—who'd stated that he was planning to stay at the boardinghouse indefinitely. The punch of relief Deborah had experienced alarmed her. Now wasn't the time to entertain an infatuation! Her life was in limbo, her future uncertain. Besides, Adam might or might not decide to make Kansas his permanent home. Judging from his comments the previous evening, he wasn't keen on staying in one place for long.

A spider scuttled from beneath the plants very close to where she knelt in the strawberry patch. She waited to make sure it was traveling in the opposite direction before resuming her task. Late-afternoon sun stroked her skin, and the agreeable smells of warm earth and grass reminded her it was nearly summer. Back home, their kitchen workers Louise and Wanda would be tending the estate gardens. The pair had treated her as an equal rather than the tycoon's graceless daughter. They'd allowed her to assist them in the daily meal preparations, provided Gerard was out of the house conducting business. A pang of homesickness struck her unawares.

Snapping off more fruit, she placed the red berries carefully into the basket beside her. Glancing around at the substantial yard behind the boardinghouse, she took stock of the generous veranda, with its wide chairs and bold-hued flowers spilling out of crates, the straight garden rows and towering trees separating this lot from the newspaper's next door. The trees and bushes lent the space privacy and blocked some of the sounds filtering from Eden Street. Deborah missed her childhood home, but this place had its own charms.

For a runaway bride, she'd been blessed with a safe place to live and friends she could count on. The Cowboy Creek community had embraced her. She thanked God every day for placing that lost train ticket in her path.

The sound of whistling drew her head up and her gaze to the low, white fence along the side street. She recognized Adam at once. Clad in a black suit, his hair slicked off his face, he walked with an air of assurance. Her pulse skipped when he caught sight of her and waved. Instead of continuing along to the front entrance, he opened the gate and crossed the yard.

He entered the narrow dirt path and came to a stop beside her.

"Good afternoon, Deborah. I see you're hard at work."

Beneath the brim of his cowboy hat, his eyes shone with excitement. He radiated a charged energy not present last evening. Why the change? Had he found land? Or perhaps a young lady had snagged his interest?

Her belly knotted. Adam was a successful businessman like her father. He'd have high standards when it came to potential brides. A poised, proper lady who could plan social events and execute them without a hitch, a perfectly behaved lady who didn't have a habit of saying the wrong thing.

She tilted her head back and blocked the sunlight with her hand. "I enjoy being outside if it isn't too stifling."

He glanced between her, the half-filled basket and the berries on the plants. "I'll be right back."

He hurried to the veranda, where he shucked his suit jacket and rolled up the sleeves of his gray-and-white-striped shirt. Back in the patch, he joined her in the dirt.

"What are you doing?" she said, an unwanted thrill shivering through her at his nearness.

He flashed a grin. "I'm hoping that by helping you, I'll get the first taste of whatever treat you're concocting."

"You make it sound like I'm a mad scientist."

She averted her attention to the plants, away from the evidence of molded shoulders and thick, muscular biceps beneath his cotton shirt. If he was indeed going to be around for a while, she had to view him as nothing more than a casual friend.

"I've only just met you," he said, humor lacing his tone. "But from what I've seen so far, there is a bit of madness to your methods."

That was a new one. She'd been called inept, thick-headed and socially incompetent. But never mad.

He must've glimpsed her frown, because his fingers closed over her wrist. "Hey, I didn't mean that in a bad way. I happen to think your approach is refreshing."

"Truly?"

His eyes softened. "Truly."

His fingers cradled her wrist with incredible gentleness. The sensation his touch wrought was both comforting and unsettling. With his handsome face so close to hers, she allowed herself to explore the jutting cheekbones and hard, square jaw, the smooth eyebrows, sensitive crescents beneath his liquid brown eyes and oh, that mouth, generous and well-shaped, able to drive rational thought from a girl's head.

Desperate for a distraction, Deborah snatched a strawberry from the basket and pressed it to his lips. "Have you ever tasted a strawberry straight from the garden? Nothing beats that burst of sun-heated flavor," she rambled. "Try it."

Adam's eyes went wide. Lips parting, he bit off a huge portion, leaving the green top suspended in her hold. He took his time chewing.

"You're right," he croaked, disconcerted. "It's delicious."

Face flaming, she snatched on to something, anything to cover her foolish reaction to his touch. "There's a fundraiser tomorrow to benefit Will Canfield's congressional run, and I've been hired to provide the desserts. I'm making individual towers of pastry, which I'll fill with strawberries in a mint and vinegar glaze—"

"Vinegar?"

"I haven't tried it yet, but I'm hopeful it will add a little zing to the mixture. Sour mingled with sweet."

"Hmm."

"You should go. The other town founders, Noah Burgess and Daniel Gardner, will be there, as well as many other prominent citizens."

He slowly nodded. "Good idea. I have a proposition for you." He gestured to the basket. "I'll help you transport and set up the desserts if you'll agree to introduce me around."

Her jaw sagged. "*Me?* I'm the last person you'd want for that job."

"Why would you think that?"

"I'm not like Lucy. My sister has an uncanny knack for remembering every name associated with every face. She recalls key details of people's lives. Once, during a dinner party my father was hosting, I put Mr. Rosenbaum next to Mr. Thatcher."

"And that was a problem because…"

"Because Mr. Rosenbaum's wife left him and later married Mr. Thatcher's *son*." She shuddered, not fond of that particular memory. "Lucy never would've done something so thoughtless."

Though his fingers made rapid work of the picking, he was careful not to bruise the fragile fruit. "Is Lucy able to create desserts that melt in your mouth?"

"No, but what does that matter?"

He raised one shoulder. "It may not matter in St. Louis, but it matters here."

Deborah fell silent, mulling his words as they worked. At least a quarter of an hour passed before he broke her concentration.

"See that gray cloud? There's a storm brewing. We'd better work fast if we don't wish to get caught in the middle of a downpour."

When they'd gotten the ripe berries into the basket and reached the welcome shelter of the veranda, she thanked him for his help. She said nothing more because Hildie emerged from the house, her lips thinning at the sight of them together.

"Adam, there you are! How inconsiderate of you to deprive us of your company the entire day." She slipped her arm through his. "Say you'll play that game of checkers with me."

His gaze sought out Deborah. "I wouldn't mind a game or two, unless you need help washing those?"

Deborah fought a swift rise of jealousy. She enjoyed his company and would've liked to have him to herself for a while longer, but she had to be practical. His time would be better spent with Hildie, not her.

"Thank you, Adam. I'll be able to better concentrate on my recipe if I'm alone."

He frowned a little. "If you're sure."

"I'm sure."

The pair went inside, Hildie's voice carrying through the house like a bird's trilling song. Deborah sank onto a chair and contemplated the clouds marching across the Kansas sky, soon to mask the sun. Once she'd fulfilled her part of their deal, she'd have to distance herself from the charming cattleman. No more informal tours and no playing liaison. She had a disgruntled groom and irate father searching for her. Soon, she'd have to make a decision. Stay in Cowboy Creek and increase her risk of being found, or purchase a ticket to the next stop on the rail line.

# Chapter Four

❧

"**Y**ou're a genius."

Adam licked the glaze from his fingers and, unable to resist, plucked another portion of pastry from the overturned dessert and popped it in his mouth. He'd helped Deborah carry her fancy concoctions into Daniel and Leah Gardner's grand parlor. Around them, the Gardners' hired staff bustled about the high-ceilinged room arranging savory snacks and cold drinks. Guests had already begun to arrive.

"I'm hardly that," Deborah denied. "A genius is someone who invents machines or makes new discoveries." Her anxious gaze swept the platters. "Did you topple that one on purpose?"

"I find it hurtful that you'd accuse me of purposefully sabotaging your display."

Grooves marred her forehead. Her mouth went slack. The brewing apology in her brilliant golden eyes strengthened his opinion that she wasn't accustomed to the back-and-forth between a man and woman.

Reaching over, he quickly righted the shell-pink bloom above her ear. "Never mind me. I was only teasing."

"Oh." She skimmed her hands over her pristine white apron.

A warning pounded at his temples. Since when did he flirt with potential suspects?

Adam hadn't encountered a woman like Deborah Frazier before. She was the epitome of earnest innocence. He couldn't decide if it was her countenance, her demeanor or a combination of both that made him want to be her protector. Was it all a clever act?

She studied him more closely. "I'm beginning to believe you're not the ideal person for this task. Kind of like having a fox in the henhouse."

He smiled. "I do have a sweet tooth."

He'd mulled over the scant personal information she'd revealed. The fact that she was from St. Louis bothered him. She could've easily met Ogden there. He could've preyed on her feelings of incompetence in order to woo her into working with him. He needed to remember the reason he was here, and find out more about her. "Who taught you to bake?"

"That credit goes to my father's trained kitchen staff. Frederica, the head cook, imparted her knowledge of herbs and spices. Louise and Wanda taught me the basics of pastry." She rescued a pastry that was too close to the platter's edge. "You should've seen my first attempt at a peach pie. Even the dog turned his nose up at it. But they were patient with me." Lost in memories, her expression turned pensive.

Who was it that had made her doubt herself? he wondered. Her father? Mother? Both?

"Your parents must've appreciated the outcome of their efforts."

"My mother died when I was ten. Unfortunately, my father does not approve of my efforts."

Any further conversation was cut off by the approach of Sadie Shriver, on the arm of a tidy gentleman with wavy, dark blond hair and blue eyes. His observant gaze swept the space in slow inventory.

"Adam, I'd like to introduce you to my particular friend, Walter Kerr."

Walter dragged his attention to Adam, who felt like a sample under a microscope. The man did a rapid study of Adam's clothing and face.

"I feel as though I've met you before," he said at last.

Adam racked his brain and came up empty. He'd traveled the country, working in multiple cities. It wasn't out of the realm of possibility that their paths had crossed. He hoped not, for the sake of his ultimate goal. "I'm afraid I can't say the same."

Sadie aimed an adoring smile at her beau. "Walter's a renowned photographer. He has an uncanny ability to remember faces."

"I would've recalled meeting a famous person," Adam said.

Walter's features relaxed. "Famous? Not quite. While Sadie's estimation of my skills is quite flattering, I'm simply a man with a passion for capturing images for perpetuity."

She patted his arm. "He's being humble."

More guests arrived, and the pair made their excuses and crossed the room to speak to the hosts, Daniel and Leah Gardner. Deborah reached for her rolling pin brooch, only to discover it wasn't there. Clouds of anxiety dulled her brilliant eyes.

"You're going to be fine, you know." He gestured to the room of guests behind him. "They won't bite."

"You never know." With a long-suffering sigh, she removed her apron and stowed it behind a squat vase dominating a side table. "Who would you like to meet first?"

"Pink is your color," he murmured, partially to knock her off balance and partially because it was true. "You should wear it every day."

Her tasteful dress was crafted of a delicate crepe fabric that lent her fair skin a pearlescent sheen. The bodice boasted a demure scooped neckline, short, ruffled sleeves and embroidered roses at the waistline. Ribbons edged the hem of the substantial hoop skirt. Her dark brown tresses were confined in a neat bun, allowing him a generous view of her swanlike nape and curved shoulders.

Her small, pink tongue darted out to moisten her lips. "Thank you. I arrived with only one satchel. Hannah Johnson—she's our premier dressmaker—made it for me."

"Only one? Most ladies I know wouldn't dream of leaving home unarmed with their entire wardrobe."

"My departure wasn't planned in advance." She must've realized her slip, for her brows drew together in a frown. "There's Hannah's father, Reverend Taggart. We'll start with him."

She led him to the opposite corner of the long, rectangular room, maneuvering around stuffed couches and intricately carved coffee tables to reach a dignified, brown-haired man peering at a painting of a ship at sea.

He turned at their approach and offered a kind smile. After Deborah introduced them, the reverend invited him to the upcoming services that Sunday. Adam accepted with sincere enthusiasm. It had been years since he'd worshipped with his family.

His breathing hitched, and he barely concealed a grimace. He *wouldn't* be worshipping with his mother or brothers. He couldn't take the chance of someone connecting the dots, especially the person in league with Ogden.

A familiar laugh drew his attention toward the parlor's main entrance, a broad doorway topped with a transom window. The papered hallway beyond was filling with guests, his brother among them. Russell chatted with the guest of honor, Mayor Will Canfield, as if they were old friends. Adam belatedly noticed the woman standing off to the side. Afternoon light shining through the many windows glinted off the silver combs in her golden-brown hair and the tasteful jewels at her throat and wrists. Her beauty and youth were enhanced by the sophisticated cut of her sapphire dress, which didn't quite hide her pregnancy. Anna Halloway, his sister-in-law, another new addition to the family.

His head still spun with all the changes. During the years of their separation, he'd given only fleeting consideration to the idea of Seth and Russell starting families of their own. Now Seth had a wife and four kids. Russell was about to become a father for the first time.

Adam recognized the flare of envy and smothered it. He may have grown weary of his solitary life, but he couldn't entertain thoughts of courtship and marriage—much less pursue them—until Zane Ogden was where he belonged. Rotting in a cell.

Deborah nodded toward the trio. "That's the lawyer I told you about, Russell Halloway. You should meet him, considering Will is grooming him to take over his job."

"He's angling to become mayor?"

"You sound surprised."

Adam chased the shock from his features. He had to be more circumspect. "Your description of him made it sound like he was devoted to his profession. I'm wondering how he'd be able to juggle the responsibilities to both his clients and Cowboy Creek's citizens if he were elected."

"He strikes me as a competent man. I'm certain he's considered the future and would adjust to the demands."

The pinch of jealousy that her obvious esteem for his brother produced was both startling and unwelcome. *Please God, I must maintain professional objectivity. Your Word promises to give us wisdom if we but ask. I'm not asking. I'm begging.*

Tucking her hand in the crook of his arm, he guided her across the room. Russell's flare of surprise was quickly masked. He moved to his wife's side while Will Canfield greeted Deborah.

"Good afternoon, Miss Frazier. I can't tell you how happy I was when I learned you'd be here today." Dark eyes twinkling, he gripped the silver handle of his walking cane. "I told Tomasina that we could easily meet our goal if we'd auction off your desserts one by one."

"I was happy to do it."

When she failed to introduce him, Will prompted, "Who's your friend?"

"Oh, I apologize for not…" Her fingers dug into Adam's suit sleeve. "This is Adam Draper. He's new to town and boarding at Aunt Mae's."

"Pleased to meet you." Adam covered her hand and gently squeezed it in a silent bid for her to release her death grip. When she did, he shook hands with the mayor, then answered his queries and, all too soon, was pretending not to know his own brother.

Russell's act was spot-on. Anna was nervous, however, and he worried she'd slip. Her green eyes were huge pools of curiosity as she placed her hand in his.

"Welcome to Cowboy Creek, Mr. Draper," she said. "What is your early opinion of our fair town?"

Adam wished their first meeting had been away from prying eyes. Welcoming her to the Halloway family would have to come later. "Very high. I've met many kind, interesting people, which helps when making a decision like the one I'm contemplating."

"Trust me, you can't go wrong with a town like ours," Will boasted. "We've got a lot to offer a man such as yourself. Opportunities to start or expand businesses abound."

"There's also an abundance of marriage-minded ladies." Russell's smirk wasn't lost on Adam. Nor was Deborah's marked reaction. Beside him, she stiffened.

Another mystery surrounding the spunky brunette.

Why would a lady averse to courtship accept a ticket for a bride train?

"I'm currently not in the market for a wife," he said. "My business requires 100 percent of my energy."

Russell curved his arm around Anna's shoulders and sent a significant glance at Deborah. "While I understand your point of view, Mr. Draper, I'd advise you not to overlook the advantages of having a loving partner by your side."

Anna dipped her head in an effort to hide a smile.

He gritted his teeth, already planning what he'd say to dear Russ the next time they were alone.

Will chuckled. "Couldn't have said it better myself." His gaze shifted beyond Adam. "Please excuse me. It appears I'm being summoned. Thank you again for coming, Mr. Draper. If you have need of further information regarding the town, feel free to stop by my office. You could also speak to my friends, Daniel Gardner and Noah Burgess. Daniel owns the Gardner Stockyards and Noah owns a ranch outside town. They can give you different perspectives."

Adam thanked the man. He was about to suggest they move on when Deborah spoke.

"I've told Adam about your work with war veterans, Russell. I had a cousin, James, who was injured and ultimately lost his right arm. He struggled for many years to support his family in the same manner as he'd done before the fighting. I'd like to believe if he'd had someone like you to help him, he wouldn't have lost hope."

Anna's lips parted. "What happened to him?"

"He abandoned his wife and children. No one has seen or heard from him for over two years." She winced. "I suppose that isn't a subject fitting for a fund-raiser."

Russell's eyes were full of understanding. "We don't

fault you for speaking of the realities of war. I'm afraid I'm all too acquainted with the unpleasant ramifications."

"What about you, Mr. Draper?" Russell inquired with faultless politeness. "Did you serve?"

Sensing Deborah's keen interest, Adam was careful not to reveal his annoyance. What game was his brother playing?

A denial was forming on his lips when he glanced at Deborah and the vulnerable light in her eyes chased the air from his lungs. Just once, he wanted to tell her something real, something true about himself. "I joined the Union army when I was eighteen."

A tiny pleat formed between her brows. "You were very young."

"There were many who were far younger. We were boys masquerading as men, pretending we weren't frightened out of our minds and longing for our mamas."

Deborah forgot about Russell and Anna. The chatter and occasional trill of laughter filling the house faded to a hum. It was as if a veil had slipped from Adam's face, and she was seeing him for the first time. Lingering anguish swirled in the brown depths of his eyes. She could only imagine what horrors he'd witnessed.

"Did you serve the entire length of the war?"

He nodded. "I've since questioned how I managed to survive when so many others weren't so fortunate."

"God preserved your life for a reason."

"Did you suffer any injuries?" Anna's voice jolted Deborah.

She blushed. They'd completely ignored the other couple.

Adam's gaze clung to Deborah's. "Nothing serious."

Had she imagined the strange flicker in his eyes? Was

he being forthcoming? Or perhaps glossing over what he might consider alarming to her and Anna?

The clink of metal against glass was followed by Daniel Gardner's booming voice welcoming everyone to the fundraiser. Most days, the stockyard owner favored cowboy gear, but for this occasion he'd donned a nutmeg-brown suit that enhanced his chestnut hair and green eyes. Since he had everyone's attention, he motioned for Will and Noah to join him at his spot beside the upright piano.

Comfortable with the spotlight, Will joined him without hesitation. The more reclusive Noah had to be encouraged by his wife, Grace, who gave him a kiss on his scarred cheek and a playful shove. That earned them a spurt of laughter as Noah meekly took his position on the other side of Daniel, who promptly began his speech.

"When we set out to build a town in the Kansas prairie, none of us could've dreamed what the outcome would be. Thanks to God's grace, and the wise direction of our mayor, Cowboy Creek has become a wonderful place to live. We've benefited from Will's leadership, and now it's time to share his time and talents with the nation." Daniel clasped Will's shoulder. "Please offer your prayers and support to him as he moves forward with his bid for Congress."

The fervent applause spoke of the residents' admiration for their mayor. He kept his speech brief and, after a tear-inducing homage to his wife, Tomasina, urged everyone to mingle and indulge in the refreshments.

Adam steered her away from Russell and Anna and toward the lone man in the nearby corner. Instead of parading him around the room, she would've preferred to go off alone and continue their conversation. She was hungry for details.

"Mr. Mitchell?"

The handsome owner of Mitchell Coal & Mining Company lowered his glass and regarded her with barely concealed disapproval. He'd been friendly, even flirtatious when she'd first arrived in Cowboy Creek. But as she'd continued to evade suitors, his manner had cooled toward her.

"To what do I owe the pleasure of your company, Miss Frazier?" he drawled.

Reminding herself that his opinion of her didn't matter, she said, "I'd like for you to meet Aunt Mae's newest boarder, Adam Draper. Adam, this is Jason Mitchell. He's in the coal business."

The men shook hands. "What brings you to Cowboy Creek?" Jason asked.

"I'm looking to buy land and set up a ranching operation."

Jason snorted. "You're a few months too late. Anything not owned by me is being snatched up by the Maroni brothers, land speculators from New York—whom I've yet to meet, by the way. Want my advice? Take the earliest train out of here."

His pessimistic attitude grated. "Your attitude stinks, Mr. Mitchell," she blurted. "Your negativity won't make Adam's decision any easier, and it certainly won't help our community prosper."

Jason arched a brow. "You're entitled to your opinion, Miss Frazier, the same as I'm entitled to mine."

His gaze slid to Adam, and she got the distinct impression he was wondering if things were romantic between them. Stung by his insinuated rebuke, she wished she'd held her tongue. Echoes of the past intruded.

*Why can't you learn to hold your tongue, young lady? No one cares to hear your opinion.*

Humiliation zipped along her nerve endings. She'd not only embarrassed herself, but Adam, as well.

Her gaze on the gleaming floor, she mumbled, "Please excuse me. I'm in need of fresh air."

Intent on escape, she ignored Adam's soft bid for her to wait.

# Chapter Five

"Tea with a splash of milk." A delicate china cup entered her line of vision, and the tantalizing aroma of Earl Grey tea teased her nose. "And we can't forget dessert. Mark my word, you'll be impressed. The two I had were equally satisfying."

Shifting on the wrought-iron chair, she reluctantly met Adam's gaze. He'd followed her to this isolated corner of the Gardners' veranda. The shade bathed them in cool relief. Beyond the railing and roofline, a profusion of tall trees absorbed the unrelenting sun. It was a pleasing vista of varying shades of green and vivid blue, broken by patches of purplish blue wildflowers.

Adam smiled in a gentle, coaxing way, and his dark eyes were kind. She accepted the tea. "Two? Did you sneak another one without telling me?"

He set the dessert plate on the oval side table beside her. Sinking into the chair opposite, he stretched his legs out and hooked one ankle over the other. He adopted an innocent expression. "In Aunt Mae's kitchen. I couldn't help myself."

She took a grateful sip of the fragrant brew. "That's it. You're fired."

"You're firing me?"

"Why not? I fired myself from being your guide."

Adam's brows shot up. "Don't tell me you're reneging on our deal. You don't strike me as a quitter."

Little ripples marred the hot liquid's surface as she blew on the tea. "You still want my help? I shouldn't have reprimanded him for speaking his mind."

Uncrossing his ankles, he leaned forward. "He could've been more subtle. You were upset on my account. You stood up for me and my plans."

"You're truly not angry?"

"I'm touched."

"I confess to being very curious about you."

He laughed off his initial surprise. "I'm not that interesting."

"I'll be the judge of that. Tell me about your family. Are both your parents living?"

Sobering, he ran his fingers along the crease in his pant leg. "My mother is alive and well. My father is gone."

Dangerous emotion swirled in his eyes and, for an instant, she felt the pure force of it directed at her. She blinked, and the moment was gone.

"I—I'm sorry about your father. I'm acquainted with the difficulty of losing a parent. Of course, having a sibling to share in your grief can be beneficial. Where are your brothers now?"

"I'll be honest, Deborah. I'm a private man. I don't make a habit of speaking about my family."

"I see." The birds' song didn't sound quite as cheerful as it had when she'd first sought solace in this out of the way spot.

Adam stood and moved closer. "It's nothing to do with you," he said softly.

Deborah plastered on a smile. "You don't have to explain."

His astute gaze roamed her features. "Take your time

out here. I'm going to have a word with the reverend. Find me when you're ready, all right?"

"All right."

She watched him stride the length of the veranda and enter through the side door, then set down her teacup and went to stand at the railing. If there was one thing she'd like to change about herself, even more than her tendency to speak without discretion, it was her sensitive nature. Adam hadn't been rude or condescending, even though they were recent acquaintances and she'd been poking her nose where it wasn't welcome.

With a prayer for courage, she joined him in the Gardners' parlor and resumed her duties. He remained pleasant, but there was a new reserve about him that puzzled her. His stated preference for privacy had only enflamed her curiosity, unfortunately. Why did he not like talking about his family? Had something tragic occurred? Was there a black sheep in the Draper family?

Deborah doubted these questions would ever be answered. He was here alone in Cowboy Creek, so there'd be no fishing for clues among his friends. Disappointed, not to mention confused by her interest in the enigmatic cattleman, she focused on guarding every single word leaving her mouth. To her relief, there were no more mishaps.

When the event had wound down and it was time to gather the soiled dishes, Sadie and Walter waved Adam away to mingle. As soon as he was out of earshot, Walter cornered her.

"What do you know about him?"

"Adam? Very little."

"Where's he from?"

"Big Bend, Missouri. Why do you ask?"

"I'm convinced our paths have crossed before, but I can't pinpoint the particulars. My mind won't rest until I determine whether or not I'm mistaken." His brows drew together. "Do you know if he served in the war?"

"He did."

Walter made a considering noise in his throat, then turned to address Sadie. "You know I dislike unsolved riddles. I will send for the photographs I took during those years."

Sadie paused in stacking plates. "I'd be happy to help you look through them."

"It will be a tedious process."

Admiration brightened her eyes. "To you, maybe, but I'm eager to see more of your work. Besides, any time spent in your company is far from tedious."

He flashed a rare smile and kissed her hand. "Have I told you lately how delightful I find you, my dear?"

Feeling as if she were intruding, Deborah left them, carrying empty platters through the kitchen and out to the wagon. While she was thrilled that Sadie had found happiness with the photographer, witnessing their devotion highlighted the fact that she was alone, far from home, separated from her sister and her few close friends.

She was returning to the house when something in the grass caught her eye. Moving closer for a better look, she realized it was a porcelain doll. She picked it up and brushed the dirt from its clothes and yellow curls. Judging from its decent condition, it hadn't been exposed to the elements for very long. Daniel and Leah's daughter, Evie, was far too young to be toting around a doll, and there hadn't been any children in attendance this afternoon. But there was a doll missing from Booker & Son's mercantile.

Deborah ventured farther into the yard, combing the ground for more clues. Were Seth Halloway's boys telling the truth? Had there been stowaway children on the bride train?

Holding the doll to her chest, she debated what to do. Children roaming the town without supervision were susceptible to all sorts of threats. They'd need shelter, clothing, food and water. The bride train on which the Halloway boys had traveled had arrived two months ago. Only desperation or fear would keep anyone in hiding for that long.

Leaving the doll in its original spot in case the owner came searching for it, she made plans to return that night.

"What are you doing?"

Deborah whirled. "Adam, I didn't realize anyone else was out here."

Her apron in his hands, he studied her with unsettling intensity. "I felt bad for abandoning you in the midst of cleanup. Sadie sent me in this direction."

She considered sharing her suspicions, only to dismiss the notion. He'd probably think her naive. If no one else in town had been able to solve the ongoing mystery of the petty thefts, how was she going to accomplish it?

Perhaps if she knew him better, she could ask him to assist her. They could work on solving the puzzle together, like amateur detectives.

"There wasn't much to do." She accepted the apron and put it with the platters. "Your goal was to mingle with the locals and town leaders, anyway. Would you consider the night a success?"

Walking to the house side by side, he nodded. "I enjoyed myself, thanks to you."

The words sounded forced, his customary charm worn thin.

"I'm happy to hear it."

At the door, he turned to regard the area from which they'd come. His gaze became hooded, and there was a grim set to his mouth.

For a man in town with a straightforward purpose, he seemed awfully troubled.

* * *

An innocent woman didn't hide fried chicken legs in her reticule and slink off into the night. Adam trailed her along the side street past the school and onto Lincoln Boulevard. For someone with a hidden agenda, she didn't bother to check whether or not anyone was aware of her movements. The thought that she could be taking food to Zane Ogden made his stomach churn. *Not Deborah*, his mind protested. *She's too sweet, too earnest.*

Hesitating on the corner across from the Gardners', where lights blazed in the multitude of windows, she continued at a brisk pace and took a right on Fourth Street. This direction boasted deserted woods that emptied out at the stockyards.

*Use your head, Halloway. Don't be duped by her innocent act.*

His training had prepared him to consider a problem's every angle, from the obvious to the far-fetched. He'd learned not to rule out a suspect based on appearance or behavior. Not all villains wore black and twirled evil mustaches. Some were accommodating and downright likable.

He might not want Deborah to be guilty of aiding a criminal, but in this line of work, disappointments were inevitable.

She stopped short. Adam used overgrown bushes on the street's edge as a barrier. Glancing around, she entered the copse abutting Daniel's property. He unsheathed his weapon and entered at a substantial distance behind. His quarry could be closer than he realized.

Moonlight gilded the trees in silvery essence and afforded him a view of her silhouette. The occasional hoot owl shattered the stillness. He avoided the twigs her boots crushed.

"Hello?"

The sudden sound of Deborah's voice jolted him. Slipping sideways to hunker behind a massive oak, he peered at her through a V in the branches. She removed the bundle of chicken and held it aloft.

"I've brought some tasty fried chicken," she said, turning in a circle. "You can have it, free of charge. I'd hate to leave it for the scavengers to find. Won't you come out and talk to me?"

Adam's grip on his weapon went slack. He observed her in mounting confusion. Was this some sort of code? A way for Ogden to know it was safe to emerge from his hideout?

This wasn't the best place to take refuge from authorities. The Gardners' mansion was visible from this vantage point, and the nearby street saw a lot of traffic from cowboys traveling between the stockyards and the center of town. Deborah had been studying this area after the fundraiser and had acted nervous when questioned.

But no one emerged from the shadows to greet her. Her sigh was punctuated by the slump of her shoulders.

"I'd really like to help you." She left the bundle on a tree stump and retraced her steps.

Adam edged around the trunk, barely breathing, careful to remain out of sight. He expected her to go straight to Aunt Mae's. Instead, she ventured into the Gardners' yard, her head bent as she scraped her boot through the grass. When she didn't find what she was looking for, she hurried along her way.

He let her go, murmuring to himself, "What are you up to, Deborah Frazier?"

Deborah regarded the town gossips with mounting irritation. She'd approached the two old men the next day in hopes they'd shed light on the stowaway mystery, but their claims contradicted each other.

Gus stroked his full white beard with a gnarled hand. "You're wrong. Flat out wrong, I tell ya. Those kids weren't anywhere near the livery. They were sneakin' around the telegraph office."

Slouched beside him on the bench outside Booker & Son's general store, Old Horace puffed on his cheroot and narrowed his rheumy eyes. "You're losin' your faculties, man. I remember as plain as day the boy hiding behind the water barrels."

Deborah clutched her reticule to her chest and shifted to make room for a passing cowboy. "Can you tell me what they looked like? Are they boys? Girls? One of each?"

"Well, now, it *was* awful dark," Gus mused. His gaze never ceased moving. The elderly pair made an occupation of surveying the comings and goings of Cowboy Creek's residents. It was a wonder their names weren't engraved on the bench where they sat seemingly all day and night.

"Hmm." Old Horace nodded. "The shadows *were* long."

She stifled a sigh. The sights and sounds of afternoon activity enveloped her. Wagons creaked along Eden Street. Horses whinnied. A dog's bark was thrown into the mix, as were children's laughter and mothers' stern warnings to mind their steps. The bell above Booker & Son's entrance chimed incessantly. Old Horace and Gus must be immune to it.

This had been a fool's errand, as had last evening's foray into the woods behind Daniel Gardner's home. No doubt that chicken had made a tasty meal for the ants.

*But the doll was gone, remember? Someone removed it in the hours between the fund-raiser and her late-night visit.*

At the sight of the lanky blond man heading straight for her, Deborah was reminded she had other matters to worry about. Real ones, not possibly-made-up sightings of stowaways.

"Thank you for your time, gentlemen." Squaring her

shoulders, she left the boardwalk and met Preston Wells in the shade of The Cattleman. "Good afternoon, Mr. Wells."

"Surely you agree it's time to dispense with the formalities, Deborah." His eyes bore into her, pleading and needy. "You are the epitome of summertime's best offerings in that dress."

She pressed a hand to her stomach and strove for a pleasant expression. Inside, she experienced a strange frisson of unease. A telegraph operator, Preston had become fixated on her shortly after her arrival. She'd been kind but firm in her numerous refusals of his overtures. He'd proven persistent, however. He'd even taken to badgering poor Sadie, who had to work with him, about her.

She had no objections to his appearance. In his mid-twenties, Preston wore his light hair cut very short, which emphasized his broad forehead—her great-aunt would call it intelligent—and a rather thin nose. His eyes were an interesting shade of gray, however, and he had a nicely shaped mouth. He took pride in his appearance. It was the hint of desperation in his exchanges with her that put her on guard.

"Er, thank you." She smoothed the ivory skirt printed with green and yellow flowers.

"It flatters your complexion greatly," he enthused, moving closer than was comfortable. "And your hair…" He was reaching to cup her cheek when Adam entered her peripheral vision.

"I don't believe we've met." Adam struck out his hand for Preston to shake.

Thankful for the interruption, Deborah edged out of the way. Preston regarded Adam with a mixture of bewilderment and annoyance.

"Preston Wells. And you are?"

"Adam Draper. I'm staying at the same boardinghouse as Deborah."

"Pleasure." His expression said it was anything but. His gaze returned to her. "Would you agree to accompany me for a short stroll? I'm contemplating hosting a small dinner party and perhaps engaging your services."

"Maybe another time. I have a long list of errands to complete, including picking up a few items for Aunt Mae."

"Would you believe she asked me to do some shopping for her, as well?" Adam chuckled and produced a folded paper from his pocket. "If you're going into Booker & Son's, I'll join you."

Preston gave his suit lapels a sharp tug. "I see you're preoccupied at the moment. I'll come around the boardinghouse one evening this week."

Unable to politely decline, she nodded and bid him goodbye. Adam's light touch against her back was comforting as they entered the mercantile. Navigating the aisles, they found a secluded corner near a window display of gardening instruments.

"Is he one of the men who proposed marriage?" There was a hint of humor in his dark eyes.

"No."

"But he's one of the men whose overtures you've spurned."

"Preston is nothing if not persistent." She made a show of consulting her own list. "What exactly did Aunt Mae send you here for?"

He wiggled his finger. "Uh-uh. You're not dodging this one. Tell me why you've refused to consider any of the interested parties. Were they too young? Too old? Not prone to bathing?"

"They are all decent men." Deborah inched past him to study ribbons in a variety of colors. "A-and clean."

"Are you one of those women who has a long list of qualifications a man must meet in order to be considered worthy of your hand?" His breath teased the flower at her ear. Goose bumps raced over her skin.

"What? Of course not."

"Something is preventing you. What is it?"

Deborah angled her face toward his, startled to find him so close. His nearness didn't affect her like Preston's. Instead of wanting to bolt, she yearned to move closer. His shoulders were broad and sturdy, his arms strong and inviting. He'd be a good hugger, she could tell. Someone who would hold her tight and snug for as long as she needed, not pat her awkwardly on the back and shrug free after short moments. Strangely, she was starting to view Adam as someone she could depend on. He radiated honor and goodness. She sensed he was the type of man who'd lay down his life for a stranger's.

Would it be so terrible to confide in him? Adam would entertain his own conclusions. She'd hate for him to think her snobbish, persnickety or, worse, on the hunt for a rich husband. She could've had one of those, if she'd gone through with the nuptials back in St. Louis.

In the end, she chose to tell him a partial truth. "The prospect of marriage is more daunting than I anticipated. To pledge oneself to another forever…it's a grave undertaking. Not to be taken lightly."

"You're not taking it at all, though." His smile had faded. "Despite having traveled here for the express purpose of landing a husband."

"Am I not allowed to have a change of heart? O-or lose my nerve?"

"You arrived in your wedding clothes," he said softly.

"You have the uncanny ability to question me as if I'm on trial. Were you ever a lawyer, Mr. Draper?"

"You revert to formalities when you're upset with me." He kneaded the side of his neck. "I apologize for pressing you. It's none of my business. Although, I will say I

understand the locals' frustration. You're beautiful, intelligent and talented. Any man with a scrap of sense would
make a bid for your attention."

His praise emboldened her. "*You* haven't."

Adam's lips parted. His eyes thrummed with emotion
quickly squelched. Clearing his throat, he said, "I'm not
yet in that stage of my life. There are matters that take
precedence over any desire to wed and produce heirs."

"What sort of matters? Your ranches?"

"My ranches…" His brows drew together. "Oh, yes. My
business obligations are many."

"So you've never come close to falling in love?"

He fell silent. Deborah felt as though she were swimming in that endless brown gaze as the air between them
thinned. Why had she asked such a foolish question?

"Never."

"Me, either."

The bell over the door jangled, dispelling the tension.
Adam's attention went to the entrance and immediately
the set of his shoulders changed. She shifted to get a better
view. Russell Halloway stood just inside the door, his hat
in his hands. He nodded and waved, but instead of coming over, he headed for the sales counter.

"I should let you tend to your shopping," Adam told
her. "I'll see you later."

Nonplussed, Deborah watched as he strode for the exit.
Not even one minute later, Russell left empty-handed.

The two men had met yesterday for the first time. Why
then, did she get the feeling she was missing something?

## Chapter Six

"Before you read me the riot act, stop and think." Russell held up a staying hand. "You must agree that I had to ask."

"You asked me a personal question in front of a suspect," Adam gritted, the annoyance he'd felt at the fundraiser rushing to the surface.

"I'm a lawyer who specializes in assisting veterans. It would've raised suspicions if I *hadn't* asked." His frown became an unhappy slash in his face. "Wait, did you say *suspect*? Surely you don't think Deborah Frazier is capable of consorting with a blackguard like Ogden!"

"Lower your voice." Adam scanned both sides of the alley behind the mercantile and the street running alongside the church behind them.

"She's not involved," Russell insisted, his hazel eyes confident.

"I don't know enough yet to draw that conclusion."

"You just rode into town. Anna and I have gotten to know her over the course of the last eight weeks. She's got a heart of gold."

That had been his impression, as well. His wish. But the fact was he didn't truly know her or what she might be capable of.

"Three weeks ago, I was wrapping up a case in Centerville when I got a message from one of my closest colleagues. Dayton's one of the few people I've told about our past. While pursuing a lead in a murder, he heard some cowboys grumbling about losing their jobs because their owners had to up and sell at a moment's notice. The situation sounded similar to Big Bend's, so he contacted me. Together, we did some digging and learned that an entrepreneur who called himself Thaddeus Jones had been dispensing loans to the locals."

"Let me guess," Russell bit out. "Just like in Big Bend, the locals failed to read the fine print. He charged them high interest rates and put their ranches up as collateral."

"Exactly. He'd already skipped town by the time I got there, but I did manage to locate the house he'd been renting." The sharp disappointment he'd experienced filled him anew. He'd walked through the very rooms his nemesis had inhabited with the knowledge he'd been a couple of days too late. "In the living room fireplace, I salvaged a scrap of paper that led me to Cowboy Creek."

When he explained the significance of the signature, Russell gave him a hooded look. "You suspect Deborah because her name begins with *D*? Couldn't it be someone named Diana or Desiree? David? Dustin—"

"I know it's not much to go on, all right? But the people I interviewed insisted he was in cahoots with a female. The description matches. Young and attractive, dark brown hair, elegant clothes. Unfortunately, she didn't mingle with the locals. She stuck to Ogden's side like glue."

Russell's gaze followed a buggy as it rolled past the church. He shook his head. "I'm aware of the Pinkertons' reputation. And you've proven yourself a worthy detective, otherwise you would've been cut loose a long time ago. But I urge you not to rush judgments on this one. Don't let your obsession with Ogden make you sloppy."

"I am not obsessed."

"Aren't you? Has a single day gone by these past nine years when you haven't thought about him? Imagined making him pay for what he did?"

His brother was speaking the truth, and it was difficult to hear. The implication was that Seth and Russ had moved on with their lives, while he'd remained stagnant.

Adam ripped off his Stetson and slapped it against his thigh. His older brother taking him to task hauled him back to his adolescent years. Being the youngest hadn't set well with him. He'd balked whenever Seth and Russell had tried to boss him around. That was one aspect of leaving he hadn't minded—people had treated him as his own man, not as the youngest Halloway boy.

"Adam, I've seen innocent people punished for crimes they didn't commit. I'd hate for that to happen in this case."

He met his brother's solemn gaze. "Believe me, I'm aware of the pitfalls and am making concessions."

Russell gripped his shoulder. "I want answers, too. I'll help you any way I can. Come by for supper tonight. Meet Anna proper-like."

"I wish I could, but I have to stay close to Deborah."

"You can spare an hour this afternoon, can't you?"

"I would like to speak to my new sister-in-law without worrying who's listening. Three o'clock?"

"I'll close the office early."

They said their goodbyes, and Adam headed for the Mitchell Coal & Mining Company. Jason Mitchell welcomed him into his office with polite formality. Waving him into a chair, he resumed his spot behind the desk cluttered with papers.

"What can I do for you, Mr. Draper?"

"I promise not to take up much of your time." He did a quick inventory of the cramped space. "Based on our brief exchange yesterday, I thought you might have insight into the area's property shortage. I visited the land office earlier and was met with discouraging news."

Sinking against the dull leather chair, Jason steepled his hands. "It's like I told you at the fund-raiser. The Maroni brothers are greedier than most. I've been in this business a while. Competition's normal. Even healthy." He rubbed at a coffee stain ingrained in the desk. "These men are different."

"How so?"

"First off, I've yet to set eyes on them. Only the land office clerk and the ranchers who've done business with them have spoken to them face-to-face."

Adam wet his lips. Ogden could've gotten another accomplice, a man this time. "Maybe they like their privacy."

"Maybe." Jason's eyes hardened. "Or maybe they've got something to hide."

"Don't they have a temporary office set up? Somewhere to conduct business?"

"They were staying at The Lariat, but I haven't managed to get a meeting with them." He sighed and drummed his fingers against the wood. "There have been too many ranchers forced off their land. Not a coincidence, if you ask me."

Adam adopted an expression of disbelief. "Are you suggesting the Maronis orchestrated accidents to get their hands on land they think is rich with coal?"

"I do."

"Have you gone to the sheriff with your suspicions?"

He rolled his eyes. "The new sheriff is an incompetent oaf. Folks aren't happy that the previous sheriff, Buck Hanley, abandoned the job to go into business for himself."

Adam would have to pay the sheriff a visit and make his own observations. "Not what I wanted to hear, but I thank you for your candor."

"Cowboy Creek's a fine place to live, but it won't support an operation like yours. Not with the hunt for coal. You'll have better success somewhere else."

Adam stood. "I'll take what you've said into consideration."

He was at the door when Jason spoke. "One more word of advice. Don't bother with the Frazier woman. She'll lead you on a merry dance."

Something was bothering Deborah. She'd offered little to the dinner conversation and left much of her meal on the patterned china plate. Afterward, when everyone had migrated to the parlor, she'd declined offers to join in games in favor of standing at the windows and gazing mutely out at the street.

Was her encounter with Preston Wells troubling her? Adam hadn't liked what he'd seen in the man's eyes. He was besotted with her, that much was obvious. But was it a normal infatuation or something darker? In his line of work, he'd dealt with more than his fair share of disturbing cases involving men who couldn't handle rejection. Violence was a common outcome. The idea of Deborah being a target made Adam's blood boil.

As for himself, he would never admit it aloud, but his conversation with Russ had sparked major concerns. Perhaps he'd been a shade too confident about his ability to remain impartial. If Allan Pinkerton knew what he was using this time off for, he'd knock him upside the head like an errant child. It was one of the first rules of being a detective: If you get too close to the victims or suspects, you risk letting your emotions overrule your judgment.

He was breaking the rule by investigating a crime against his family. And with Deborah in the picture, he feared he was breaking it again.

"Adam." Hildie nudged him. "It's your turn."

He stared at the chessboard and shot an apologetic look

across the table at Old Horace, who resided at the boarding-house. "I apologize, but I'm finding it difficult to concentrate. Hildie, take over for me, will you?"

Beside him on the settee, she opened her mouth to object. He stood before she had a chance to speak and started to cross the room. Deborah turned, caught his gaze and frowned.

She turned to the rocking chair where Aunt Mae sat knitting a blanket, a gift for Anna and Russell's baby. "I'm going to turn in early."

Aunt Mae's hands stilled. "It's not even nine o' clock yet."

"I have a headache." She fiddled with the rolling pin brooch.

"Oh, you poor dear." She patted her hand. "Perhaps some extra rest will make you feel better. The kitchen was hotter than usual today."

"Thank you."

Adam changed course and met her in the doorway. "Is there anything I can do to help? Prepare you some tea or warm milk?"

Her wide gaze centered on him. "Do you know how?"

He smiled. Her blunt nature didn't bother him. He found it refreshing. "I know enough to keep you from getting thirsty."

"Well, I thank you for the offer, but I don't require anything at the moment."

Adam would've found a way to detain her longer, if not for her pale complexion and the pinched skin around her eyes. Was she truly ill?

He watched her ascend the stairs, his disappointment stemming from the missed opportunity to delve for more answers.

*Are you sure that's the only reason?* a voice wheedled.

*Or is it that you find her fascinating and desire to be in her company?*

Shoving those thoughts aside, he rejoined the others, aware that Deborah's absence put a damper on the evening. The boarders retired to their rooms about an hour later, and Adam sat at the desk inside his and studied his compiled notes. It was nearing eleven when he thought he heard a noise from across the hall.

Deborah.

Dropping his pen into its cylindrical container, he tugged his suspenders into place and shrugged on his vest. Padding over to the door, he eased it open just far enough to afford a sliver of a view. Her door was closed, and the strip beneath was dark. Farther down the hallway near the stairs, the floorboards creaked.

Adam grabbed his boots and slipped into the hallway, his stocking feet whispering against the narrow boards. He paused at the top of the stairs, ears straining to separate the natural groans of the large house from man-made sounds.

*There.* The grind of a metal knob.

Someone was leaving through the kitchen door, and he was certain that someone was Deborah. He didn't have time to return to his room for his weapon. Heart hammering, he descended the stairs, praying he'd catch up to her.

If she was assisting Ogden, she was in danger. A criminal like him used people to get what he wanted and might decide to dispose of anyone he considered no longer important.

He'd stepped into the kitchen when a lamp flared to his right.

"Going somewhere, Adam?"

Clad in her nightdress with her hair covered by a mobcap, Aunt Mae held a lamp high and studied him with eyes of steel. Her room was the only one on the first floor, ostensibly to be close to the kitchen. Adam was convinced it was to also prevent any shenanigans from occurring beneath her roof.

He shifted his boots behind his back. "I confess, I was hungry for more of Deborah's blueberry and basil tart."

"Were you now?" She arched a brow and gestured for him to have a seat at the small, round table in the corner. "You don't mind if I join you, do you?"

Defeat punched at his temples. "Not at all."

His gaze strayed to the far door, feeling the lost opportunity shudder through him and worry congeal in his gut. *What have you gotten yourself into, Deborah?*

## Chapter Seven

Why would Adam try to follow her? Deborah glanced over her shoulder at the light flickering in the kitchen window. Fortunately for her, Aunt Mae had emerged in time to forestall him. She'd heard their voices but hadn't been able to make out the conversation. Tucking beneath her arm the basket she'd prepared after supper and placed in a rarely used cabinet, she walked at a brisk pace until she turned the corner onto Lincoln Boulevard. She would return to the same empty lot behind the Gardners' home once more. If she didn't find a trace of the stowaways, she'd focus her search elsewhere. Or give up and leave the issue to the professionals to solve. That would be the prudent thing to do, but as a runaway herself, she was familiar with the myriad difficulties associated with being far from home. Fear and uncertainty. Sadness. And she was an adult. How much more daunting it must be for children.

The figures of a man and woman melted from the shadows. Deborah recognized the blacksmith and his wife and tried to think of an excuse for being out at such an hour.

"Deborah, is that you?" Beatrix Werner called as they drew closer. Walking beside her, Colton held their son, Joseph. The dark-haired baby rubbed his eyes and yawned widely.

"Hello, Beatrix. Colton." She smiled brightly. "I see I'm not the only one having a restless night."

Beatrix shot a concerned glance at her son. "I believe he has a tooth trying to push through. He's been irritable all week."

Colton rubbed the baby's back in a soothing motion. "We thought Bea's harmonica music would soothe him. When that didn't work, we decided to take a stroll through town."

Though a mountain of a man, Colton looked at ease holding the baby. Deborah had heard the story of how he'd married Beatrix moments before she gave birth to Joseph for the sole purpose of giving the child a name. Midwife Leah Gardner and one of the town's doctors hadn't thought Beatrix would survive long enough to hold her baby. The Austrian woman wasn't as delicate as she looked, however, and she'd pulled through. The pair may have married for an unconventional reason, but they'd fallen deeply in love with each other.

Would she ever experience a deep connection like theirs? Would she even recognize it? She hadn't had a mother to guide her in such things, hadn't had the benefit of parents after whom to pattern a loving marriage. Adam Draper was the first man to breathe hope into her life, the first to inspire a yearning to love and be loved. From the moment he caught her in that ridiculous blindfold, something inside her had strained to get to know him better. It was confusing and frightening and a tiny bit exhilarating. But Deborah wasn't convinced he felt the same way. There were times when he regarded her with what she thought was admiration. Other times, he acted suspicious of her. She didn't blame him. The circumstances of her arrival and her continued evasion of suitors were cause for skepticism.

*Oh, Lucy. I wish you were here so we could hash this out together.*

"Are you sure you should be out alone?" Beatrix asked.

"I couldn't sleep." That was true. "I thought it would be better to get some fresh air and exercise than toss upon my bed for hours."

Beatrix eyed the basket Deborah held, then looked back at her. "Cowboy Creek is safe enough, I suppose—"

"I don't plan on going far." She pointed to the next street corner. "That's my stopping point. Besides, I can scream loud enough to scare the dead."

Colton chuckled, earning a playful swat from his wife when Joseph started fussing and trying to cram his whole fist into his mouth.

"Keep your wits about you," Beatrix advised. "We're going to keep walking. He doesn't seem to like it when we stop."

"I hope he lets you rest at some point."

"As do I," Colton said.

The couple bid her good-night and continued along toward the school. At the corner, Deborah hesitated. But they weren't paying her any attention. She hurried on her way and was soon blocked from view by the Gardners' mansion. Her thoughts strayed to Adam. It was too easy to imagine him cradling a baby to his chest. But he wasn't ready for marriage, he'd told her, much less children. He had other priorities.

A noise in the woods to her left startled her. Edging closer to the trees, she tried to peer through the darkness.

"Shh! She'll hear us!"

Deborah's pulse picked up speed. That was a child's voice.

"But I'm hungry," a second, higher voice whined. "I'd rather go back to Lakewood than starve."

"You don't mean that."

"Hello?" She ventured into the woods, twigs snapping beneath her boots. "I've brought food for you."

Silence greeted her announcement. Somewhere in the distance, an owl hooted.

"I have smoked ham, cheese and fresh baked bread. Molasses cookies, too."

She picked her way closer, still unable to make out their shapes. Without a lamp, the shadows beneath the tree canopy were opaque.

"My name is Deborah." Her skirt caught on a fallen log. "I'm the chief dessert maker for Aunt Mae's boardinghouse."

There was a rustle in the distance, followed by the drubbing of feet. They were running away.

"Please, don't leave! I only want to help!"

She tugged her skirt free and rushed ahead. Her foot sank into a shallow hole, wrenching her ankle. Pain arced up her leg. Sucking in a sharp breath, she managed to keep hold of the basket. Disappointment squeezed her lungs. There'd be no catching them now.

Using a tree trunk to brace herself, she called, "I'll leave the basket here." Her voice trailed off. "In case you decide to come back."

But that wasn't likely.

Deborah limped over to the log and sank onto it. Reaching down, she attempted to massage her sore ankle through her boot. The throbbing ache made the walk back to the boardinghouse seem extralong.

"I like ham."

Deborah whipped her head up. She could barely make out the outline of a small girl.

"Lily! What are you doing?" A slightly larger child, a boy this time judging by the voice, crashed into the clearing. He reached for the girl, but she dodged him.

"I'm hungry, Liam! She has food. And she's nice. She brought us chicken, remember?"

"You found that?" Deborah said, pleased it hadn't gone to waste.

At her question, Liam marched over and seized Lily's arm. "We're leaving. We can't trust her, remember? We can't trust anyone."

Deborah rifled in the basket and located the matches and a candle. The wick caught flame, illuminating the few feet separating them.

She stifled a gasp of dismay. The children were young. Too young to be fending for themselves. They looked alike, with tousled dark hair and thin faces dominated by large, distrustful eyes. Their clothing was tattered and dirty.

Holding out the basket, she urged them to take it. "I don't mind if you eat the cookies first."

Lily's grin transformed her face. "Did you hear that, Liam?" Her hand closing over the handle, she crouched on the ground. "It's been ages since we've had anything sweet besides berries."

Still staring at Deborah, he stopped Lily from rifling through the contents. "We're not eating it here." He craned his neck to peer around them. "She could have the sheriff waiting to haul us off."

Lily nibbled on her lower lip.

"Please don't go." Deborah held up her hand. "No one knows I'm here. I've been looking for you since I heard the rumors about two stowaways. You were on the train that wrecked, right?"

The girl nodded.

"I'm a runaway, too."

Liam sneered. "Grown-ups don't run away." Grabbing the basket, he urged Lily to follow him.

Deborah got quickly to her feet. She moaned.

Lily stopped. "Did you hurt yourself?"

"It's nothing serious." She gestured to their surroundings. "Look, I understand you're scared. I'm certain it's no fun sleeping outdoors. Why don't you accompany me to the boardinghouse? The proprietress, Aunt Mae, wouldn't turn you away. She can be grumpy sometimes, but she's a kind, sympathetic woman. You can have baths and sleep in real beds. There's more food there, too."

"I bet the covers are warm and soft." Lily sighed.

Liam's eyes gleamed in the darkness as he took Deborah's measure. She sensed his hesitation, but ultimately, he jutted his chin and grasped Lily's hand.

"We're leaving."

Deborah couldn't physically compel them to Aunt Mae's, even without a sore ankle. "I wish you'd reconsider."

"And let you send us back to—" He clamped his lips shut. "Uh-uh."

He marched Lily between the trees and deeper into the gloom.

"Thanks for the food, miss," Lily called to her.

"I'll bring more tomorrow night," she answered, holding the candle high.

Feeling bereft, she tarried there for a while in hopes they'd circle back. She finally gave up and limped home. If only she'd been able to persuade them. Given the boy's suspicious nature, she wasn't convinced he'd risk returning to that spot. She may have ruined any chance she had at helping them.

Deborah was alone in the kitchen the next morning when Adam strolled in. The instant he stepped into the room, her body reacted. Her skin prickled. Her face heated. A rush of excitement swept through her.

Adam's presence charged the air with energy.

"Good morning." Somehow, she managed to sound normal and completely unaffected. She focused on flipping the sausage patties one by one in the sizzling skillet. "Aunt

Mae's feeling under the weather this morning, so I have breakfast duty."

"I'm sorry to hear that. How can I help?"

Deborah pointed to the hutch. "You could set the table."

He whistled under his breath as he moved between the kitchen and dining room. By the time he'd finished with that chore, she was transferring the sausage to a serving dish. He came close and flashed a smile that made her knees weak. "That smells delicious."

"Don't steal any," she warned with a wave of the spatula, trying to avoid looking directly into his warm brown eyes.

He was especially inviting today in a cream collared shirt beneath a paisley brown, cream and blue vest and chocolate-brown slacks.

"Hurry up with those flapjacks," he said, nodding to the bowl of batter, "and I won't be forced to."

She twisted around to the stove and winced, the breath hissing through her teeth. The cool compress she'd applied last night hadn't eased the tenderness in her ankle. She'd awoken to find it still swollen and mottled.

"Did you hurt yourself?" Adam circled the table and advanced toward her.

"I wrenched my ankle, that's all. It'll be fine in a day or two."

Frowning, he touched her arm. "Come and sit down. Let me take a look at it."

"No, thank you." The mere thought of Adam's sure fingers removing her boot, then examining her limb made her giddy.

"I'll be gentle, I promise."

"It's not a good idea."

"Why not?"

Deborah waved her hand to encompass him from head to toe. "Because you're too handsome for my peace of

mind, that's why not! When you come near me, I get fluttery inside. I don't wish to add swooning in your arms to
my expanding list of faux pas."

A variety of emotions flashed over his face. Astonish-
ment. Amusement. Longing.

Wait. What?

Before she could determine if she was imagining what
wasn't there, his gaze shifted to the floor beneath their feet,
and his hand passed over his hair and came to rest against
his neck. He swallowed hard. "Deborah…"

Belatedly, she accepted that she shouldn't have admitted those things to him. If Lucy were here, she would've
pull her aside and admonished her.

"I've stunned you speechless, haven't I?" She seized
the bowl of batter from the work surface and went to the
stove. "All I can say is, it's a good thing you're not a doctor. Your female patients wouldn't stand a chance."

She mentally cringed. Like *that* was going to help
smooth over her embarrassment.

"I never aspired to be a doctor," he said at last, his voice
smooth and husky.

The circles of batter expanded and popped in the skillet. "You dreamed of raising cattle instead."

There was a long pause. "I suppose you could say that."
He closed the distance between them. "Deborah?"

"Hmm?" She kept her gaze on the skillet.

His fingers skimmed her cheek, urging her to turn her
head. His expression was solemn. That didn't bode well.

"Deborah, I'm flattered." His gaze roamed her features
as if memorizing them. "But, I—"

"I wasn't angling for an invitation to supper, if that's
what you're thinking. I know nothing romantic can develop between us."

*Do not look at his mouth*, she sternly threatened. *Do*

*not think about how it might feel to be kissed by him. Or held by him.*

"That's not what I was going to say."

"Oh."

"I was going to offer a word of advice. I happen to find your candor refreshing. I like knowing your thoughts and opinions. However, some men might be tempted to take advantage. Do you understand what I'm trying to say?"

Why did his concern have to make her eyes well up with tears?

Footsteps heralded another boarder's arrival and she stepped back, the pain shooting up from her ankle.

"Is something burning?" Sadie entered the kitchen and stopped short. "Oh, excuse me. I apologize if I'm interrupting."

"You're not." Deborah turned to see that the flapjacks were indeed black around the edges. "Well, I've made a mess of these."

Adam stepped close beside her. "Here, let me." He held out his hand for the spatula. "Sadie, would you mind helping me finish breakfast? Aunt Mae is indisposed and Deborah has injured her ankle."

"I thought you could only manage drinks," Deborah said, reluctant to hand over the utensil.

"I know a bit more than I let on." He shrugged. "I learned to cook the basics while in the army."

"Go sit down, Deborah." Sadie's skirts swished as she hurried over. "How did you hurt yourself?"

Adam's features sharpened, and he seemed particularly interested in her answer.

Sinking into one of the chairs, she folded her hands atop the table. "I couldn't sleep last night, so I went outside for a while. I stepped into a hole."

Adam's profile was to her as he scraped out the ruined flapjacks and dropped more batter in the skillet. His lips pursed. Did he suspect she wasn't telling the whole truth? Part of her yearned to tell him about her discovery and enlist his aid. Another part rejected that idea. What if he scared the kids off for good? Or insisted on taking them to the sheriff?

More than likely it was they who had stolen items from the local business owners.

Hildie bounded in the room then, refreshing in a light-weight blue printed cotton dress, and pitched in. Deborah found it difficult to watch the other woman cozy up to Adam. To his credit, he didn't let her marked attention inflate his ego. He was kind without encouraging her.

Once they'd had their fill of coffee and food, Adam asked the others to clean up while he took Deborah to the doctor.

Her hand flew to her throat. "That's not necessary."

"I'd feel better if you got his opinion." The set of his mouth brooked no argument, giving the impression that whenever Adam Draper set his mind to something, there was no swaying him.

"Don't take her to Doc Fletcher," Sadie advised. "Take her to see Marlys Mason. She's a holistic doctor who's done wonders for many in our community."

Placing his cloth napkin beside his plate, he stood and, retrieving his suit jacket from the back of his chair, sunk his arms into the sleeves. He walked around to her chair and rested a hand on the rung. "Which one will it be, Deborah?"

"If I must go, I choose Dr. Mason."

He assisted her through the house, into the front yard and past the gate leading to the boardwalk. Her pace was slower than usual. She tried to mask her discomfort, but he was too perceptive not to notice.

"That's it," he announced suddenly. "I'm carrying you." Before she could protest, he'd hooked one arm behind her back and the other beneath her knees and hauled her into his arms.

"Adam!" Her arms went automatically around his neck, the fine hairs above his collar tickling her skin. "Put me down."

He cocked a brow at her, his brown eyes dancing. "I'd like to get there before noon."

"So you're not doing this to spare me pain?" she demanded, offended he'd shattered her romantic ideals. "You're simply impatient?"

Chuckling, he strode along Eden Street as if carting her around town in his arms was a common occurrence. They passed Sam Woods Mason's newspaper office and the jail. As expected, people gawked. Thankfully, the streets were less crowded on Saturdays.

"You're going to start rumors about us," she told him.

"As long as we know the truth, what anyone else thinks doesn't matter."

Deborah closed her eyes and tried to squelch the disappointment his words engendered. But with the world shut out, her focus switched to Adam's wide, hard chest anchoring her, the absolute strength of his arms around her and the imprint of his hand curved around her ribs. The clean, woodsy scent clinging to his clothing teased her. If she opened her eyes, she'd get a close-up view of his smooth, close-shaven jaw and tanned neck.

"Is this the doctor you want?"

She forced her lids up. "No. Turn right. Marlys has her practice on this street."

They passed several cowboys outside the bathhouse.

"What's this, Miss Frazier?" someone called.

"You're breaking our hearts, you know!"

"What's he got that we don't?"

Adam's stride didn't falter. "Did you ever consider saying yes to one of them? What could one outing hurt?"

What hurt was that the prospect of her being courted by another man didn't faze him in the slightest. She'd obviously gotten the signals wrong. He didn't long for her. He saw her as a fellow boarder, that's all.

"You know, you're right. I shouldn't let my misgivings prevent me from having a little fun."

He slowed. His gaze flicking to hers, he shifted her higher. "On the other hand, you should be careful not to rush into anything serious."

They entered the yard. Adam was out of breath by the time they climbed the porch. He gently set her on her feet.

"Adam, can I ask you something?"

"Of course."

"Have you ever wanted to help someone, but you weren't sure you should?"

The stiffening of his spine was almost imperceptible. "Are you referring to someone undeserving?"

"No, not at all." She regretted broaching the subject. It was just that, of all the people she'd met in Cowboy Creek, Adam was the one she felt closest to. "I meant, what if you wound up making matters worse?"

"I would say it depends on the situation. In my experience, you can't force others to accept your help. But if they're willing, and you're positive you aren't breaking the law by doing so, then I don't see why you shouldn't."

Deborah bit her lip. *Was* she breaking the law by not reporting Liam and Lily? What if their parents were frantically searching for them?

"Deborah?" Adam leaned closer, his gaze consuming her. "If you've gotten yourself into a predicament, you can tell me."

"I—"

The image of Liam's dirt-streaked face, the hollows beneath eyes too mature for his age, gave her pause. First, she had to earn the boy's trust. Only then could she think about involving Adam. "I appreciate your advice. I was asking in theory."

The door swung open and a patient exiting greeted them. "Dr. Mason is in her office."

Adam was quiet as he accompanied her inside. Once Marlys had greeted them and ascertained the problem, he turned to Deborah.

"I'll wait for you outside."

He looked disappointed about something. And worried.

Deborah almost caught his hand and asked him what was bothering him. She dearly wanted to be his friend, someone he could confide in. But how could she expect that from him when she wasn't willing to offer it herself?

## Chapter Eight

He'd thought coming to church would make him feel better. The worship hymns, the gathering of people under one roof to learn about God, the reading of His Word... those things *had* offered him a modicum of comfort. But the knowledge that Zane Ogden was walking around free and hurting other innocent people made it impossible to truly know peace.

Adam glanced beside him. Deborah, fetching as usual in an elegant dress of lavender trimmed in darker purple, sat with her hands folded atop the open Bible on her lap. Her skin was pale and soft-looking. The gold bracelet around her wrist winked in the sunlight slanting through the high windows.

Was Deborah one of Zane Ogden's victims? Had she been tricked into assisting him?

The more time he spent with the delightful baker, the more he began to doubt she'd knowingly assist in an illegal scheme. But she might've fallen prey to Ogden's deceit. Her question yesterday had painted a troubling picture.

After escorting her back to the boardinghouse, he'd spent the rest of the day in various establishments chatting with the locals in the full persona of Adam Draper, enterprising cattleman. He'd attempted to ascertain if there was another woman fitting Deborah's description who might've spent time in Centerville in recent months. He'd eaten lunch at The Lariat, browsed the aisles in Hagermann's and Irving Furniture, pretended interest in a new pair of boots at Godwin's and finished off the fruitless search with supper at The Lariat. That last stop hadn't been without merit. From the porter, he'd gleaned an invaluable tidbit—a pair of brothers from New York City were still in residence. The curious thing was they'd never been seen together.

Time to park himself at the hotel.

Deborah closed her Bible. Amid the congregants' shuffling that signaled the end of the service, a middle-aged gentleman stood to his feet.

"Before we dismiss, I'd like to ask for your prayers."

Reverend Taggart immediately looked concerned. "What's happened, Ezra?"

"Yesterday morning, my hay stores were deliberately set on fire. I lost it all." His weathered face was haggard, but there was a determined glint in his eyes. "I have enough savings to purchase supplies for the winter, but with the recent accidents, I'm worried I'll continue to be targeted."

Grumblings erupted. Adam surreptitiously scrutinized Deborah's reaction. She exuded sympathy for the man's plight, nothing more.

"Accidents, my foot," another man said. "We aren't stupid. Someone's got coal fever, and the ranchers are at risk."

Jason Mitchell caught Adam's gaze and arched a brow. Then he addressed the crowd. "What we should be asking is how come Sheriff Getman hasn't managed to capture the culprits."

"If Noah was still sheriff, he'd have ended this mess already."

Noah Burgess left his pew and strode to the front. "I understand your concerns and frustrations, folks. As a rancher myself, I share them. We have to be patient, however, and let the new sheriff do his job. You can help by keeping your eyes and ears open. He can't be everywhere at once." He turned to Ezra. "Do you have proof that fire was set?"

He nodded. "My hired hand saw someone riding away from the barns right around the time we noticed smoke. We also found the remains of a kerosene-soaked cloth."

Noah's jaw tightened, causing the scarred flesh on one side to pucker. "Can he describe this person?"

Ezra shook his head in defeat. "He was too far away."

Deborah shifted close to whisper in his ear. "This sounds dangerous, Adam. What if you settle here and become a target like the others?"

The light-as-a-feather touch of her cool fingers on his hand coupled with the sweet fan of her breath across his cheek scrambled his thoughts. He willed himself not to turn his head. They were in church, after all. Not alone on Dr. Mason's porch. Holding her in his arms had shifted his mind toward nonprofessional avenues. Her scent had enveloped him, her silken hair teasing his chin, her warm curves tucked against his chest filling him with the yearning to continue holding her indefinitely.

Deborah made him think about the future and how he was no longer content being alone.

*Why her, Lord? Why now?*

There'd been a couple of female Pinkerton agents he was sure had been interested in more than friendship, but he hadn't been of the mind-set to entertain such possibilities. Now, when he was closer than ever to capturing his prey, would his single-minded purpose falter?

Praying for strength, he answered her. "It's not my habit to cower when obstacles arise."

Her delicate fingers curved around his. "I didn't intend to question your courage. I'm simply concerned for your well-being."

Adam couldn't resist. He shifted their clasped hands to the pew between them, where her skirt folds would prevent anyone from seeing, and brushed his thumb over her inner wrist in a slow, repetitive motion. He couldn't look at her, though. If he looked at her, he'd be sure to see the same longing waging war inside her. And he'd be hard-pressed not to kiss the surprise from her beautiful face.

"I'm not offended," he murmured. "I'm grateful you care."

He heard her soft inhale. Was he out of his mind? Hadn't he already told her that romance was out of the question?

His behavior surely confused her. And guilty or not, she didn't deserve to have her feelings trampled.

With immense regret, he released her and busied his hands with his own Bible. Reverend Taggart concluded the service, and conversation replaced the silence. He intercepted Seth's gaze from a nearby pew. His brother's raised brows and pointed nod toward Deborah meant Adam would soon be facing an inquisition.

"The rumors are true, I see," Hildie spat. "You really were biding your time in order to hook a fat fish."

The blonde had trailed after Deborah and Sadie, catching up to them beneath the massive oak in the far corner of the churchyard.

Deborah hugged her Bible to her chest. The heat of the June day closed in on her, causing her nape to become damp. "Excuse me?"

"Don't play coy. You haven't given the cowboys the time of day, and you broke poor Preston's heart." Hands on her hips, disdain twisting her features, she tapped her foot against the hard earth carpeted with lush grass. "And now that a wealthy entrepreneur has come to town, all of a sudden you're interested in courting!"

A man and woman passing by exchanged glances.

Sadie shushed her. "Keep your voice down, Hildie."

"Why should I when I'm speaking the truth?"

Deborah's hand tingled with the remembered imprint of Adam's touch. That stolen caress had sent an exhilarating charge through her. She searched the yard, settling on his familiar profile as he stood talking with a rancher, Seth Halloway. Adam looked solemn. Was Seth warning him against buying in Cowboy Creek?

The thought of him leaving, of never seeing him again, filled her with sadness.

She schooled her features. "Adam and I aren't courting. We're friends."

"You've hoarded his attention from the start."

"Hildie, jealousy isn't becoming of you," Sadie said, drawing a gasp from the other woman. "You can't force Adam and Deborah to cease being friends any more than you can force him to take more than a passing interest in you."

Hildie's cheeks blazed. "I thought we were bound by the same aspirations. I see I've misjudged you both." Whirling on her heel, she flounced off, her wide skirts swinging like a brass bell.

Deborah sought the tree trunk as support. "I hate the idea of being the subject of rumors."

Her friend turned toward her, sympathy wreathing her. "I hate to add salt to the wound, but Hildie has a point. Plenty of people saw Adam carrying you down Eden Street. And the pair of you seemed awfully cozy in there." She gestured to the church building.

"He was carrying me to the doctor," she denied. The poultice Marlys had given her had greatly reduced the swelling in her ankle. The initial pain had lessened into a dull ache. "And we walked over from the boardinghouse. It was natural for us to sit together."

"I see the way you look at him, Deb." Her eyes were

soft with worry. "He intrigues you like no other man in Cowboy Creek has."

Lowering her gaze, she ran her fingers over the uneven bark. "He's not keen to find a wife, at least not yet. And even if he does purchase land, his stay will be temporary. Missouri is his permanent home."

"You sound as if you'd dearly like him to make Cowboy Creek his home."

"This is all very confusing," she admitted, her focus on a grasshopper as it sailed from a tall weed to land beside her boot. "I've never felt this way before."

"You weren't serious about anyone in St. Louis?"

"No."

"Why did you leave?"

Deborah pressed her lips together to keep the tale from spilling out. She'd held it in for two months, shouldering the burden alone. Lucy had always provided a sounding board. Without her to confide in, she was bursting at the seams.

"Why were you dressed in your wedding finery?" Sadie persisted. "You clearly weren't keen to marry. And you've been closemouthed about your life there. I've entertained several scenarios. The most likely one is that you were running from something."

Deborah whipped her gaze to Sadie's. Something in her expression must've clued her in. "What chased you from your home?"

"Not a what. Who." Deborah pushed off the trunk and paced to the edge of the tree's leafy bower. Adam and Seth were both gone. "I was scheduled to be married the day the bride train pulled into the station. I was running from my groom and my father."

Sadie tugged her gently around to face her. "You must've been desperately unhappy to do something so rash."

There was no judgment in her friend's eyes, only the need to understand. "My father betrothed me to his friend and colleague, Tobias Latham. Not only is he the same age as my father, I barely know him."

The entire story came pouring out, including how, after leaving home with nothing but a single satchel, she was walking the streets of St. Louis and came across a discarded train ticket. Desperate to escape, she'd seized the opportunity presented. Sadie listened without interrupting. When Deborah was finished, she pulled her close for a hug.

"I'm glad you told me," she said, easing away. "I do have a question, though. Why are you so afraid of your father finding you? You're a grown woman. He can't force you to marry Tobias or anyone else."

She plucked a leaf off the tree and rubbed the smooth side. "You haven't met my father. He's a forceful man. I've always had difficulty denying him. Add to that the fact that I've been a disappointment my entire life, I find myself searching for ways to earn his approval."

"Let's say you stayed and married the man he chose for you. Would that have been enough? Or would he have asked more of you?"

Deborah's shoulders slumped. "I'm not sure."

But she had a sinking feeling Sadie had a point. Gerard Frazier would've expected her to transform into a brilliant hostess for Tobias and their business associates. He would've also expected her to provide heirs for his friend. A shudder worked its way through her.

Sadie laid a hand on her shoulder. "I've learned that some people are beyond pleasing."

"My sister doesn't struggle the way I do."

"Different children have different relationships with their parents. Deborah, you have to be true to yourself. Follow your own hopes and dreams. Your father may continue to try to control you, or he may ultimately realize that he's wrong. Who knows? In choosing your own path, you might win his grudging respect."

An impossible goal, she feared. "All I know is that I'm not ready to face him."

Nor was she ready to put distance between herself and Adam, despite the speculation swirling around them. She'd simply have to be ever mindful of the many reasons they could only be friends. A future with Adam was about as likely as her father bestowing his love and approval upon her after a lifetime of dissatisfaction.

Sadie linked their arms. "I'll be praying for you, my friend. God will grant you wisdom. All you have to do is ask."

They returned to the boardinghouse and helped Mae prepare the noon meal. Hildie did not appear, and neither did Adam. Had Hildie invited him to dine with her at one of the hotels?

Deborah shoved the thought out of her head. She had more important things to worry about. Namely, two children wandering the town without supervision.

To fill the hours until sunset, she and Sadie went berry picking. After her friend left to meet Walter at The Cattleman, Deborah sat in the parlor and wrote her sister a letter. The big house was quiet. While Aunt Mae rested, she experimented with a new dessert idea. The task invited thoughts of Adam and their first meeting. She hadn't known him long, and yet he'd made a profound impact on her.

He didn't show for supper. Hildie hadn't yet returned, either. The meal was a subdued affair. Deborah insisted on doing the cleanup herself, which would give her a chance to pack another basket for Liam and Lily.

The moment the sun slipped below the horizon, she set out. It didn't take her long to reach the woods where she'd first encountered them. This time, she carried a lamp. She didn't want to aggravate her injury.

But they didn't show. After a half hour of pacing and jumping at every sound, she decided to expand her search. The temptation to quit assailed her more than once. She ignored it. Liam and Lily needed her.

Another hour passed as she explored the vacant, overgrown lots closer to the smelly stockyards. Her ankle began protesting in a major way. Her oil was getting low, too. When a cloud passed in front of the moon, discouragement filled her.

*God, please lead me in the right direction. These kids are hungry and dirty and scared. They're runaways, like me. Help me help them.*

She stood in the midst of a small clearing, unsure which way to turn.

The clouds glided beyond the moon, and there in the pale light stood a tent.

She'd found their hideout.

## Chapter Nine

"It's too early to go to sleep, Liam. Please light a candle."

"Someone might see us," he said, his voice strained and thin.

Hearing their voices, Deborah crept closer, trying to formulate a greeting that wouldn't send them screaming into the night. They were inside the tent, the flaps pinned back to admit air.

"I don't want to stay in here anymore. It's dirty and there are bugs."

She pictured the slight girl crossing her arms in a huff.

"I know." Liam's tone softened. "But this is better than—"

"What is it?"

"Shh. I think I heard something."

Deborah took a steadying breath and stepped forward. "Hello? Liam? Lily? It's me, Deborah. I've brought more food for you."

The kids spilled from the tent and gaped at her.

Setting her basket and lamp on the ground, she removed an old tablecloth she'd unearthed in Aunt Mae's pantry and smoothed it on the grass. "I've already eaten, but I'd like to keep you both company. I've never had a moonlit picnic."

Lily inched forward. "Did you bring more cookies?"

Deborah smiled. "I brought something better. Dried apple and walnut cake."

"Did you hear that, Liam?"

The boy stood silent and still, his fists bunched at his sides, his expression unreadable. The sight broke her heart. Someone had acted atrociously toward these kids to engender such distrust.

Acting as if her welcome was assured, she unloaded the shallow pails and thin dishes. "I hope you like beef. Aunt Mae made a roast with carrots and potatoes."

Someone's stomach growled. Ignoring it, Deborah continued in a cheerful tone. "There are yeast rolls, corn on the cob and pickled okra. I'm not sure if you like pickled okra. Personally, I prefer to eat it coated in cornmeal and fried." Once everything was arranged, she sat back on her haunches and regarded them with a smile. "You don't have to eat everything. Just take what you want."

Lily fell to her knees on the cloth and snatched a roll. "This is so good!" she groaned. "Liam, you have to try one."

"Why are you helping us?" he said.

She got more comfortable and clasped her hands atop her legs. "Because, like you, I'm far from my home and family. I didn't plan to come here. I found a discarded ticket and used it for the same train you were on."

Lily polished off her roll. Deborah handed her a plate and spoon. After initial hesitation, she took them and eagerly dished out hefty portions. Liam didn't move. Beneath the messy fringe of his hair, his big eyes were fixed on Deborah.

"Unlike you, I have a nice room to call my own. I have plenty of food. And I have friends. I'd like to be your friend, if you'll let me."

"My sister and I don't need nobody but each other."

"You've done a good job taking care of her." Reaching

across, she chose a roll, tore off a small bit and popped it in her mouth. "That tent's a great shelter for summer. I once slept in a tent with my sister. I was nine." She smiled in remembrance. "We begged our parents to let us sleep in the garden. My mother agreed, even though my father was against the idea. We had the best time." They'd spent the night in relative comfort, having toted their bedding outside, along with books and dolls. Their mother had asked cook to prepare an assortment of treats. Deborah recalled her father's ill mood and frowned. "That was our last summer with her. She passed away a couple of months later."

Lily stopped midchew and tossed a glance at her brother. "Our ma's gone, too. She and Pa died of the sickness."

It was as she'd expected. They were orphans. But what had led them to hide on a train to Cowboy Creek? "I'm sorry to hear that."

Liam trudged closer until the tips of his boots met the blanket. "Why did you run? Was someone mean to you?"

"No. I had a disagreement with my father." It sounded ridiculous put like that. And immature. "Instead of staying and sorting it out, I bolted."

"Does he know where you are?"

"Um, no. I've been in communication with my sister, however." She picked up the second plate and held it out. "Eat up, Liam. Before your sister eats it all."

To her surprise, he did as she suggested. Her heart softened like room temperature butter as he gobbled down the meat and vegetables.

"You know, that tent is great during summer. Once it turns cold, it won't be enough to keep you warm."

"We'll manage somehow," the boy replied.

"How long have you been on your own?"

The pair's forks ceased moving, and they shared matching expressions of foreboding.

"I want to help you," she told them. "I can't do that if you refuse to tell me what brought you here."

"Do it, Liam." Lily looked at Deborah with eyes full of hope.

"You won't turn us in?" Liam asked.

"I'll promise not to go to the sheriff if you promise not to run away again."

Emotions warred on his face. He didn't trust her. Not completely. "Okay." The boy's head dipped, and he set his plate aside. "We're Liam and Lily Quinn. After our parents died, our great-aunt and -uncle took us in. They didn't really want us. They made us clean from dawn to dusk and wouldn't let us go to school." His hands balled. "I overheard them making plans to ship us off to new families who'd pay handsomely for us."

"They were going to separate you?" Sell them off like prized cattle? Her dismay leached into her voice.

He lifted his gaze, swirling with fear and fierce determination. "I couldn't let them."

"Of course not." Her spirit heavy, she studied their disheveled appearance. "How long ago was this?"

"A little more than two months."

This boy had been forced to shoulder adult responsibility, to lose his childlike innocence far before his time. "So you left your guardians and found your way onto the train."

He nodded, guilt pinching his features. "I know we did wrong, not paying for the ride. But we had to get away from there."

"Thank you for telling me." Deborah was quiet as they finished their meal. Inside, her mind was spinning. What should she do? She'd made a promise not to involve the sheriff. She couldn't tell anyone about her discovery until she'd formulated a plan.

Adam had snuck into countless hotel rooms and private homes during his Pinkerton career. Not once had his conscience balked. Being in Deborah's room without her knowledge was having a strange effect on him, however. He felt dirty, as if he was a criminal himself.

*It's because you like her. You've developed feelings for her. Deep down, you believe she's innocent.*

If she was innocent, where did she go at this time of night?

"Let's just get this over with," he muttered.

Calling forth his professional training, he lit one wall sconce and began his search. The hulking wardrobe opposite the bed contained nothing more than dresses, blouses and skirts. Her floral scent surrounded him, distracting him. Quickly moving on to the walnut dresser beside the window, he skimmed the drawers' contents and pulled them out to check for items adhered to the inner panels. There was nothing.

His relief was hampered by the fact that he was in here in the first place. She'd be horrified if she knew. And hurt.

He glanced at the dark night visible through the patterned curtains. Was she with Ogden at this very moment? Denial warred with worry. Was she safe?

Beneath the bed, he spotted a large black trunk and maneuvered it onto the oval rug. The house's occupants were in their rooms, having retired over an hour ago. Occasional creaks and groans echoed through the space. Grateful there was no lock, he eased open the lid and received a shock. He choked back an indelicate exclamation.

With unsteady hands, he lifted the white silk and lace creation and laid it atop the maroon bedcovers. A wedding dress. *Deborah's* wedding dress.

Adam's gut churned. While he'd heard of her bride train attire, he hadn't fully entertained the ramifications. All sorts of crazy thoughts assailed him. Deborah had her quirks, it was true, but she was a rational woman, and rational women didn't hop onto a train wearing an immaculate wedding dress.

Had Zane Ogden proposed marriage as a way to enlist her aid? His gut churned. Perspiration dotted his forehead. Were they already married?

No. She couldn't be that good of an actress. Could she?

He was personally vested in this case's outcome. Russell was right. He'd become obsessed with discovering what truly happened to their father. Was his judgment trustworthy?

Adam was so wrapped up in his thoughts, he didn't at first hear the approaching steps. By the time they registered, he had mere seconds to stuff the dress into the trunk, shove it into place and duck into the wardrobe. His heart throbbed against his chest as Deborah entered the room.

If she discovered him, she'd scream the walls down and never speak to him again.

Through a pencil-thin slit, he watched as she sank into the desk chair, removed a parchment and began scrawling a message. She sniffled. Swiped at her eyes. Witnessing her distress and not being able to offer her comfort bothered him.

*What if she's crying over Ogden?*

He'd heard rumblings of a former Pinkerton agent who'd gotten entangled in a suspect's web. Adam couldn't let a failure like that sully his reputation and cancel out the good work he'd done until this point. He couldn't let Ogden ruin this part of his life, too.

Ten, maybe fifteen minutes passed. Perspiration dotted his skin. His legs and back started to protest his hunched position. *Lord, let her realize she's hungry and needs a late-night snack. I have to find a way out.*

She dropped her writing utensil and folded the missive with clean, even lines, then stood and arched her back, reaching behind to massage the stiff muscles. What now? Would she cross to his hiding spot in search of her night-clothes? He considered his options. Wait here in this spot and give her a fright she'd never forget? Or abandon his hiding place and attempt to curtail her scream in order to deliver a believable explanation?

The only believable one was the truth. He could imagine how well that would be received. *Trust me, Deborah, I don't make a habit of hiding in women's rented rooms. I'm simply here to spy on you and ascertain whether or not you're colluding with the enemy.*

To his amazement, she curled onto her side atop the bedcovers without bothering to snuff out the lamps. Time slowed to a crawl. Any minute now, she was going to get up and prepare for the night.

Her deep, rhythmic breathing reached him after some time had passed. He gripped the wardrobe door's edge. She'd fallen asleep?

Adam waited another interminable amount of time to be certain before easing the doors open. The waft of cooler air was most welcome. Moving stealthily, he righted the wardrobe doors and started for the entrance to the room. But the letter beckoned him. The single bit of parchment could unlock her secrets.

Changing course, he was at the desk when he made the mistake of glancing over at her. Every misgiving receded at the sight of her in repose. Sleep enhanced her innate air of vulnerability. Her beauty ensnared him, lured him closer. Almost before his steps registered, he was at her side, his fingers outstretched to test the softness of her cheek.

At the last second, he snatched back his hand. What he was he doing?

He had to leave. Now.

Snaring the thin blanket from the footboard, he laid it over her and left her room, wondering if he would ever regain his professional footing or if this case would prove his downfall.

## Chapter Ten

"Can we, Uncle Adam?"

Adam set his glass between his plate and the basket of dwindling biscuits. He looked at the mischievous-eyed boy seated directly across from him. "You'll have to forgive me, Harper. My mind was elsewhere. What is it that you're keen to do?"

The five-year-old glanced uncertainly at his new parents, Seth and Marigold. Perhaps he wasn't accustomed to apologies from adults. There'd been a couple of young drummer boys in the war. Other than that, Adam hadn't spent much time in the company of children. He was fascinated and—dare he say it—slightly intimidated by the three little brothers whom Seth had "inherited" from a former friend.

"I'm new to this uncle business. I'm counting on you and your brothers to guide me." His smile encompassed the boys as well as Violet, Marigold's young niece. The child had recently lost her only living parent and come to live with Marigold before being adopted by the couple.

The oldest and most serious of the boys, Tate, nodded sagely. "You can count on us, sir."

Little John, the three-year-old, leaned into Marigold's side and hid his face. Marigold curved her arm around his thin shoulders and hugged him close. Adam caught the affectionate smiles she and Seth exchanged and experienced a stirring of longing.

Thoughts of Deborah taunted him. His mouth went dry. He couldn't stop thinking about that wedding dress. After that close call in her room Sunday, he'd kept busy the past three days, spending as little time in her presence as possible. If she'd noticed, she'd made no indication. In fact, she'd been more distracted than usual.

Contemplating the food remaining on his plate, he wondered how he'd manage to finish it.

Seated beside him, his mother tapped his wrist. "Is everything all right, Adam?"

All right? No. Nothing had been right since he'd arrived in Cowboy Creek and encountered a woman who'd upended his world.

"The meal is delicious. I've simply lost my appetite."

Evelyn's hazel eyes communicated concern.

He patted her hand. "I'm fine, Ma. Out of sorts, that's all."

"What are sorts?" Harper looked to Seth for an explanation. "Did he lose them? I can help you look, Uncle Adam."

As Marigold chuckled and Seth's eyes twinkled, Adam replied, "Marigold will explain it while you help your grandmother wash the dishes."

The meal ended soon after, to Adam's relief. His brother invited him out to the barn. The sun was an orange-yellow ball hanging above the horizon, yet the stifling heat lingered. Seth stopped at the corral closest to the barn and offered a small carrot to the sorrel mare who ambled over to greet them.

"What's troubling you, Adam?"

Propping his arms on the top fence rung, he gazed across the verdant fields. "This case. I paid a visit to the newspaperman, Sam Woods Mason. He proved too discerning for me to get anywhere."

"Not surprised. He's a professional through and through."

"I'm not making progress with the ranchers, either. I'm an outsider."

Seth nodded. "It was the same way in Missouri, remember? We didn't welcome strangers with open arms. Not until we took their measure."

"I remember."

Being on this ranch was bringing memories to the forefront. While this spread was considerably smaller than their previous holdings, it was a prime spot to ranch and raise a family. For a brief moment, he entertained thoughts of the future, beyond the capture of his most elusive prey. He hadn't even heard of Cowboy Creek two months ago, but it was growing on him. He'd lived apart from his family for too long.

"You're part of the community," he told Seth. "The locals trust you. Would you consider asking around to see if anyone can give a good description of the Maroni brothers?"

"Of course." His jaw firmed. "I want Ogden behind bars as much as you do."

"I know. I'm sorry for the things I said all those years ago."

"No more apologies or lamenting the past. Let's focus on the present."

The horse nudged Adam's elbow. Straightening, he rubbed her neck and mane. "I don't have any treats for you, old girl."

Seth crossed his arms. Beneath his battered Stetson, his eyes assumed an indiscernible gleam. "Now that you've told me about the case, why don't you tell me what's really put that glum expression on your face?"

"I don't know what you're talking about."

"I've never known you to turn away Ma's cooking." One brow inched up. "Is a certain baker giving you problems?"

"You've spoken to Russell, haven't you?" Adam let out an exasperated sigh. Confidentiality hadn't ever been their strong suit. "He told you about my suspicions."

"He was upset that you suspect Deborah."

"How can I not when she keeps slipping out of the boardinghouse after dark and acts jumpy if anyone questions her?" The frustration he'd wrestled with for days leaked into his tone. Never before had he yearned for someone to be innocent.

"You could tell her the truth about why you're here. Gauge her reaction."

"And risk destroying my biggest case?"

His face wreathed in sympathy, Seth said, "You're not getting paid. No one hired you. The Pinkertons aren't counting on you. If you've developed feelings for this woman, I wouldn't blame you for being tempted to give up the chase."

"Give up?" The notion was foreign to him. "And let Ogden go unpunished?"

"You've devoted years of your life to hunting him. He's the inadvertent reason you joined the army. When will it end, Adam? When will you cease letting Ogden dictate your decisions?"

"I'm not doing this just for me. I'm doing this for you and Russ and Ma." His gut churned. "Pa deserves justice. We all know he didn't run off in shame. Ogden murdered him. He hid the body, cheating him of a proper burial, and spread lies that tarnished the Halloway name. I won't stop until Ogden is either behind bars or six feet under."

His brother looked torn. "I respect your commitment to our family's legacy. I admire your grit and single-minded determination. And I know that as long as he's free, other innocent people are at risk at falling victim to his schemes. But you're my little brother. I hate to admit this, but I wish someone else could assume responsibility. I'm afraid this worthy cause has become an obsession."

Overwhelmed, Adam's mind emptied of rational argument. Seth's praise meant a lot. Before he could protest the obsession accusation, a lone rider appeared on the lane leading from town.

"You expecting company?"

"No." Seth squinted into the distance. "I see the glint of a badge. Must be the sheriff. Can't imagine what would bring him here."

Alarm skittered along Adam's spine. "We're not supposed to know each other."

Seth shot him a sideways glance. "Allow me to have a try at pretense."

The sheriff rode into the yard in a cloud of dust. His brief greeting was accompanied by marked curiosity. Adam had yet to make the man's acquaintance and had planned to stop in his office later that day. The sheriff's unexpected visit would save him a trip, but would he accept whatever explanation Seth cooked up?

Seth gestured in an offhand manner. "Sheriff Getman, have you met Adam Draper? He's in town to survey available land parcels for his ranching business."

Looking Adam up and down, the sheriff gripped the saddle horn. "I've seen you around. Welcome to Cowboy Creek."

"In light of recent incidents, he's not sure settling here is in his best interest."

Adam nodded. "That's assuming I can even find land. Rumors are it's scarce."

Something flickered in the older man's gaze, something that aroused Adam's suspicions. "You're thorough,

I give you that. Are you riding around interviewing all
the ranchers?"

"Would that be a problem, Sheriff?"

He spat a stream of tobacco juice into the dirt. "They're
an unsettled group. Some, like Mr. Halloway here, might
not be disturbed by a stranger poking his nose into town
business. Others might get spooked. I'd rather you direct
your inquiries to me."

His conviction that the sheriff was dirty deepened. "I
understand. The last thing I want is to cause further trouble. However, you'll understand my motives. An ounce of
prevention is worth a pound of cure."

"Cowboy Creek has become a popular place. The rumors are true. There's little land to be had at the moment.
If you'd like, I can contact my associates in Centerville to
see what the ranching landscape is like there."

Centerville. The same town Ogden and his female accomplice had been. Interesting.

"That's thoughtful of you. I'd appreciate any help you
can give."

The house door slammed, followed by the pattering of
feet. "Pa, can we go riding now with Uncle—"

"Go back into the house, Harper." Seth angled toward
the porch, his demeanor casual but firm. "I've got guests.
I'll be inside in a few."

Adam focused on keeping his muscles loose and his
face blank, all the while praying the new sheriff hadn't
snagged on that one condemning word. When Harper complied, Seth turned to Adam and extended his hand. "Nice
to talk with you, Mr. Draper. I wish you well in your business venture."

Adam shook it. "I appreciate your time."

"For a fellow Missouri man, of course," Seth replied.

Bidding both men goodbye, Adam crossed to the hitching post, the weight of the sheriff's stare burning into his

back. He left Seth's property with a heavy spirit. He wished his brother hadn't mentioned Missouri. If Ogden got wind that his past had collided with his present, he could very well fly the coop.

Deborah hadn't intended to enter Mr. Lowell's bakery. She'd used it as a means of escape. Hiding behind a dusty hutch, she watched Adam stalk past the windows. Only when she was certain he was gone did she release her breath and turn to find sisters-in-law Anna and Marigold Halloway watching her from their table.

"Is everything all right?" Marigold inquired, her red-gold brows lifted high.

Feeling ridiculous, Deborah nodded. "Quite right. I, ah, was simply overtaken with the urge for a cinnamon bun." She pointed to the half-eaten pastry on Marigold's plate.

Anna rested her hand on her gently rounded middle, her wedding ring winking in the light. "Was someone bothering you, Deborah? If so, I'm sure Russell would have a word with the gentleman."

"That's thoughtful of you to offer, but there's no need."

Deborah glanced out the window once more, hoping her inner turmoil didn't show on her face. She wasn't sure what had spurred her to evade him. He hadn't been around much the last few days, and when he had, he hadn't acted like himself. She missed their talks, missed the warmth in his eyes and his smile. Deborah had gotten the sense that he was angry with her, but she hadn't mustered the courage to confront him.

When she'd glimpsed him headed her way with that unsettling, intense expression marring his handsome face, she'd acted without thought. And now the Halloway women were concerned she was being harassed.

They invited her to join them. She accepted, thinking

some time spent in their company would distract her from her own problems.

But as soon as the pleasantries were exhausted, Marigold mentioned Adam.

"We're aware you haven't been interested in any one suitor yet, but you should know about the rumors swirling around town. You're being linked to Adam Draper."

Deborah wasn't ignorant of the rumors. She simply didn't know how to respond because, deep down, she wished they were true.

She sipped the weak tea and grimaced. It appeared Mr. Lowell also needed instruction on how to brew a proper cup.

"Mr. Draper and I are acquaintances." Until Sunday, she would've labeled what they had as a budding friendship. Now, she wasn't certain that was the case. Not with his wavering mood and mystifying behavior. "He's a gentleman, and that's the only reason he was carrying me to the doctor."

The sisters-in-law exchanged what looked to be silent but significant communication.

A crease dug between Marigold's brows. "You don't harbor romantic inclinations for him, then?"

Anna leaned forward in her chair. "He strikes me as a good man. However, he's not a local. Who knows where he'll wind up once his business in Cowboy Creek is concluded."

"We don't want to see you get hurt," Marigold tacked on.

There was something beneath the surface, some hidden meaning that eluded her. Deborah replaced her cup in the chipped saucer. "I appreciate your concern. I realize my reluctance to be courted is confusing everyone. I thought I was ready to leap into marriage, but I'm not."

Anna patted her hand. "I understand. Although Russ

and I already knew each other when we wed, I was nevertheless apprehensive about entering into a marriage of convenience."

"Looking at the two of you now, one would never guess you didn't marry for love," Marigold declared, her smile sentimental. No doubt she was thinking of her own husband, as well.

Deborah refused to feel sorry for herself. The twinge of longing was unexpected, however, especially as it was centered around the one man who didn't want a bride.

She lingered for another quarter of an hour before excusing herself. Not ready to return to the boardinghouse, she decided to head to the river by way of alleys and side streets. On the edge of town, she was passing the cabinetmaker's place when she collided with a wall of muscle.

Her gasp was swallowed by surprise. The mountain of a man who'd rounded the corner was a stranger to her. Wearing an expensive suit and black bowler hat, he had a narrow, craggy face with pronounced nose and jutting chin. His eyes flared with irritation.

"E-excuse me. I didn't see you."

His scowl deepened. "Watch where you're going next time."

"Don't mind him," a feminine voice chimed. "He's grumpy because he missed the noon meal."

Deborah turned to the young woman joining him. Slight of frame and short like Deborah, she also had fair skin and dark hair. The similarities between them ended with the other woman's eyes and oddly shaped mouth. Still, from a distance, they could be mistaken for sisters. How curious.

The brunette didn't seem to notice. Or perhaps she was in a rush to find sustenance for her companion. "Sorry to disturb you." Linking arms with him, she urged him along the street.

The man allowed himself to be led away, but he glanced

back at Deborah. Her scalp prickled. She couldn't decipher his expression. Was he intrigued by their resemblance?

Something about him bothered her, which didn't make sense. Shaking off the strange encounter, she continued on her way.

Adam hid in the trees behind the boardinghouse. Tonight, he would wait for Deborah to leave the house. He would follow her. He would finally discover her secret.

He was out of patience.

Did she think he hadn't seen her duck into that bakery? Did she think he didn't know she was avoiding him?

A burning sensation crawled through his chest and up his throat. He was going to develop an ulcer before this case was over.

He glanced at the stars in all their glory. *Is it so wrong to want answers, Lord? To seek justice? My family needs closure, Father. I need to know what Ogden did to my pa.*

Only then could Adam find peace.

The minutes ticked away. One by one, the lights in the windows winked out. From his vantage point, he had a clear view of the veranda and kitchen door. Deborah had used this exit the last time. If she chose a different route, he'd be hard put to follow her.

No matter. He'd stand out here every night until Christmas if it meant solving the puzzle.

The creak of the porch slats reached him. There, bathed in weak moonlight, was his primary suspect. His beautiful, fascinating suspect.

Adam massaged his temples to try to relieve his headache.

He pressed against the tree trunk as she neared, his gaze soaking in every detail. When she'd passed the yard, he sidled between the trees and left through the gate, making sure no one was around to see him trailing her.

Adam followed at a safe distance, the anticipation racing through his veins at odds with the dread making him break into a cold sweat. He had opposing goals, his desire to capture his enemy warring with the desire to protect Deborah.

Once again, she walked in the direction of the Gardners' home. But this time she continued toward the stockyards. When she veered into the copse on her left, he removed his revolver from its holster.

Deborah wove through the woods as if following a mental map. How many times had she visited Ogden?

Her wedding dress flashed into his memory, fueling wild speculation. Were they more than coconspirators? Was she infatuated with a cold-blooded killer? Although intelligent, Deborah was a bit naive.

Adam gritted his teeth. This wasn't helping.

In a little clearing, she paused and looked around. Then she bent low and, ducking beneath a branch, entered a lopsided, tattered tent.

Adam's grip on his weapon became slippery. His throat dried. Getting a better grip on the handle, he prayed for the strength to do what needed to be done, even if it was difficult. Even it damaged his soul in the process.

"This is for you, Pa," he whispered.

He crept closer and, with one final plea, pushed his way into the tent.

What he was expecting to see didn't align with what he encountered.

A pair of kids took one look at his gun—aimed directly at them—and screamed. Deborah twisted to face him, her face as white as a sheet. Her basket slammed to the ground, contents spilling across the dirt.

"Adam!" Her eyes went wide with fright. "What are you doing?"

The boy seized the girl's arm and, pulling aside a slit in the rear panel, pushed her through it. He scurried after her.

Deborah scrambled on her hands and knees. "Lily! Liam! Wait!"

Adam grabbed her arm. "Deborah, who are those kids?" *Where's Ogden?* The words echoed in his mind.

She wrenched free and glared at him. "Orphans who were just beginning to trust me, that's who."

Leaving the tent the same way the kids had, she didn't offer further explanation. Adam holstered his weapon and dashed outside. It didn't take long to catch up to her.

The stench of hundreds of cattle slammed into him. Not far in the distance, he could see the fences that kept them contained and the sharp, pointed horns that lent them their name.

"No, don't go in there!" Deborah was yelling, her breath coming in uneven pants.

Adam saw the boy glance back and, registering their pursuit, pump his legs faster. Together, the kids sprinted toward the pens, straight for a mass of longhorns that could trample them within the space of a minute.

## Chapter Eleven

Liam and Lily were headed into danger. Disregarding her warnings, they flew toward the fences holding in cattle with razor-sharp horns and enough bulk to crush a child. Deborah knew Adam wouldn't hurt them, but they didn't. All they knew was a stranger had invaded their hideout and waved a gun in their faces.

Adam owed her answers. But first, they had to stop the siblings. If the children managed to escape the pens unharmed, they'd run and not stop. Her chance to help them would be lost.

Deborah's layers upon layers of undergarments hampered her progress. Adam didn't have that problem. His longer legs gave him an advantage, too. He was closing in on Lily.

The girl noticed the distance diminishing and screamed for her brother. The antsy cattle lowed their displeasure. Liam yelled for her to hurry. He lunged, grabbed her arm and hustled her beneath the fence and into the pen.

"Stop!" Adam called, his steps slowing. "I'm not going to hurt you!"

Deborah reached his side, her breath coming in short bursts, fear sending icy shards through her veins.

The kids didn't listen. They ran into the midst of the

heavy-footed animals. Deborah noticed the instant Lily registered the sheer size of the cattle. Liam became aware of this new danger around the same time, his thin face strained, his mouth sagging.

The cattle were moving in erratic circles, their lows becoming a cacophony as they tried to get away from the intruders.

One bumped into Lily, nearly knocking her off her feet. She clung to her brother's arm and started crying. They kept inching farther away from the fence, increasing the distance between them and safety.

Deborah must've made a sound, because Adam turned to her, his eyes gleaming like coals in the near-darkness. "What are their names?"

"Liam and Lily. They're siblings."

He pushed his hat into her hands.

"What are you—"

He didn't wait for her to finish. Climbing over the fence, he dropped into the pen. On the edge of the mass, animals pushed and strained to get away. If they broke into a full-out stampede, all three would be in grave danger.

"Liam? Lily?" Adam spoke in a firm, low tone. He walked with measured steps. "I'm Adam, Deborah's friend."

Two animals trapped the kids between them.

Lily cried out for Deborah. Hiking up her outer skirts, she planted one boot on the fence. Adam whipped around and jerked a finger at her. "Don't."

"She needs me."

"I'll get them out."

Torn, Deborah gripped the post. Adam was an expert on cattle. He worked with them every day and would be able to anticipate their behavior. As she watched him weave through the crowded pen, her heart shuddered with dread.

*Please, God, guide his footsteps. Bring all three to safety.*

Somewhere near the stockyard offices, raucous laughter rang out. Gunshots rent the air. The successive blasts reverberated through the night, spooking the already nervous longhorns.

Their legs became a blur of movement. Dust stirred in choking clouds. Bits of earth and grass were dislodged.

Adam didn't flinch. Instead, he continued into the fray.

Deborah felt helpless and she hated it. She couldn't see Liam and Lily, couldn't hear them over the noise. She kept her gaze pinned on Adam, who was getting knocked and jostled. At one point, a horn tip scraped his face.

Above the rumble of thundering hooves, she thought she heard his voice.

Then he was gone from view. Deborah clambered onto the fence.

"Adam!"

Had he been pushed to the ground?

A lone cow veered toward her, but her attention was focused on the last spot he'd been. She jumped into the fray. Her pulse thundered loud enough to be heard above the noise.

He couldn't be trampled. Who'd tease her about her desserts? Comfort her when she was sad? Boost her confidence?

*God, please...*

One second, all she could see were horns gleaming white and deadly in the moonlight. The next, Adam loomed out of the morass, Liam and Lily on either side of him, tucked in the haven of his arms.

As they neared, Adam noticed her new position and scowled. Blood dripped down his cheek.

"I thought I told you stay put."

"I thought you'd been trampled."

Though she was tempted to throw her arms around his neck, she turned her attention to the kids. They looked fine aside from scrapes and bruises. Adam boosted Liam and Lily over the fence. Then his hand closed over Deborah's.

"You okay?" he asked gruffly.

"I'm fine."

Once on the other side, Lily latched on to Deborah's waist and sobbed.

She smoothed the girl's hair. "You're safe now, sweetheart."

Liam took another step, his right leg buckling. A gasp of pain ripped from his lips.

Adam crouched beside him. "What hurts?"

He cradled his leg. "My knee."

"It's a long walk to the boardinghouse," Adam told him. "Let me carry you."

"You promise not to turn us in to the sheriff?"

"You can trust us," Deborah cut in. "Isn't that right, Adam?"

His features solemn, he retrieved his hat from where she'd dropped it. "That's right. I apologize for scaring you."

Lily swiped at her eyes. "And for ruining our supper?"

Surprise lifted Adam's brows. The corner of his mouth curved.

"All she ever thinks about is her stomach," Liam grumbled.

Adam hefted the boy into his arms. "I did make a mess of your meal. Not to worry, we'll remedy that as soon as we reach Aunt Mae's."

Relief combined with exhaustion kept Deborah off balance. Ascending the rarely used staircase on the rear west corner of the house, she marveled at the sudden twist of events. Adam knew about the Quinn orphans. She wasn't alone. Their well-being didn't fall squarely on her shoulders anymore.

Liam and Lily were safe. She was willing and eager to fill the role of nurturer. First, she had to convince Adam that keeping their presence a secret was vital for the time being.

Easing open the door to her room, her arms laden with a tray of food, she discovered a sight that made her heart melt. Liam was perched on the lone cushioned chair, the high back and wide arms emphasizing his frail, small body. Adam knelt before him, one knee balanced on the floor as he examined the boy's bruised knee.

Lily stood off to the side. Dust smudged her nose and forehead, her brown hair was a nest of tangles and her already ratty clothes had sustained a tear. When the aroma of the meat and its juices reached her, she raced over, her blue gaze fastened onto the plates piled with leftovers.

Deborah led her over to the desk. Lily dug in without waiting for permission or pausing to say a blessing.

Tears stung her eyes. What hardships they must've endured these past months.

"Go ahead and eat your fill. Now that you're with me, you won't have to worry about going hungry."

"I've never had meat like this," the girl enthused between bites. "Aunt Laura usually gave us pinto beans and stale corn bread."

Across the room, Adam lifted his head and observed them both. It was impossible to guess his thoughts. He looked as if he'd survived a barroom brawl. His hair was mussed. Dirt coated his boots and pants. There was a rip in the side seam of his shirt. The gash across his cheekbone had ceased bleeding, but already the skin around it was turning an awful purple shade.

She wouldn't soon forget his actions. He'd set his own

safety aside for a pair of kids he'd never met. The cattle-man possessed a heroic heart.

Deborah brought Liam's food over to him. Adam took up position beside the window and folded his arms across his chest as he surveyed the trio.

"Who wants to tell me what the three of you have been up to?"

Since neither of the kids dared look at Adam, Deborah sucked in a deep breath. "Liam and Lily fled an untenable situation and wound up here."

Liam found his voice. "If you try to send us back, we'll run away again."

"I can't help if I don't know details."

Deborah crouched beside the chair. Liam's blue eyes latched on to hers. She could see the battle waging inside him, the wariness forged by mistreatment, the drive to protect his younger sister, the unspoken cry of a boy who simply wanted to be a kid again.

"You can't run forever, Liam." The hypocrisy of her own words made her throat seize.

His gaze roamed her face for long moments. Frowning, he put down his fork.

"Our parents died on the same night, about an hour apart."

Sympathy flickered in Adam's steady gaze. "I'm sorry to hear that."

The story poured out in fits and starts. The weeks of being cared for by the elderly pastor and his wife, their future uncertain as they awaited word from relatives. The move to their great-aunt and -uncle's home and un-just treatment. The news they were being sold off like prized bulls.

Deborah found herself wanting to confront these strang-ers who weren't acquainted with compassion.

Adam's growing frown indicated he felt the same.

He checked his pocket watch and nodded at Liam's un-eaten food.

"You finish up while Deborah and I go to the kitchen and fetch some cloths and soap to clean your hands and faces. Since everyone else is in bed, baths will have to wait until morning."

Lily watched their short walk to the door with trepidation. "Will we have to return to the tent?"

Adam shook his head. "I was thinking you could stay here. What's your opinion, Deborah?"

"Lily can sleep in the bed with me, and I can fix a soft pallet on the floor for Liam."

Lily eyed the bed with longing. "Say we can, Liam. I can't remember what sleeping on soft ticking feels like."

When Liam agreed to the plan, Adam accompanied Deborah downstairs. In the darkened dining room, she clasped his hand, preventing him from entering the kitchen and possibly waking Aunt Mae.

Placing the kerosene lamp on the mantel, he turned to regard her with solemn eyes. "How did you get involved with a pair of runaways?"

"Remember the bride train?" At his nod, she said, "There have been rumors of stowaways since our arrival. Seth Halloway's boys claimed to have seen them on the train. Gus and Old Horace insist they've seen them around town. Then there were the stolen items that didn't fit the typical pattern. Food, mostly, but also toys. I found a porcelain doll outside the Gardners' home the night of the benefit."

"That's why you've been sneaking out at night."

"I couldn't help wondering if the rumors were true. What if there were children in our midst who were fending for themselves?"

He rubbed his hands down his face, wincing when his

fingers came in contact with the gash. "Why didn't you tell someone when you found them?"

"You've seen how they react to strangers. The only reason they talked to me is because I appealed to Lucy's stomach."

His mouth twisted into a half smile. "Smart approach."

Deborah crossed her arms. "My turn to ask questions. Why were you following me? And why did you point a gun at us?"

His gaze skittered away, and he shifted on his feet. "I was walking home tonight when I saw you. I was afraid for your safety."

"So you took it upon yourself to nose your way into my affairs?"

"Cowboys are unpredictable." He shrugged. "You know that. More than half of the crimes committed here can be attributed to them. Those gunshots you heard tonight? Those were cowboys who'd likely had too much to drink. I don't want to think about what could happen to a beautiful woman alone in a deserted part of town late at night."

He thought she was beautiful?

"While I appreciate your concern, I wish you hadn't burst in there with abandon. It will be difficult for you to earn their trust." She glanced out at the quiet street. "One good thing can be said about your involvement. They're finally here, where I can keep them safe."

"We don't know whether or not their story is true," he said. "And if they've stolen from local stores, some of the owners might call for some sort of punishment."

"They're children," she retorted. "What do you suggest we do? Turn them over to the sheriff and let him lock them up?"

"Nothing so extreme. But they might have to do odd jobs to pay for the things they stole."

"When the time comes, I'll cover the costs."

His brows shot up. "You're awfully invested in these kids. They could've been taught to swindle unwitting adults."

Dismay shivered through her. "How did you get to be so cynical?"

"I'm being practical."

"I'm not as naive as you think."

"You've got a huge heart. I don't want you to get hurt."

"You haven't spent time with them." She'd looked into their eyes and seen their need. "Promise me you won't tell anyone. Not until they've had a chance to recover from their ordeal."

A muscle ticked in his jaw. "Deborah—"

She laid her open palm against his chest. "They've been on their own for at least two months, living in fear of the elements, wild animals and adults who'd do them harm. They need food and clothing, but above all, they need a friend. I aim to be that, with or without your blessing."

His chest was sleek and hard beneath her hand, his heartbeat slow and steady.

"I won't say anything," he finally said.

"Thank you."

"It won't be easy keeping their presence here a secret," he warned.

"We'll manage it somehow."

The kids were counting on her. She wouldn't let them down.


"I thought you preferred to fill your grooming needs over at the bathhouse."

The note of suspicion in Aunt Mae's voice was unmistakable. Adam replaced the hot kettle on the stove and set the empty basin on the floor by his feet.

Plastering on a smile, he turned toward the woman. "I

volunteered to carry this up to Deborah's room. Her ankle isn't fully healed."

Hands on her hips, she narrowed her eyes. "You should know that nothing gets past me, Mr. Draper. I've seen the way you look at her."

Shock chased the smile from his face.

With a knowing smirk, she wagged her finger. "Deborah has many fine qualities, but she's not wise to the ways of the world. See that you don't break her heart."

What *exactly* had this woman seen to warn him off Deborah?

"I'm not looking for a wife."

"Does she know that?"

"Absolutely." He thought back to that moment in church when he'd made the mistake of caressing her hand. "I've spoken to her about it."

"See that your actions match your words." With that parting warning, she removed a handwoven basket from its peg and headed to the garden.

Her chastisement wormed into his conscience, unsettling him. Last night, as he'd pursued Deborah through town, he'd been 100 percent convinced she was leading him to his long-hunted quarry. So convinced that he'd drawn his weapon and waved it in innocents' faces.

He'd spent a restless night, replaying the horrible scene and thanking God no one had gotten seriously hurt. He'd acted like an inexperienced agent. Rash judgment could get someone killed.

His mood grim, he ascended the stairs to her room. She opened the door with a smile that wrought a reaction that made a liar of him. His interest in Deborah had started out professional. The more time he spent with her, the more he was drawn to her. The discovery that she'd been helping needy children—not a criminal—made it more difficult to restrain his attraction.

"Good morning, Liam. Lily."

They were scarfing down the breakfast Deborah had snuck up soon after the boarders had finished theirs and dispersed from the dining room. They watched as he placed the basin in the corner and poured in steaming water.

"How did you sleep?"

"The bed was like a dream," Lily piped up.

Liam shrugged, his wariness a barrier between him and the world. Despite Adam's inclination to question everything first, verify later, he was inclined to believe the children's account of events. Their eyes bore evidence of haunted memories and grief he could identify with. The impact of losing a parent wasn't easy to fake.

Deborah's bell-shaped skirt swished against him as she scraped soap shavings into the bath. She looked fetching, as always, this time in a tasteful dress the hue of a blue jay's wing. Her rich brown hair was arranged into an understated twist. Tendrils had escaped to caress the line of her jaw.

"And how did you sleep?" he asked her.

Her big topaz eyes locked on to his. "I have no complaints." She gestured behind her. "They're safe now."

Decreasing the distance between them, he pitched his voice low. "I'd like to discuss their case with Russell Halloway."

Her eyebrows puckered. "They're orphans, Adam. Not a court case."

"Information is vital. I can ask him to dig into their relatives' past. We can't help them if we can't prove their claims of neglect and mistreatment."

Her fingernails made crescents in the scented soap. "I don't know."

"You have to think about their future, Deborah. You can't hide them in this room forever."

Looking pained, she nodded. "You're right. Russell is a compassionate man. I believe he'll do his best to help them."

"I want to see their situation change, too."

"You aren't even sure you believe them."

Adam looked over and caught Lily licking the gravy from the plate. Her arms were frail, her shoulders a sharp line beneath the thin material. Liam's face was gaunt.

In his line of work, he'd seen the worst of humanity. He'd also witnessed the best. People who forgave those who'd wronged them. People who helped others without expecting anything in return.

"I believe they're in a bad spot and that you're the best person for this task."

She pressed her lips together, uncertainty surging. "I hope you're right."

"In this instance, I am." He withdrew his money clip and offered it to her.

"What's this?"

"After their baths, I'll stay with them while you procure suitable clothing."

"I can't ask you to do that. I have enough to cover it."

"You're planning to pay the boarding expenses they incur. And you didn't ask. I offered."

When she didn't reach for the clip, he gently unfurled her fingers and pressed it into her hold. "You'll have to be circumspect about your purchases." He thought of Seth and Marigold's little girl, Violet. "In fact, why don't you worry about Liam. I have an idea where I can get something for Lily."

His family would be curious, but they were used to his reticence on certain subjects.

"I'll take care of my errand first to give them time to clean up. Will an hour suffice?" Adam asked her.

She cast a dubious glance at the kids. "Give me an hour and a half."

Chuckling, he let himself out. And almost smacked into Hildie.

"Hildie," he said in an overly loud voice, hoping the sound carried through the door as a warning. "I apologize. I didn't see you there."

Casting a glance at the closed door, she sneered at him. "I misjudged you, Adam."

"Excuse me?"

"I thought you were too astute to fall for her innocent act. You deserve whatever she dishes out." With a disdainful sniff, her head high, she marched for the stairs.

Alarmed, Adam caught up to her. "Hildie, I'd like to know to what you're referring. What is the nature of pretense you're accusing Deborah of?"

"Ponder the fact that she has ignored every interested male overture until you came along."

The sudden vise squeezing his chest loosened. "We're not courting."

"I've seen the way she looks at you."

Her words were an almost exact repetition of Aunt Mae's. "You're mistaken."

"I don't think so." Leaning close, she tapped Adam's shoulder. "You should know that those other suitors didn't have padded pockets like you."

Adam watched her descend the main staircase. He'd deliberately given the impression that his assumed persona, Adam Draper, was a wealthy cattleman. Hildie had decided that Deborah had befriended him in hopes of landing a rich husband. He was sure jealousy played a role in her behavior. Hildie wanted a husband, and it appeared any willing gentleman would do.

While he didn't share her convictions, he was forced to acknowledge that he'd failed to gather intelligence on his prime suspect. His lips pursed in a frown. That label may have worked in the beginning, but now… He found it impossible to view the warm, generous woman he'd gotten to know as a potential criminal. The orphans' presence alone challenged his previous theories.

He'd been wrong about her clandestine outings. What else was he missing?

He had to dig deeper. He'd gleaned scant details about her past, and that needed to change starting today.

## Chapter Twelve

As a child, Deborah had been scolded for eavesdropping. Turning away from the door, she wished she hadn't overheard Hildie. Granted, she hadn't heard the entire conversation, but it had been enough to confirm she was repeating her hateful opinion. Would Adam believe her?

"He's a nice man, isn't he?"

At the hope tinged with doubt in Lily's big blue eyes, Deborah set her own worries aside.

She smiled. "Yes, Lily. He's been a wonderful friend to me. You can trust him."

His arms crossed over his chest, Liam turned from the window overlooking Eden Street and faced her. "We thought we could trust Aunt Laura and Uncle Jeremiah. Turned out their nice act was for the pastor's benefit. As soon as we left town, they told us how things were going to be."

Lily bowed her head. Going to her, Deborah put her arm around her and hugged her close to her side. "Adam isn't pretending. And neither am I. Together, we'll make sure you never have to worry again."

It was a vow she fully intended to keep, but to these kids, they were empty words. They'd have to see proof of her devotion, and that would take time.

Praying for discernment, she situated Liam at the desk with paper and pen. Moving the privacy screen into place, she ushered Lily into the bath and tackled her hair. Then it was Liam's turn. He was old enough to see to his own grooming, so the girls left him to it. Deborah lent Lily a plain white blouse that, on her slight frame, looked more like an oversize dress. Humming to herself, she combed the last of the knots from her waist-length hair. Lily seemed engrossed in their reflection.

Deborah caught her gaze in the mirror and ceased humming. "Feel better?"

Lily nodded. "Yes, ma'am."

"When it's dry, I'll braid it for you. Would you like that?"

Her smile was tinged with sadness. "My ma used to hum a lot, too. Pa teased her about it."

"I know you miss them." Setting aside the comb, she gently squeezed her shoulder. "You won't ever lose the precious memories you have of them."

Adam returned not long after Liam finished his bath. One look at the siblings' clean countenances and tidy hair evoked a whistle of appreciation. His grin transformed his features and lent a sparkle to his brown eyes.

"Don't you two look spiffy. I hardly recognize you." He placed two bulging flour sacks on the desk and started unloading items. "Lily, these are for you."

Her eyes widened at the growing pile of dresses and undergarments. "For me?"

"I'm afraid they aren't new."

She tested the texture of a navy blue dress. "I don't mind," she said shyly.

Switching to the second bag, he said, "Deborah is going to take care of your clothes, Liam. But I was able to locate something I thought you'd like."

He gave the young man a set of marbles and jacks. Liam

reverently held the square tin to his chest. His voice gruff, he thanked Adam.

"I didn't forget about you, little lady." As he pulled a new porcelain doll from the sack, Lily gasped aloud and reached with hesitant fingers to caress its brown curls.

"She has the same color hair as me," she said, the wonder evident in her face. "And same color eyes."

When she burst into tears, Adam's smile vanished. He turned a troubled gaze to Deborah.

With a helpless shrug, she bent to the girl's level. "Sweetheart, what's the matter?"

Lily's hands covered her face. Instead of answering, she cried harder.

"I don't understand," Adam murmured. "I thought she'd like it."

"She probably wants Sally," Liam explained, "the doll our ma and pa gave her last Christmas."

"Does Sally have blond hair?" Deborah asked.

"How'd you know?" Liam said.

"I saw it in the Gardners' yard one day," Deborah explained. "I thought you'd recovered it, because the next time I looked, it was gone."

Lily dropped her hands, revealing tearstained cheeks and a pink nose. Her eyes were awash in despondency. "Sally's lost!"

Adam laid the doll on the desk. "I can't promise we'll find her, Lily, but we can certainly try."

"Truly?"

Adam handed the girl a fresh handkerchief and awkwardly patted her head. "I'll search the woods in that area."

Deborah's heart felt full. He'd been beyond understanding about this whole situation. Purchasing the toys was a sweet, thoughtful gesture. He couldn't have guessed the doll would touch on a sore spot.

Liam picked it up and made a show of inspecting the

frilly dress and painted face. "I'm sure Sally wouldn't mind if you cared for this one while Mr. Draper conducted his search."

Lily considered that for a long moment. "Can I see her?"

Liam handed it over and waited. Adam seemed to be holding his breath.

Finally, she hugged the doll to her chest. "I'm going to call her Sarah. She and Sally can be sisters."

"That's a fine idea," Deborah declared.

Adam's breath left him in a relieved whoosh. The little girl's happiness mattered to him.

Deborah was certain she wouldn't mind staying in this room for at least a week. There'd be no reason to leave. Watching Adam navigate their interactions was a delight. The orphans had given her a sense of purpose, a validation that her hasty, ill-thought-out retreat from St. Louis hadn't been futile, after all.

Adam hadn't been in charge of kids before. This pair didn't need diapers changed or milk heated, but they acted as if he might toss them from the window at any moment. The fact that he was completely out of his element probably didn't help. He dealt with unsavory types. People who had secrets to hide. Not kids missing their parents and childhood home, kids who were very aware of their vulnerability.

He'd masked his nervousness during Deborah's absence by keeping them busy. They were on their fifth checkers game, and he was losing. If his fellow agents could see him now, they'd never let him live it down.

"You won," he announced with an exaggerated sigh. "Play again?"

The checkerboard between them, he and Liam sat on the bed. Lily sat near the footboard with her doll.

Liam's mouth quivered. For a second, Adam thought

he might be awarded a genuine smile. But distrustful blue eyes met his and the chance was lost.

"No, thank you."

"I'm not a worthy opponent. Is that what you're trying to say?" he teased.

His head jerked back. "I didn't mean to imply... That is—"

Adam lifted a hand. "I was only joking. Besides, I'm perfectly aware of my poor skills. My army comrades liked to torment me about it."

"You weren't letting me win?" Liam hesitantly inquired.

Laughing, he replaced the board and disks in the cloth bag. He'd borrowed the game from the parlor and would have to return it. "You won fair and square, young man."

"Papa used to let him win," Lily said. "Mama scolded Papa, but he didn't stop."

"Did Deborah mention she lost her mother?"

The siblings regarded him with serious expressions. "Yes, sir."

"I lost my father when I was eighteen."

Lily frowned. "Did he get sick, too?"

"No, he wasn't sick."

He probably shouldn't have mentioned it, but he'd wanted to form a connection with them. Earn their trust. Standing to his feet, he dragged the desk chair to the middle of the floor.

"Have you made a fort out of furniture before?" he asked them.

They weren't familiar with the game. Since they didn't express disgust for his idea, he enlisted their aid using blankets and other items. By the time Deborah returned half an hour later, both brother and sister were caught up in the pretense.

On his hands and knees, his hair falling in his eyes, he

lifted the blanket serving as an entrance and greeted her with a sheepish smile.

"I hope you don't mind we've made a mess of your room."

Lily pushed into the space beside him. "Come into our fort, Miss Deborah."

Deborah paused on the threshold, surprise lighting her features. "You've been busy, haven't you?"

"We'll put everything to rights," Adam promised.

She placed her single parcel on the bed. Indicating her voluminous skirts, she grimaced. "Are you certain there's room for me?"

"We'll make room."

He and Lily retreated into the far edges of the blanket-draped furniture. Deborah had trouble squeezing into the low, cramped space. Her laugh had a self-conscious lilt. "This isn't very ladylike, I'm afraid."

Liam sat off to their right, his knees pulled up to his chest and a scowl on his face. "There's not much difference between this and our tent."

Lily tossed her head. "This is much better, Liam. There are no bugs. It's clean except for a few dust balls under the bed."

Deborah's brow furrowed. "That reminds me. Aunt Mae will want to clean the rooms first thing tomorrow morning."

"Why do we have to hide in here, anyway?" Liam charged. "I thought you promised to help us."

Unable to ignore Deborah's silent appeal, Adam spoke up. "Before we can tell the townspeople about you, we have to be armed with proof."

His hands fisted. "You don't believe us?"

"Of course we do," Deborah responded. "It's just that sometimes adults will believe other adults before they will children."

"It's unfortunate," Adam said. "But it's the way of our society. We're planning to engage a lawyer's services. His name is Russell Halloway, and he will gather information about your great-aunt and -uncle."

"He won't tell them where we are, will he?"

The boy's terror was plain. Adam's doubts evaporated. He decided then and there to do whatever it took to protect these children, no matter the specifics of their case.

"No. Our utmost priority is to keep you safe." He chose his next words carefully. "Liam, would it be possible to make a list of items you and Lily took from the local shops?"

The boy's cheeks flamed. "Yes, sir."

"Are you sending us to jail?" Lily wailed loud enough to attract attention if anyone had been around. Fortunately, it was midmorning and most boarders were either working or tending to errands.

"We don't put children in jail," he said. "I simply think it's a good idea to make a list. You know it's wrong to take things without paying, right?"

Sucking in her lower lip, she nodded.

"Our parents taught us right from wrong, but I couldn't let my sister go hungry," Liam said hotly.

"I understand. Most of the shop owners will, too. Some might expect you to work off what you owe, however."

He jutted his chin. "I'm stronger than I look."

Adam smiled. "I'm convinced you'd be a great asset to any business."

"I'm a good sweeper," Lily managed in a small voice.

Deborah smoothed the girl's unbound hair. "Try not to fret over it. We'll figure everything out." She angled her face toward Adam. "What about Aunt Mae?"

"We should probably tell her."

"She won't like it."

He dredged up his most charming smile. "Leave the cantankerous proprietress to me."

## Chapter Thirteen

As Adam entered the boardinghouse later that afternoon, he was jerked into the storage room behind the kitchen. He stared at Deborah, who closed and latched the door.

"A little warning would've been nice," he whispered. "You're fortunate I didn't mistake the situation and strike out at you."

She turned to face him. It was then he noticed the narrowness of the room. The floor-to-ceiling shelves wouldn't allow for two people to stand side by side. Like in their furniture fort, he was close enough to touch her, to explore the promise of her fair skin, glossy tresses and inviting mouth. Only now Liam and Lily weren't around to mute his attraction.

They were alone in a storage room. Suddenly the many, many reasons he must keep his distance—not to mention professional objectivity—didn't seem important.

"I apologize," Deborah said softly. "I had to get you alone. Sadie and Hildie have stationed themselves at the dining table with a very large pot of tea and enough cookies to feed a passel of hungry cowboys." Grimacing, she reached up to fiddle with her pin. "What did Russell say?"

Adam tugged at his shirt collar. His brother had had plenty to say, none of it easy to hear. Russell insisted this development proved Deborah's inherent goodness and that she couldn't be aiding Ogden. He'd demanded to know when Adam planned to inform her that they were related and reveal his true reason for being in Cowboy Creek.

She obviously mistook his silence to mean he bore bad news. "Did he refuse to help us? He won't involve the sheriff, will he?"

Her clear distress pained him. Adam shifted closer, lifted his hand and cupped her cheek. Her lips parted on a sudden inhale.

"Don't fret," he murmured. "He and I are going to work together to fix this."

Her eyes were wide and trusting. She covered his hand with her own, holding him fast. The dark hair at her temple tickled his fingertips. The sensation of her small, smooth hand and cool, satiny cheek flooded him with longing.

He rested his other hand on her waist. The pale blue cotton of her bodice was stiff and unyielding, whereas the layers of skirts were as filmy as a cloud. This woman confounded and delighted him in equal measures. She made him question his view of the world and made him dread returning to his solitary life. When she didn't protest the possessive contact, he lowered his head inch by inch, ignoring the warning inside his head telling him that this was his stupidest idea yet.

"Adam." His name on her tongue vibrated with yearning and caution.

His lips hung a breath from hers. "Deborah?"

Her hands found their way to his chest. There was no mistaking their message.

She wasn't ready.

"I have to tell you something."

Adam released her.

Deborah lowered her hands to her sides. "I can identify with Liam and Lily's predicament because I ran away from my own problems."

His throat closed. "Was someone mistreating you?"

"No. Nothing like that." Her lashes swept down. "I ran away from an arranged marriage."

"You told me you weren't married. That first day in the kitchen. Remember the pepper cake and the blindfold?"

Her arrested gaze shot to his face. "I told you the truth. I fled St. Louis a few hours before the wedding." She pressed her hands to her cheeks. "My father and I have had a tumultuous relationship for as long as I can remember. It got worse after my mother died. He doesn't understand me." A harsh laugh devoid of true humor escaped. "He certainly isn't proud to claim me as his daughter. I've done everything in my power to please him, and every time I've fallen short. When he promised my hand in marriage to his dearest friend, I couldn't find it in me to refuse."

"Do you care for this man?"

"Tobias? I barely know him. He's my father's age. Very stern. He was married many years ago. There have been rumors that he mistreated his first wife, who died from consumption."

Adam would've liked to have a few words with Mr. Frazier. The man had to have known Deborah's desire to earn his approval would influence her to agree to a loveless marriage.

"Your father manipulated you, Deborah."

Judging by the look in her eyes, she hadn't considered that angle.

"Why didn't he approach Lucy?" he pressed. "She can do no wrong in his eyes, right?"

"I'm older."

"Would Lucy have agreed to the match?"

A furrow dug into the skin between her brows. "She never had trouble opposing him."

Adam gave her shoulder a light squeeze. "You did the right thing. Marrying someone for the wrong reasons would've made you miserable."

And rendered her untouchable. Out of his reach. If she'd gone through with the wedding, their paths wouldn't have crossed.

"I let people purchase wedding gifts. I let my father spend an exorbitant amount of money on everything from flowers to food. I was a coward, Adam. I hate to admit that to you, of all people. I didn't have the courage to stand my ground."

"Don't sell yourself short. Look at what you're doing for those kids."

"Speaking of Liam and Lily, what exactly did Russell say?"

At the mention of his brother, Adam wrestled with guilt. She'd revealed private information. Trusted him enough to share what she viewed as a humiliating experience. But he could not tell her who he was. Not yet.

"He suggested they stay with Seth, Marigold and the boys."

The corners of her mouth turned down. "They would have plenty of space to roam, I suppose. And four playmates. And Seth and Marigold have more experience with children."

"I told him no."

"You did?"

"They're happy with you. They trust you."

Joy brightened her face. "I like spending time with them. Liam is a bit prickly, but he's a good boy. He loves his sister and watches over her like a loyal guard dog."

"An apt description."

"And Lily is a darling. She wouldn't say it, but she's aching for someone to love her. To take the place of her ma."

"You're going to be good for them."

She blushed scarlet, as if he'd gifted her a bouquet of flowers and handwritten poetry. "Thank you, Adam."

He meant it; he realized. Russell was right. Deborah Frazier possessed a heart of gold. If she'd gotten lured in by Ogden's deceitful charm, and he wasn't convinced she had, it would be due to her desire to help others.

"Oh! I completely forgot!" she exclaimed. "Would you have time to stay with them while I prepare tonight's dessert?"

"I'd be happy to."

Adam didn't want to examine too closely why it didn't bother him that he was spending his time watching a pair of orphans instead of hunting his nemesis.

They both jerked when the doorknob rattled.

"Who's in there? Open the door this instant." The command was muffled but insistent.

Deborah's eyes went wide. "Aunt Mae."

Adam shuffled past her and, pasting on a bright smile, opened the door with a flourish. "Aunt Mae, we were just on our way to find you. Did you realize your sugar stores are running low?"

Having relocated to the rear veranda, Aunt Mae faced them with arms crossed over her bosom and a serious expression on her face. "You ushered me out here to inform me that you're making this romance official, I hope." She quirked a brow at Adam. "I've seen a lot of things in my time, but the storage room is a new one. I don't know whether to be impressed or appalled."

Embarrassment seared Deborah's skin. She waved a limp hand between them. "It's not what it appears, Aunt Mae."

Adam's dark chocolate gaze cut to her, and the memory of their almost-embrace sent goose bumps along her arms. She'd wanted his kiss with a feverish desperation. Only the fact that she was hiding her greatest humiliation from him prevented her. She'd had no choice but to confess.

To her amazement, Adam hadn't faulted her. Hadn't ridiculed her. He'd offered support and encouragement as a devoted friend and confidante. More than his kiss, she yearned for his high opinion.

"Deborah and I weren't engaging in the sort of clandestine meeting you're imagining," he said. "You see, we've encountered a delicate situation. We've attempted to handle it ourselves but have come to the conclusion that we need your assistance."

Aunt Mae's brows hit her hairline. "It's not romantic in nature?"

Adam's features clouded. "I harbor the utmost respect for Deborah and wouldn't dream of treating her in a cavalier manner." There was a hint of reproach in his voice. "She's a lady, and I was taught to be a gentleman."

The irascible proprietress actually had the grace to look ashamed. Deborah's already healthy admiration for the cattleman deepened.

Aunt Mae's wrinkles bunched and stretched. "I'd be happy to help if I can. What's the problem?"

"We've taken in two new boarders," Adam told her. "They're currently stationed in Deborah's room."

"Excuse me?"

Deborah spoke up. "We weren't intending to cheat you. I'll pay for room and board."

Aunt Mae's eyes sparked. "Who are they, and why am I just now finding out about them?" she barked.

Adam's fingers grazed Deborah's spine, and she turned to him as he asked her, "How about we introduce her first?"

"Good idea." Maybe if she saw Liam and Lily, her ire would be less intense.

The trek to the second floor was a quiet one. Deborah entered first. The kids were seated on the bed with a book between them. Liam's voice trailed off once he noticed their visitor.

"Liam, Lily, I'd like you to meet the owner of this boardinghouse, Mae—" She looked over at the proprietress, who was gaping at the kids in awe. "I apologize. I've just realized I don't know your last name."

"Livingston-Jones. Maeve is my birth-given name." She shuffled closer to the bed. "Everyone calls me Aunt Mae, and you can, too."

Lily snuggled closer to her brother. "You're a good cook, Aunt Mae."

"Why, thank you, young lady. My grandma taught me when I was about your size. Do you have much experience in the kitchen?"

"No, ma'am. My ma died before she was able to teach me."

Mae sobered. "I see. Well, perhaps you'd like to learn how to bake bread sometime."

"I'd love to!"

Liam studied the newcomer with his customary cynicism. "You're not angry?"

"While I've never cottoned to deception, I'm guessing you've got a valid reason for being here."

Adam chose that moment to explain their circumstances. Aunt Mae patiently listened, her gaze returning repeatedly to the siblings. She seemed especially intrigued with Liam.

"Well, it seems as though there are a few things that need sorting," she said. "While we're waiting, you're welcome to stay here as long as you'd like."

Aunt Mae summoned Adam and Deborah downstairs to the kitchen, where she set about preparing a snack.

"Have you been feeding them enough?" She placed two apples on the plate, along with hunks of ham and cheese.

"You should've told me right away, you know. From now on, they join us for meals."

"But the other boarders—"

"Do you honestly think you can keep a pair of kids holed up in that room?" She jammed her fists on her hips. "Hildie has already reported suspicious sounds."

Deborah looked at Adam, who merely shrugged. Had Hildie been spreading more rumors about them?

"And don't think I hadn't noticed your unusual behavior, missy." She pointed at Deborah. "No, this can't be hidden any longer."

"What if someone tries to take Liam and Lily away?"

"I won't allow it," Aunt Mae announced with authority. When she noticed their reaction, she said quietly, "I have a son. His name is Vincent, and he's twenty-nine. I haven't spoken to him in many years, since he joined the army at the beginning of the war."

Adam's jaw tensed. "You haven't heard from him since? No letters?"

"Nothing." A sigh shook her. "He blamed me for his father leaving. My first husband died not long after our fifth anniversary. I'd known Marcus for years, so when he proposed marriage, I accepted even though I didn't love him. We soon discovered our temperaments didn't suit. We held on, though, for Vincent's sake. Then one day I woke to find my husband and his stuff gone. He didn't bother to say goodbye."

Deborah leaned toward her. "I'm so sorry."

"Liam reminds me of Vincent. He was always a serious child. He felt things deeply."

"Thank you for being understanding," Adam said.

"You might not think so when I tally your bill," she shot back.

Deborah saw her prickly demeanor for what it was— armor to protect a wounded heart. Aunt Mae's woeful tale, added to Adam's earnest support, lessened the burden she'd been carrying since sneaking out of that St. Louis church.

She had the right to refuse a groom who wouldn't suit her. She didn't owe her father her future. Wasn't she carving out her own future now? One that wouldn't earn Gerard's approval but that made her happy?

Adam snagged her attention and winked. Her heart thrummed against her chest, straining for him. Adam had become a fixture in her life. A raft in a storm-tossed sea. A ray of hope in a dismal sky.

Would he become part of her future? Or would he do as he'd promised—get a ranch up and running in Cowboy Creek before moving on to the next challenge?

## Chapter Fourteen

"Have you met Seth's wife, Marigold?" Deborah braced her hands against the wagon seat and soaked in the prairie landscape. "She and I were on the bride train together, but she wasn't on her way to meet a groom. She'd accepted the position as the town's teacher."

Beside her, Adam kept tight control of the rented horses hitched to the borrowed wagon. "I've made her acquaintance," he said without looking in her direction.

"And their children? Tate, Harper and Little John? Oh, I forgot Violet. She's Marigold's niece."

His brows pulled together. "Them, too."

Shifting to check on Liam and Lily riding in the back, she pondered Adam's strange mood. When she'd brought his attention to the kids' restlessness earlier that morning, he'd been the one to suggest taking them for a ride in the country. A mile or so outside town, she'd noted the Halloway ranch was nearby and suggested they drop by for a visit.

The closer they got, however, the more drawn his features became and the less inclined he was to talk. Was all this open land mocking him? He'd yet to locate a proper plot for his enterprise. She didn't think it had anything to do with Liam and Lily. The boarders had been astonished, of course, but they'd welcomed the siblings with genuine kindness. Well, Hildie hadn't been overly friendly. No surprise there.

He'd been supportive of her, and she wanted to repay the favor.

"Is something bothering you, Adam?"

He angled his face toward hers. The glimmer of guilt was unexpected.

With a heavy sigh, he guided the horses to a stop beneath a lone tree on this stretch of road. Lily immediately popped up.

"What are we doing here? I thought we were going to see animals and play with kids our age."

Her hair was neatly braided and her face fresh and clean. Her cheeks were rosy, and her eyes bright. It was wonderful to see the change in her.

Adam set the brake and wound the reins around it. "That plan hasn't changed," he said. "I'd like to talk with Deborah for a few minutes first, though. Why don't you and your brother explore this field? I'd guess there are all sorts of treasures to find."

"Like caterpillars?"

He smiled. "And ladybugs."

Liam studied them both. "Snakes, too."

Lily and Adam lost their smiles. Adam hopped to the ground and scanned the grassy patch. "You're right, Liam. Better stick to the edge here."

"Yes, sir."

Adam swung Lily down before coming around to assist Deborah. The delicious sensation of his hands on her waist was fleeting. He took her elbow and guided her to the shaded area on the far side of the giant tree.

Removing his Stetson, he drew the brim through his fingers several times. "You revealed something about yourself the other day, and it's my turn to do the same."

"You can tell me anything."

Putting his hat back on, he shrugged out of his navy suit jacket and draped it over a limb. He rolled up the sleeves of his crisp white shirt. Whatever was on his mind must be of great import.

"In my line of work, I've had to obscure certain pieces of information. It hasn't been an issue until now." His brown eyes bored into hers. Daring her. Imploring her. "Until you."

Butterflies unleashed in her stomach. "You're the first cattle rancher I've met, so I'm not acquainted with the workings of your business. Why would you have to hide aspects of yourself? To disarm your rivals?"

He grimaced, revealing a flash of white teeth. "That's the problem. I'm not a cattleman."

"You're not?"

"I used to be a rancher, before the war. Before other things happened to break up my family."

The butterflies transformed into nervous bees. "What are you then?"

"I work for a national agency whose aim is to garner justice for the wronged." His gaze roamed her face intently. "My last name isn't Draper. It's Halloway."

"Halloway." Deborah felt weightless. Not anchored to the earth. "Like Seth and Russell Halloway?"

"Yes." Apology softened his mouth. "They're my older brothers."

She gripped the bower arching above her head. "I introduced you to Russell at the fund-raiser. Your own brother." Unable to look at him, she searched for and found the siblings. They were crouched at the field's edge, their dark heads together as they observed something in their hands. "I feel stupid."

"No." He was suddenly very close to her, his hands cupping the backs of her arms. "Don't say that. I'm a professional at making others accept whatever persona I've dreamed up. It's what I was trained to do."

Longing thundered through her veins, clashing against her right to be outraged. She may have kept part of her past hidden from him, but she hadn't played out an active deception.

His fingers flexed on her flesh, his heat seeping through the pale green cotton sleeves. His expression was one of entreaty. His eyes were molten, his jaw hard, his mouth set in silent appeal.

Her eyes filled with tears. "What else do you make people believe, Adam?"

Glancing sideways to make sure the children weren't watching, he pulled her against his broad chest. She couldn't find the strength to object.

"Whatever this is between us isn't pretense. Not on my part."

Deborah believed him. Maybe she was naive. Maybe she was desperate to find the good in others. Maybe she didn't want to think his friendship had been a ruse.

"You need to release me."

He did so at once. Stepping back, he sunk his hands deep in his pockets and regarded her with an indiscernible expression.

"I'm sorry for upsetting you. I haven't been in this position before, and I'm making a muddle of it. Forgive me," he implored.

"Who's your employer?"

"I'd rather not say."

"You're here not to buy land, but to solve a mystery."

"A crime, actually."

"And once you've accomplished that goal, you'll move on to the next case."

Shadows darkened his eyes. "That's typically how it works, yes."

"I see."

Wrapping her arms around her middle, she turned her back and blinked the moisture from her eyes. *I don't understand, God. He's the first man I've felt comfortable enough to be myself with. He's seen the good and bad, and he didn't run. He's become a treasured friend.*

She cared about Adam. How deeply, she wasn't aware until this moment. There was no question of him staying. He traveled around helping victims and their families.

Deborah angled back. "How can I know for sure this isn't another ruse? Perhaps you're not on the right side of the law. Maybe you're a wanted man."

He flinched as if her accusations caused him physical pain. "My family can vouch for me."

Russell was an upright man, a lawyer who made it his mission to aid those unable to help themselves. Seth was good to the core. Hadn't he taken in a trio of orphans simply because it was their mother's dying wish? And what about their precious mother, Evelyn? Deborah had had several delightful conversations with the lady during church socials and other events. The Halloways didn't strike her as gullible or willing to overlook unlawful behavior.

"I can't show you my credentials until this case is solved. If you can't trust me, trust my family."

Deborah let her gaze roam freely over his dear features. Her faith in him, her conviction that he was honorable and heroic, had been shaken. Could it ever be restored?

Her response was cut off by Lily, who rushed up in a panic. "A baby bird fell from its nest and can't fly back. You have to do something!"

"Show me," Adam said.

Lily seized his hand and drew him past the tree. Deborah trailed behind them. There in the flattened grass beside the rutted dirt lane was a baby bird flopping about.

His small body was covered in downy feathers, his beak wide-open.

Liam's frown was deeper than usual. "He'll get eaten if we don't return him."

Adam crouched to examine the bird. "Have you seen the nest?"

Liam pointed to the mass of twigs and debris that served as the bird's home, visible in a gap between the leaves.

"Won't be easy to get to," Adam observed.

Tears pooled in Lily's eyes. "You're giving up?"

He gently swiped at a lone tear that escaped down her cheek. "I haven't even started, my dear girl. Now, we'll need gloves on before we handle him." Striding to the wagon, he retrieved his gloves from beneath the seat. "A shame we don't have anything here to use as a stepping stool."

Liam approached Deborah. "I'm a decent climber."

"I'm sure you are. Let's go see just how high off the ground it is."

Together, they moved beneath the branches. From this angle, the limb was higher than she'd first thought.

Liam stuck his chest out. "I'm not afraid of heights."

"Let's see what Adam says, all right?"

Adam carefully scooped the baby bird into his hands and carried him over. "I wonder if he needs water. He isn't closing his beak."

Deborah thought for a minute. "Do you have a handkerchief? We could use water from our flask to moisten it."

While his eyes hadn't lost their guardedness, admiration shone in the dark depths. "Good idea. It's in my pocket. Liam, would you mind?"

Liam fished out the white square. Deborah hurried to the wagon for the flask. When she'd moistened the end, she squeezed tiny drops of water into the bird's mouth. He gulped it, his little black eyes batting rapidly. Lily crowded close and stared in wonder.

"I wish we could take him home," she breathed. "I mean, to the hotel room."

Deborah's heart ached for what the kids had lost. *Lord Jesus, You see their deep need. Help me provide for them. Help me not to be selfish, however. I want the best outcome for Liam and Lily, and I understand that might not include me. But I hope it does.*

"He needs his ma," Liam told her.

"Indeed, he does," Adam said. "Now, who wants to hold this little guy until I can reach the spot?"

"Let me go up there, sir."

Adam regarded Liam with raised brows. "You sure you're up to the task? What about your knee?"

"The soreness is mostly gone. You can count on me."

Adam gave him a nod of acquiescence. The boy took his time climbing, measuring distances and testing the weight of each limb. Deborah's heart stuttered when his shoe skidded from its nook and he almost fell. But he quickly caught himself. The relieved grin he shot down to them filled her heart with joy.

It was the first time she'd seen him smile. All because of a baby bird in distress, and Adam's willingness to give the boy a chance to prove himself.

"Uncle Adam!" Harper left his younger brother and their miniature wooden trains spread out beneath the old maple tree and ran over to greet him. Looking at the others, he stopped short. "Oh, I wasn't supposed to call you that, was I?"

"It's all right," Adam said. "They know we're related."

He risked a glance at Deborah, who was keeping ample distance between them. Her pretty features bore the stamp of unhappiness. He'd felt compelled to tell her the truth, the partial truth anyway, but now he was experiencing reservations. Had he done the right thing? Because she didn't look at him the same as before, and it hurt.

Deception was intrinsic to his work. Not in every case, but some demanded it. And capturing Zane Ogden required all the ammunition at his disposal.

His mother and Marigold had been reclining in the shade with sewing projects. Setting those aside, they approached with wide smiles and unveiled curiosity.

"What a nice surprise," Evelyn enthused, her gaze zeroing in on Deborah and the children with a calculating gleam that made him uncomfortable. "It's good to see you, Deborah. Who've you brought with you?"

Gesturing to Lily, who stood very close to her side, and to Liam, who was busy inspecting the farm, she made the introductions.

Little John tugged on his mother's skirt. Marigold scooped him into her arms and smiled at the newcomers. "Welcome to our home. Would you like to play with Harper and Little John here? I'll bring out glasses of raspberry shrub I made this morning."

The promise of a treat, even if it was only something to drink, hooked Lily. Liam looked bored.

Adam touched his shoulder. "I'm going to find Seth. Want to stick with me?"

"Yes, sir."

Evelyn pointed past the house. "He's in the barn with Tate. They were going to muck out stables."

"I'm sure they'd appreciate some help," Adam said. "Enjoy yourselves, ladies."

Evelyn grinned. "No question about that."

Adam shot her a warning look that only enhanced her glee. No doubt she would steer the conversation with Deborah toward the topic of romance and suitors. He prayed his name would be left out of it. His and Deborah's relationship was complicated enough without his mother's interference.

During the short walk to the barn, he told Liam the story of how Tate, Harper and Little John came to be with his brother and Marigold.

"Tate's the oldest boy. Maybe you'll discover common interests."

"I'll be eleven soon," he said quietly.

"Oh? When's your birthday?"

"July 18."

"That's next month."

Liam didn't comment. Squinting into the sun, he kept his gaze on the horizon and the wooden fences surrounding lush fields. They passed a grouping of apple trees, and the large barn came into view.

"Thanks for saving the bird," he said, striving for nonchalance. "Lily would've been upset if we'd left it to fend for itself."

Lily wouldn't have been the only one, Adam guessed. "I happen to like animals. It's important to respect God's creation."

"Our uncle would've sooner squashed it beneath his boot than waste his time rescuing it. And he would've railed at Lily for crying."

Adam's hands fisted. He'd like a one-on-one encounter with the monsters who'd accepted responsibility for the siblings when they clearly weren't qualified to parent children.

"Your parents would be proud of you."

Liam stumbled, although there were no obstacles in the grass. "Sir?"

"Absolutely. It took a lot of courage to endure such mistreatment and to ultimately make the decision to get your sister out of there."

Liam's lips quivered, and his cheeks bunched. "I was scared. Didn't know whether to stay or leave."

Adam nodded. "I would've been, too." Stopping, he turned and put his arm around the boy. "You did the right thing. I believe God was watching over you, and that He led you to the right person."

"Miss Deborah?"

"She cares about you. She'll do whatever is necessary to help."

Liam blinked and stared at the ground.

"I want you to know you can count on me, as well."

"Thank you, sir."

Adam hadn't taken the time to envision what it might be like to be a father. Standing here with Liam, a kid who'd borne more burdens than the average adult, a kid who hid his fear and uncertainty for the sake of his little sister, he understood finally the drive to protect and nurture. He understood what had inspired his oldest brother to take on three orphans and Russell to love an unborn child that he hadn't sired.

The desire to be a father, to have a family to provide for, struck him out of the blue. It was fierce and demanding and specific.

Adam didn't want just any family, he realized.

He wanted Deborah, Lily and Liam.

He wanted the impossible.

## Chapter Fifteen

"Making bread is fun!" Lily pounded the dough with her tiny fist. Flour dusted her nose and chin and much of the apron she'd borrowed from Evelyn. "I want to do this every day forever."

Assembled in the Halloway kitchen, Deborah, Marigold and Evelyn laughed. Then, as she placed her stack of shallow bowls on the kitchen table, the elder Halloway shook her head. "You say that now, young lady. Wait until you have a hungry bear of a man to feed and a passel of youngsters whose bellies are always grumbling."

Marigold gave a hearty nod, her pretty hair catching the sun's rays brightening the farmhouse's central room. "Isn't that the truth? I've learned to adjust the amount of food I prepare. Violet and I didn't require nearly as much." She gave the fragrant stew another stir and, as was her habit, did a visual inventory of the room for Violet.

During those initial weeks in Cowboy Creek, Deborah had heard the sad tale of Marigold's young niece. After having helped raise Violet nearly all her life, Marigold had believed she'd be Violet's permanent guardian following her sister's death. That changed when her brother-in-law returned out of the blue to claim the child.

Already Deborah would miss Liam and Lily if they

were no longer in her care. She could only imagine the depth of grief and loss Marigold must've endured after years of being Violet's substitute mother.

In a surprise turn of events, the child was returned to her when her dying father could no longer offer her care. Now, with the four adopted children, Marigold's family was off to a booming start. There was no question in Deborah's mind that she and Seth would eventually add to their brood.

Marigold's body relaxed the moment she saw that Violet was content with her miniature tea set laid out on the rough-hewn table by the sofa. The girl ignored Harper and Little John's rowdier play with toy ponies and hand-carved farm buildings.

"Speaking of families, Deborah, the man who claims your heart is going to reap sweet rewards." Evelyn circled the table laying out silverware. Her eyes sparkled with mischief.

Deborah stood beside Lily to oversee her progress. Sensing that Adam's mother wasn't actually talking about her baking skills, she searched for an appropriate response. "I appreciate the sentiment."

"Do you have any prospects on the horizon?" the Halloway matriarch asked.

Marigold wagged her spoon at her mother-in-law. "Evelyn."

"Can't I be curious?" She adopted an innocent air. "Were you aware that Preston and Hildie have been seen about town?"

"I wasn't." Hildie no longer spoke to her. "Hildie is eager to get hitched. For her sake, I hope she doesn't rush into a commitment without thinking it through."

Evelyn's gaze turned speculative. "It does pay to be cautious, especially in matters of the heart." Something outside the window snagged her attention. Her features softened with familial affection. Pressing her hand to her heart, she sighed. "It's wonderful to have Adam with us again after years of separation. I'm grateful God saw fit to bring him home to us."

His confession still fresh in her mind, she entertained a dozen questions. She didn't pose a single one. No way could she interrogate his mother about his character.

Instead, she prayed for God's wisdom and discernment in the matter. Adam had given her the benefit of the doubt. She couldn't forget that.

When he entered the house half an hour later, laughing with his brother and including Liam and Tate in their good-natured teasing, her intuition said he was a trustworthy man who wouldn't disrespect or mistreat her.

*He lied about so many things, though.*

He wasn't a cattleman. He wasn't in Cowboy Creek in search of land.

He was a man of pretense.

Adam's intent gaze searched the room, bouncing over the occupants until landing on her. Emotions kicked up inside her like a mile-wide twister—disappointment, apology, longing—before being snuffed out.

*He's on the side of justice, though.*

*He puts lawless men behind bars, preventing them from enacting their evil on others.*

If there ever was a reason for deception, that was it.

Evelyn ushered everyone to the table. Despite being manipulated into the chair beside Adam, Deborah found it easy to relax and enjoy the meal. The Halloways enjoyed each other. They liked each other. The pleasant atmosphere was in direct contrast to that of the Frazier household.

Afterward, the kids went outside to play beneath the elm trees. Evelyn placed a cup of coffee in Deborah's hand and ordered her onto the porch where Adam and Seth had retreated to a pair of rocking chairs. Adam immediately gave his up for her, going to the porch railing and propping a hip against it. She hid her consternation by focusing on the children. The younger boys and the girls were involved in a game of tag, while Tate and Liam sat off to themselves in the grass with the family cat, Peony. It appeared they were comfortable in each other's company, for which she was grateful.

"Did Adam ever tell you about the time he rescued our neighbor's young son from drowning?"

"No, he didn't."

Seth relayed the details. Throughout the story, Adam fiddled with his cup or watched the kids. When Seth was finished, Adam aimed an arch look at his brother. "You think she doesn't know what you're trying to do?"

Seth's innocent air mimicked Evelyn's. "You'd rather I tell her the embarrassing stuff about you? Because I can. I have a lot to choose from."

His chin dipped. "You're trying to paint a flattering picture that isn't reality."

Deborah sipped her coffee, intrigued by the exchange.

Seth fixed his brown gaze on her. "Adam's got his faults, okay? He's stubborn and bullheaded. But he's also loyal to a fault and one of the most selfless people I know."

She risked a glance at the man in question. His cheeks were flushed a dull pink. His discomfiture was obvious.

"You're trying to convince me to trust him," she said to Seth.

"You may not understand his process," Seth continued, "but he devotes his life doing what few people are willing to do. He scours the nation for the worst examples of humanity at the cost of his own happiness."

Adam held up his hands. "Who said I wasn't happy?"

"You're alone, aren't you?"

He pushed off the railing and stood to his full height. *"Seth."*

The tall, well-built man popped out of the rocker and edged to the door. He flashed a boyish grin. "I think I heard my wife calling for me. Better go see what she wants."

The door hinges whined and creaked, the wood slapping against the frame.

Adam huffed his irritation. "My family doesn't know the meaning of tact or subtlety."

"I'm not offended." Standing, she smoothed her voluminous skirts and crossed to the railing. "You're fortunate you have a good relationship with them."

After a minute, he nodded. "You're right, especially considering how I went off to fight and rarely made time to pen letters."

"Do they know the details of your current case?"

He looked wary. "Yes."

What type of person was he searching for? A bank robber? A horse thief? A murderer?

"Your work is dangerous."

"You sound surprised."

"I was more focused on the deception aspect of your revelation than anything else." She was thinking about it now. Most criminals wouldn't willingly submit to their punishment, would they? Oh, no, they'd be desperate to avoid capture. Desperation made men reckless. "Have you been shot at before?"

"I've dodged everything from knives and rocks to broken bottles. One man knocked me unconscious with a carpetbag full of bricks." At Deborah's gasp, he shrugged. "I hate to say I'm used to the violence, but it's what I've known for too many years. First in the war, then in my occupation."

"Aren't you tired?"

His eyes narrowed. Shifting his gaze to the distant prairie, he said, "Putting outlaws behind bars is fulfilling work."

"Lonely, too, I imagine."

"Sometimes."

"But you're still planning on leaving Cowboy Creek once you're finished here."

"My agency is counting on me," he said with a slight wince. "There are too many criminals and not enough of us."

"You're never going to settle in one place and build a life?" Didn't he want a wife? Children? Stability? A familiar place to lay his head at night? Adam's previous excuses marched through her head. "Expanding your empire isn't the challenge. It's each new case."

"This one's my biggest yet. I can't afford to fail."

She didn't point out that he hadn't answered her question. She would've fished for answers if not for Lily, who scrambled up the porch steps and begged to be shown Peony's litter of kittens.

He agreed with an indulgent smile that made Deborah's heart skip. Taking the girl's tiny hand in his large, suntanned one, he led the way across the porch, listening intently to her chatter. Once they reached the yard, the other children rushed to join them.

He shot Deborah a beseeching glance. "I'm outnumbered. Won't you have mercy on me?"

"Come on, Miss Deborah!" Still latched on to Adam's hand, Lily bounced on her toes. "You can't miss kittens. They're the best!"

"After cookies and pie, of course," Adam added.

"Of course!"

Deborah couldn't hold back a smile.

Adam would make a fine father. A shame he didn't realize it.

But that was none of her business. His future didn't include her.

* * *

"When can we go back to the Halloways' ranch?"

Liam was snug in his pallet on the floor. His query surprised her, as did the unabashed excitement in his blue eyes. His tousled hair spilled across his forehead, making him appear younger than his ten years.

Smiling, Deborah smoothed the coverlet. "Perhaps next week."

"Next week!" Lily wailed from the bed. "Why can't we go tomorrow? Adam promised we could ride horses."

"Tate said he'd show me his bug collection."

"That was nice of him." Liam could use a friend. And like him, Tate understood what it meant to lose his parents and move to an unfamiliar place.

Straightening, she dimmed the lamp and crawled beneath the covers beside Lily. "The ranch requires a lot of hours of work each day. That's why we can't visit again tomorrow."

"We could pitch in, couldn't we?" Lily countered. "Like I helped with the bread and you peeled potatoes and carrots?"

Liam sat up. "Adam and I mucked out some of the stables."

"I enjoyed our time there as much as you did," she said. "However, I have to help Aunt Mae with the meals." At their crestfallen expressions, she said, "We can speak to Adam about it in the morning. But I'm guessing Aunt Mae would appreciate it if you two could weed the vegetable garden."

They agreed to the idea. Resting against the pillows, Deborah folded her hands in her lap. "It's my habit to pray before bed. Do either of you have something you'd like to pray about?"

Lily's lips puckered. "I'd like to have one of Peony's kittens. The one with orange and white stripes."

"You can't," Liam said. "Not in a boardinghouse."

She jutted her chin. "Then I'm also gonna ask for a house."

Her throat constricted. Their future was so uncertain. "There's nothing wrong with that. Liam? How about you?"

He opened his mouth to speak, then thought better of it. He slowly shook his head. "I don't have anything."

She was sure there was many things weighing on his mind. He simply wasn't ready to share. She'd pray for him in the quiet of her heart. God knew his needs and desires, just as He knew Lily's and Deborah's. While she was at it, she'd pray for Adam, too.

His deception yet bothered her, but she understood his reasons.

"Miss Deborah?" Lily bit her lip. "Would you mind if I asked God to make you our new ma?"

"Oh, sweetheart." Hugging her close, she stroked the girl's unbound hair. "You can certainly ask Him anything."

"Maybe she doesn't wanna be our ma." Liam's head bowed, and he nibbled on his fingernail.

"Come join us on the bed for a minute, Liam."

He did as she bid, hunkering against the footboard, his knees pulled up to his chest.

"I'll be honest," Deborah said, "I have no idea how to be a parent. I traveled here to avoid marrying a man I didn't love. Until I heard about the possibility of orphans hiding among us, I was focused on my problems and what I'd do if they caught up to me. But that changed as soon as I met you." Her voice wobbled.

Lily patted her hand. "It's okay to cry if you feel sad. My ma taught me that."

Deborah's heart swelled with tenderness. "She was a wise woman. But I'm not sad. I'm grateful God brought you into my life." She looked at Liam. "I enjoy having you with me, and I'd like to keep you around for a long while."

"Truly?" Lily breathed.

Deborah smiled. "Truly."

She bowed her head and prayed aloud, asking for God's will to be done in their lives and for the willingness to accept His answer.

## Chapter Sixteen

The streets were quiet Monday morning when Adam made his way to Russell's house. Overhead, a thick layer of clouds masked the sun. His front-door knock wasn't immediately answered, so he tried again, louder this time.

The door jerked open and a surprised Russ looked out. "Is this an emergency so early in the morning?"

Adam took in his stocking feet, unbuttoned shirt and tie dangling from his fingers. "Nothing's on fire, if that's what you mean, but it's important."

Russ granted him admittance, grumbling, "Wait until you're married and you've had a long night with an uncomfortable pregnant wife and I show up unannounced before you've finished breakfast."

"You'll be waiting a long time." Adam smirked as he trailed his brother down the hallway. "I'd forgotten how grumpy you are in the mornings."

Russ paused in the dining room entrance, his expression turning smug. "With a certain baker in the picture, the prospect of your nuptials is not that far off."

"I'm going to pretend you didn't say that." Brushing past him, Adam greeted his sister-in-law, who was enjoying a boiled egg and toast with marmalade.

"Good morning, Anna. I apologize for intruding."

"Nonsense. You're family." She gestured to the place across from her. "Let me get you a plate."

"I appreciate the offer, but Aunt Mae's expecting me to join the other boarders." He glanced at Russ. "I wouldn't mind a cup of coffee, though."

His brother fetched him a mug and filled it to the brim with steaming, rich brew. Adam settled in the chair across from Anna and beside Russ.

"What's the pressing issue?" Russ forked a bite of sausage.

"Liam and Lily Quinn."

Swallowing, Russ passed the napkin over his mouth. "If you'd been patient, I would've come to see you later this morning. During office hours."

"I'm not patient."

"I know that." He sipped his coffee. "I've received confirmation from the postmaster in Lakewood that a Jeremiah and Laura Jackson do in fact live there. While long-term inhabitants, they're rather reclusive. They attend church sporadically and rarely take part in community events."

His gut tightened. "You didn't mention the kids, did you?"

He gave him a dry look. "Of course not. In order to dig deeper, the next step is to hire someone to travel there and investigate in person. I can supply you with a list of names of men I trust."

Lakewood was a two-hour train ride from Cowboy Creek. "Not necessary. I'll go."

Russ exchanged a surprised look with his wife. "What about Ogden? You've had your hands full the past few days. Can you afford to divert your energy to the orphans' plight?"

It was true. He hadn't made progress in the hunt for Ogden. "Our quarry doesn't know I'm on his trail. He's enjoying success here, so there's no reason to leave. It won't take me more than a day or two to find the answers I seek in Lakewood."

Anna's smile was tender. "You care about Liam and Lily, don't you?"

He recalled his conversation with Liam on Saturday and the time they'd spent with Seth and Tate. "I care enough not to rely on anyone else to do the job. This is too important."

When Russell walked him to the door, he caught Adam's sleeve. "You don't still suspect Deborah, do you?"

"How can I? I've seen no evidence."

"Forget your analytical approach for a second," he scoffed. "What does your heart tell you?"

He wasn't sure his heart was reliable. He did know that the thought of Deborah engaged to another man filled him with despondency. He knew that it was getting increasingly difficult not to kiss her and shower her with affection.

Russ whistled low and long. "You're smitten with her."

Adam waved him off. "I'm not having this conversation."

"Why can't you admit it? She's a wonderful person. Anna likes her. And I think she'd make a fine addition to the family."

"I'm leaving. Thanks for looking into the Jacksons." Outside on the porch, he turned back. "While I'm gone—"

"I'll keep an eye on Deborah and the kids."

Ignoring his brother's catlike grin, Adam waved and headed for the depot. He had an important mission to complete, one that took precedence over his years-long crusade to catch a crook. Was the success of both too much to hope for?

The thin telegram paper crinkled beneath the pressure of Deborah's fingers. Lucy had reached out to inform her that their father had hired an investigator. Not just any investigator, either. Lyle Canton was a Pinkerton agent with a reputation for success.

Around her, folks bustled about their business. Like yesterday, clouds lent the day a gloomy quality that dampened her mood.

*But it isn't the weather affecting you, is it? It's Adam's absence. And now this troubling news.*

Worry nipped at her like a riled dog. Was Adam all right? Would he find answers that would aid the kids? Would her father's new bloodhound discover her whereabouts? What would she do if Gerard showed up and demanded she return home and marry his friend?

Shoving the paper into her reticule, Deborah retrieved her parcels from the bench and hurried along the boardwalk, dodging other shoppers. Aunt Mae had offered to watch Liam and Lily while she completed a few errands. It hadn't taken long for the boardinghouse proprietress to take a liking to the kids and assume the role of stand-in grandmother. Still, she didn't possess endless patience, and Deborah had been gone longer than she'd anticipated.

She was passing Hannah's dress shop when a hulking figure bumped into her. Her parcels went flying.

The man muttered an apology and retrieved her things with jerky movements. "Sorry about that," he said, his face obscured by his hat.

She noted he had overly large feet. The black, round-tipped shoes were the size of toy boats.

When he straightened, she recognized him as the same man she'd bumped into before, the one who'd been with the woman who could pass for her from a distance.

Wearing an inscrutable expression, he tipped his hat and continued on his way.

"Who was that?"

Deborah turned to find Hannah at her elbow. "I have no idea. You haven't seen him before?"

"Not that I recall." The willowy brunette frowned at his retreating figure. "I hope you didn't have anything breakable in those sacks."

"Fortunately, no."

"Well, I'm glad I saw you through the window. I've got those dresses you ordered for Lily ready." She waved her into the shop's cooler interior. "How's she and her brother doing?"

Deborah waited at the counter. "They're coping as best they can, considering their uncertain circumstances."

"I saw the four of you at church," she called from the storage room. "They seem comfortable in your and Adam's company."

Deborah glanced around, relieved there were no other customers to overhear.

Liam's reserve melted a little more each day. It was like watching a flower slowly open to the sun's rays...a touching experience. Adam had a lot to do with that. The boy clearly admired him.

Hannah returned with two dresses, a Sunday dress of buttercup yellow with white ribbon trim and an everyday dress of whimsical mint green with tiny pink roses.

Deborah made a sound of appreciation. "Lily is going to be ecstatic! You've done a wonderful job, as usual."

Since she'd purchased new clothes for Liam, she couldn't resist giving new dresses to Lily.

"It's my pleasure." When she'd accepted Deborah's payment, Hannah proceeded to package the dresses. Her face clouded like the sky outside. "I don't like to repeat gossip, but you should know there've been rumblings that concern the merchandise Liam and Lily took."

"Oh? The sheriff didn't act concerned when Adam and I approached him the other day." In fact, he hadn't given them more than five minutes of his time before announcing he had other pressing concerns to tend to. There was something about the man that struck her as insincere.

"Some of the shop owners are willing to overlook the losses, considering the situation. Others may not be as compassionate." She named one in particular. "Mr. Hagermann's threatening to hold them responsible."

"We'd intended on having the kids visit each affected proprietor. We simply haven't gotten around to it. That's our mistake."

"I'm sure you and Adam will find a way to appease everyone."

The way Hannah said it made it sound like she and Adam were a real couple, partners caring for the siblings. But that wasn't the case. Or it wouldn't be for long.

Adam shouldn't be this excited to see Deborah and the kids. Nor should he have allowed them to dominate his thoughts during his brief sojourn to Lakewood. He should be strategizing. Trying to predict Zane Ogden's next move.

Instead of stopping at Russ's office to discuss the information he'd uncovered, he strode down Eden Street with one object in mind—speak to Deborah. He couldn't wait to share everything he'd learned, to see her reaction and together decide what the next step should be.

It was a unique experience, this feeling that they were partners. How ironic that the woman he'd suspected of wrongdoing had become so important to his happiness!

Adam passed through the gate, climbed the porch steps and entered the boardinghouse through the main door. His anticipation built, perspiration dampening his collar. His heart beat against his ribs with sudden force. Would she be in the kitchen baking something unusual? He could hardly wait to see that winsome smile of hers. No doubt Liam and Lily would be there, too.

Lily would greet him with a hug because she was unreserved with her affection.

Liam would probably want to hug him, too, but would hold back. Not only was he determined to guard his bruised heart, he was in a peculiar place between boyhood and manhood.

Voices drifted from the parlor. Changing direction, Adam charged inside.

Hildie and Preston, seated close together on the sofa, looked at him in surprise. "Adam." Hildie's eyes held a note of censure. "Where's the fire?"

Preston didn't bother to hide his dislike. Adam wondered if the man was spending time with Hildie because he truly liked her, or because he was angling to get close to Deborah.

"No fire. Sorry to bother you."

Swiftly retreating, he passed through the dining room, certain his footsteps would summon Deborah. But no one appeared in the doorway.

"Deborah?" he called as he entered the kitchen.

The scene was chaotic. Liam and Lily flanked Aunt Mae at the stove. Every surface was crammed with utensils and dishes.

"Adam!" Circumventing the worktable, Lily rushed up and threw her arms around his middle. "I missed you!"

Lifting her head, she looked up at him with shining, hopeful eyes. His fondness for this little girl grew each day. Despite her hardships, she hadn't lost her zeal for life.

He gently patted her back. "I missed you, too, sprite." He angled toward Liam, who'd approached them but hung back. "I suppose you're too old for hugs?"

Lily giggled. "No one's too old for hugs! Come on, Liam."

The boy shuffled closer. Lily seized his arm and tugged him into their shared embrace. He relaxed after barely a second, his arms squeezing tight around Adam and Lily before he removed himself.

Aunt Mae's soft-as-butter expression mirrored Adam's insides. These kids had endured enough sorrow. They deserved kindness. They deserved guardians who'd care and provide for them, who'd make them feel safe and loved.

If he wasn't on the trail of Ogden, if he wasn't in the employ of the Pinkertons and was free to do as he pleased, he'd be the first to volunteer. Second, actually, after Deborah.

"Where is she?"

Aunt Mae's eyes took on a knowing gleam but she asked, "Where's who?"

He couldn't hide his impatience. "Deborah."

"She's outside picking snap beans."

Lily grabbed his hand. "I'll take you to her."

Aunt Mae chuckled. "I believe the adults would like to speak privately, little missy. Besides, I need help with this chicken if we're to feed everyone at a reasonable hour."

Adam forced himself to take a sedate pace through the kitchen, past the storage room and out to the shaded, rose-scented veranda. He scanned the vegetable garden, spotting her almost immediately. A yellow blossom was tucked behind her ear, contrasting with her chocolate-colored tresses. He studied her profile, the pert nose and elegant line of her jaw.

His mouth dried. He felt almost queasy.

What was wrong with him?

It wasn't like he was fighting for his life on a bloody, chaotic battlefield or hemmed in by a crook's bullets.

Telling himself he was being childish, he left the veranda and strode across the short grass, halting at the end of her row and drinking in her beauty. She was a ray of summer sunshine in her yellow dress.

Unable to think of a thing to say, he cleared his throat.

Surprise flitted over her features, followed by a surge of joy.

Was she as happy to see him as he was her?

Bolting to her feet, she dashed straight for him. Holding his arms out in silent welcome felt like the natural thing to do. When she stepped into his arms, it seemed as if she'd found a home in his embrace, burrowing against his chest, her cheek pressed to his heart.

"Oh, Adam." She released a sigh that indicated she hadn't breathed properly while he was gone. Funny, he could identify.

He stroked between her shoulders and along her spine. The cotton fabric of her bodice was supple and warm with her body heat.

"I feel like I've been gone a month," he murmured, unable to keep from kissing her temple.

"More like a year," she whispered.

Meeting his gaze, she slowly twined her arms around his neck and focused on his mouth.

Adam hugged her closer, his head swimming with intoxicating anticipation.

There were no more words as their lips touched and sparks exploded. This wasn't a tender exploration. They'd waited too long. Dreamed too long.

Adam held her tight, his hands spanning her waist, keeping her close.

She was everything he'd hoped. Giving. Daring. Passionate. Sweet.

Her floral scent enveloped him, imprinting this moment on his brain.

He never wanted to let her go. Never wanted to be separated from her again.

Deborah suddenly broke contact, her breath uneven and fanning his tingling mouth.

Her topaz eyes whirled with wonder. "You're the first man I've kissed."

Grinning, he inched his fingers over her cheek and jaw, glorying in the silken skin stretched over fragile bone. "This is new for me, too."

"If I'd had any inkling how amazing it would be, I'd have kissed you a long time ago."

Adam chuckled and kissed the tip of her cute nose. "Don't ever lose your candor, Deborah."

She didn't respond. Taking her cues from him, she framed his face, her thumbs stroking his lips and chin. The expression on her face made his heart tumble over itself.

"If you continue in that vein," he murmured in a thick voice, "I'll be forced to kiss you again."

Her smile was bright enough to banish the darkest shadows. "Would that be so terrible?"

"Not if I could be sure a pair of orphans wouldn't discover us."

His emotions—heightened by his absence—had edged out common sense. He couldn't ensure that neither of them would be hurt. He couldn't offer her a future.

With that fact fresh in his mind, Adam let her go.

# Chapter Seventeen

Something had changed. Deborah couldn't pinpoint exactly what.

Longing burned in Adam's molten gaze, but his countenance had lost its easy lines from moments earlier. Smoothing his hair—she vaguely recalled threading her fingers through the short locks—he glanced at the windows. *Ah.* He was worried the kids might see them.

She pulled her thoughts to where they should be. Not a light task, considering her nerve endings danced with the thrilling aftermath of his touch. Adam's kiss had confirmed that what she felt for him wasn't fleeting or inconsequential. She wasn't sure what to label it, exactly. Perhaps it was best not to. Not until his case was solved, which would then allow him to entertain thoughts of his future.

The sun broke through the clouds. The brightness was almost blinding. She started walking toward the veranda.

"What did you find out?"

He fell into step beside her. "I interviewed several townspeople first, including the owner of Lakewood's only mercantile, the livery owner and the pastor. They had little good to say about the Jacksons."

His grim tone chased the last of her giddiness away. In

the shade, she located the pitcher she'd brought out earlier and poured water into glasses before choosing one of the wicker chairs.

Adam sank into the one across from her and removed his tie. "They haven't witnessed any questionable behavior. However, what interactions they have had left them with poor impressions. Jeremiah and Laura moved to the area a decade ago, but according to Pastor Lund, you'd be hard-pressed to find anyone who claimed to have a relationship with them."

"We suspected they were recluses. Did you have better results with the neighbors?"

"One was a surly old bachelor who ordered me off his property."

"With rifle in hand?"

His smile was part grimace. "I obliged him without hesitation. I had better success with the Rands, a couple in their early sixties whose property borders the Jacksons'. They confirmed Liam's story about how they wound up in Lakewood. Six months ago, Mr. Rand paid Jeremiah a visit to discuss farm business and was surprised by the kids' presence. Apparently, Jeremiah and Laura have an adult son who rarely comes around. Mr. Rand's seen him only once or twice in the decade they've lived there."

Anger bubbled up inside her. "If they treated him like they did Liam and Lily, I'd imagine he has good reason."

"Jeremiah made sure Rand didn't see much of the kids." His jaw hardened. "What he did see troubled him."

Deborah left her chair and began to pace. "Why didn't he go to the sheriff?"

"Sadly, there's not much he could do unless he had a witness to attest to outright cruelty."

Her hands fisted. "There should be laws protecting children like Liam and Lily."

"I agree."

"Did you meet Laura and Jeremiah?"

"I didn't introduce myself, if that's what you mean. I thought it best not to arouse their suspicions."

"You spied on them, didn't you?"

"I did."

"And?"

"I didn't have time to do a thorough examination. Even so, what I saw leads me to believe that the kids were right to leave. The place is a ramshackle mess. Jeremiah takes no pride in his property or his animals. Several of his horses looked in need of medical attention. The stalls hadn't been cleaned for weeks, gauging by the awful stench."

"Probably because he didn't have Liam to do it for him," she muttered. Finding a place at the railing, she splayed her palms atop the ledge. A stray splinter poked at her.

"He has a hired hand. I would've liked to ask the young man a couple of questions, but there was never a good opportunity."

"Did you see her? Laura?"

His lips thinned. "Didn't strike me as the browbeaten type."

"You're trying to say she's just plain mean, same as her no-good husband."

She peeked at the sky. "Thank you, Lord, for rescuing them from a life of torment."

"Amen."

Her eyes met Adam's as she said with conviction and without hesitation, "I want to petition for temporary guardianship."

Surprise tugging his brows together, he replaced the glass on the side table and rose to his feet. "You're already their guardian."

"Not officially. I want a legal document stating my rights. If the Jacksons were to discover their whereabouts,

I wouldn't be able to prevent them from taking Liam and Lily."

"We'll speak to Russ about it at once." He joined her at the railing. "What about your father? And the man you pledged to marry?"

Her skin flushed hot. The words, uttered so soon after their intimate embrace, stung like a hundred bee stings. "I broke that pledge the day I left St. Louis. Besides, what do Gerard and Tobias have to do with the kids?"

"I got the impression you were hiding here."

Deborah shifted her focus to the garden and trees beyond, humiliation making her nauseous. He was insightful and observant—two valuable qualities for an undercover agent. What must he think of her? That she was a scared little girl inside a grown woman's body, too cowardly to stand up to her own father?

"In order for a judge to grant you guardianship," he said, "you'll need a permanent place of residence. He'll want to ensure the kids have stability." Crossing his arms, he openly assessed her. "Deborah, do you plan on staying in Cowboy Creek? Or returning to St. Louis? Or somewhere in between?"

She wished he was asking for himself. "When I arrived in April with the other brides, I had every intention of moving on down the rail line. To what town or city, I had no idea. But the longer I stayed, the harder it was to think of leaving. For the first time in my life, I wasn't the tycoon's graceless daughter. I wasn't Lucy Frazier's inept sister." She tried to blink away the gathering tears. Adam's hand covered hers, a sweet gesture of comfort. "I didn't have to hide in the estate kitchens anymore. In Cowboy Creek, people love my desserts. They admire my talents. I have something valuable to contribute here."

Tipping her chin up, he gazed deeply into her eyes. "Don't allow your father or anyone else to make you doubt your worth, Deborah. God made you special, with your own unique strengths and gifts."

Joy took root in her heart. This was it. She was falling in love with Adam Halloway, and there was nothing she could do to stop it.

"I want to stay in Cowboy Creek."

"You're certain?" he said. "What about Lucy? Your friends?"

Deborah missed her sister, and there were certain things she missed about her home. The magnificent library where she'd passed countless winter afternoons curled up with a book, and the manicured garden with its man-made pond. The kitchens that were either too hot or too cold but always cheered by the staff who treated her as a part of their group.

The estate house had been built by her great-grandfather, utilizing the finest materials shipped from all over the world. The furnishings were grand and expensive. It was stunning and breathtaking. It was also a constant reminder of her inadequacy, her inability to meet Frazier standards, her grief over the loss of her mother and futile wondering if things might have been different if she'd lived.

But the place couldn't hold a candle to the cowtown she lived in now. She knew that for certain.

"I'm content here," she told him. "This is my community."

He slowly nodded. "Okay."

Deborah wasn't staying for Adam. She wasn't even staying for Liam and Lily. She was staying for herself.

Part of Adam's job involved sitting around observing people and eavesdropping on conversations. He'd hated it in the beginning. A waste of time, he'd told his superior, when he could be out in the middle of the action, *doing* something. The other man had been patient with him and taught him the value of collecting data, from the seemingly inane tidbit to the obvious. Over the years, he'd honed his skills and accepted that this part of being a Pinkerton might not be glamorous, but it formed a foundation on which he could build his theories.

He'd come to The Lariat earlier that morning in hopes of spotting the elusive Maroni brothers, or as he figured it— Zane Ogden and yet another cohort pretending to be brothers. The hotel's reception area had been bustling until an hour ago, so he moved to the restaurant and nursed an endless cup of coffee while pretending to read the newspaper.

So far, he'd observed a scruffy cowboy failing spectacularly to charm a pair of young ladies, an elderly couple meeting their grandchildren for the first time and hotel staff gossiping instead of dusting the fixtures as their manager instructed.

He was about to leave when the blacksmith, Colton Werner, and the newspaperman, Sam Woods Mason, chose a table nearby. They nodded in greeting before ordering the lunch special. The waitress, by this time annoyed by Adam's presence, asked if he wished to order something to eat. He surprised her by saying yes.

While awaiting his roast quail and vegetables, he noticed Noah Burgess entering the restaurant. The rancher scanned the room's occupants and headed straight for Colton and Sam. He delivered news that suffocated Adam's appetite.

Pushing to his feet, Adam approached the trio. "I apologize for interrupting, but I couldn't help overhearing. Did you say another rancher has met with an accident?"

Noah assessed him with steel blue eyes. "That's right. You're the cattleman from Missouri?"

"Yes, sir. Adam Draper." They shook hands. "Is he going to make it?"

"It's not good." Sam and Colton looked somber as Noah outlined what happened. "Floyd had climbed onto his windmill last evening when it collapsed. He fell from a height of about twenty feet, and part of the structure landed on his legs."

"Was it tampered with?" Colton asked.

Noah's scar bunched as his jaw hardened. "Looks that way."

"How long is this going to continue? Until someone dies?" Sam threw down his napkin. "I need to get out there and gather information. This will need to go in the paper tomorrow. I'll have to skip lunch."

The blacksmith gestured toward the entrance. "I understand. We'll meet another time."

Adam tossed coins on his table to cover his meal, bid a hasty farewell to the pair and caught up with Sam. "Mind if I tag along with you?"

"Suit yourself."

"My horse is at the livery."

"Mine, too." The man fell silent as they walked, obviously processing this new development. When a stray dog bounded toward them and pushed between them, Sam collected himself and shot Adam a sideways glance. "I suppose you're rethinking your decision to stake a claim here."

"I've been informed the town hasn't always seen troubles like these. If the sheriff finds his culprit, there won't be anything holding me back."

Sam made a noise that cast doubt on the possibility.

"I gather you don't have much faith in his abilities?" Adam probed.

"That's yet to be determined."

"Do you have any idea who might be behind all this?"

"Surely you don't expect me to answer that." Winding through the knot of men outside the livery, Sam entered the welcome shaded interior.

"You've got a broader view of Cowboy Creek and its

happenings than most folks. I know you've got an opinion," Adam coaxed.

At the stall containing his horse, Sam turned. Humor hovered about his mouth. "One I can't share with anyone other than my wife."

"Of course." Adam knew when he'd hit a wall. The newspaperman was too much of a professional to let crucial information slip.

They rode out to the Rocking J beneath the searing June sun. Waves of heat were visible at ground level. By the time they reached the house, Adam's hair was wet beneath his Stetson and his shirt stuck to his skin. There wasn't a single cloud in the sky to offer a reprieve.

Sam dismounted and mopped his face with his handkerchief. "Floyd's wife is shy, even in the company of people she knows." He gestured toward the house. "I suggest you hang around out here until I've had a chance to speak with her privately."

Adam agreed, inwardly grateful for the chance to explore on his own. He waited until Sam was inside to head for the outbuildings. The barn and surrounding paddocks were deserted. No one was around to challenge him, so he continued on his way, taking mental notes to record on paper later. Unlike the Jacksons, this couple took pride in their home. The structures were old but sound. The fences were sturdy. Troughs clean.

As he passed yet another storage shed, the remnants of Floyd Gains's windmill came into view. Two men stood outlined by the vivid blue sky—one beanpole thin and with wiry silver hair, the other young and doughy—surveying the damage. They both turned and scowled at him.

The thin one settled his hand on his pistol. "State your business here, mister."

"I'm Adam Draper. Rode over with Sam Woods Mason."

He gestured behind him. "He's at the house speaking with Mrs. Gains."

"We don't appreciate gawkers."

"I'm not here to gawk, I assure you. I'm in town looking to purchase property for my own ranch. Guess I chose the wrong time to visit Cowboy Creek."

The doughy one spat a stream of tobacco in the dust. "Guess you did."

Adam met the silver-haired man's gaze. "How is Mr. Gains doing?"

His hand lowered to his side, away from the pistol. "Only God knows if he'll survive."

"I'll be praying for his recovery." That was the truth, too, not an insincere bid to gain this ranch worker's trust.

"Appreciate it." His gaze lost its hostility. "You from Kansas?"

"Big Bend, Missouri."

The doughy one shifted his bulk. "I got kinfolk from there. You know the Whitfields?"

He didn't bother hiding his surprise. "Went to church with a Nora and Lincoln Whitfield."

"Nora's my cousin." He grinned and extended his hand. "I'm Bob Polanski."

"Have you been to Big Bend in recent years?"

"Nah, not since before the war."

They conversed for another ten minutes before Adam felt comfortable introducing the topic of Floyd's accident again. Tension reignited in the air. He sensed they had more on their minds than they were willing to admit. Sam eventually joined them.

While he didn't look thrilled that Adam had gone exploring on his own, he didn't call him out. To his relief, the other men returned to the house. Maybe now he'd get a chance to nose around.

When Sam began inspecting the crippled windmill,

Adam walked along the fence line, his gaze trained on the ground. The newspaperman met him on the far west side of the enclosure.

"You looking for anthills?"

Adam's lips compressed. "I'm looking for items like this." Halting, he showed him the handkerchief he'd found nestled against a fence post. "If this doesn't belong to Mrs. Gains, it might belong to our suspect or an associate."

Sam took the square and studied the dainty purple flowers embroidered along the outer edge. He lifted his gaze. "*Our* suspect?"

"As a rancher, I take attacks like this personally." He pretended to be preoccupied by the jagged wooden stakes jutting from the ground. If Floyd died, the person who did this would be hanged for murder.

Sam considered him for long moments before gesturing behind him. "Let's ask her."

At the house, Adam waited on the porch, pacing the length of it and praying for a break in this case.

Sam's features were difficult to read. In his line of work, Adam had practice hiding his feelings. He could relate.

"Well?" he asked when Sam stepped outside.

"It's not hers."

"Looks like you have a puzzle to solve. Will you involve the sheriff?"

He examined the handkerchief. "Not yet. I'd appreciate your silence on this."

"You have my word."

Adam wasn't going to tell anyone about the discovery. He was going to refocus his efforts, however. Instead of searching for Ogden, he would hunt for a beautiful brunette whose name started with a *D*. His heart and mind were in agreement on one thing—the woman he sought was not named Deborah.

# Chapter Eighteen

"Deborah, do you have a minute?"

Sadie hovered in the hallway near the dining room, her hands tangled at her waist.

"We were about to take care of important business. Can it wait until after supper?"

"It's an urgent matter." Her gaze skittered to Adam, who was holding the door open for Deborah.

Her friend had been acting strangely throughout the noon meal, so Deborah could not ignore her request.

She looked at Adam, who gestured out to the porch swing, where Liam and Lily had gone once the table had been cleared and the floors swept. "Go ahead," he said. "We'll wait for you outside."

"All right." When the door closed behind him, she extended her hand. "Will the parlor be suitable?"

Sadie's brow crinkled. "Not private enough. Let's go to my room."

Deborah's imagination churned as they ascended the stairs. Were Sadie and Walter having problems? The pair seemed closer than ever during the Sunday service a few days ago. Or was the other woman concerned by how much time Deborah was spending with Adam?

"I have something I need to show you." Sadie bustled

to the desk beneath the window and presented her with a photograph. "Look at this."

A wartime photo, the scene depicted soldiers amid a sea of tents. It captured everyday activities...men playing cards, cooking in cast iron pots over small fires, cleaning weapons and laundry.

"What am I supposed to be looking for?"

Sadie drew closer and tapped the image of a gentleman who stood alone. His army uniform hugging his lean frame, he surveyed his world with a grimness that broke her heart.

Lifting the paper, she studied his features, mostly hidden by a thick beard. "It's Adam."

"Yes."

She met Sadie's troubled gaze. "Where did you get this?"

"Walter was certain he'd met Adam before, remember? He sent for his collection, and I've been helping him sort through them." Gently turning the photograph, she said, "Deborah, his last name isn't Draper. It's Halloway."

"I know."

Sadie's jaw sagged. "What? How?"

Going to the bed, Deborah sank onto the edge. "He told me."

"Why aren't you upset? I've been worried sick since the moment we discovered his deception. What explanation did he give you?"

"I'm not at liberty to say." Pacing to the window, she glanced out at the porch but was unable to see Adam or the kids.

"You've allowed your feelings for him to cloud your judgment."

The memories of their embrace encompassed her, calling forth the soul-deep ache that hovered near the surface. "I trust him."

Sadie laid her hand on Deborah's arm. "You wouldn't be the first to succumb to the wiles of a handsome charmer."

"He's not a bad person, Sadie."

"Why can't you tell me what's going on?"

Deborah turned to her friend. "I wish I could."

"Is he related to the Halloways of White Rock Ranch?"

The expression on her face must've given her away, because Sadie's eyes grew wide. "He is, isn't he?"

Taking her hands in hers, Deborah pleaded for her understanding. "You're right. I've come to care a great deal for Adam. I may not have experience with suitors or men in general, and I admit I can be naive at times, but I'm not reckless when it comes to my affections. And I would never allow anyone to take advantage of two vulnerable children, no matter how handsome or charming."

"Deborah—"

"Adam Halloway is the finest man I've ever known, Sadie."

"You're in love with him."

Deborah couldn't admit it to herself, much less to another human being.

Sadie sighed. "I pray you know what you're doing. I'd hate for you to be hurt."

"What are you going to tell Walter?"

"I'll ask him to keep this information to himself."

"Will he?"

Sadie gave her a half-hearted smile. "For me, I believe he will."

Deborah hugged her. "You're a wonderful friend."

"I try to be."

It didn't take training to figure out something had upset Deborah. As they navigated the busy boardwalk a short while later, he felt her arm tremble beneath his light hold.

Instead of wrapping his arm about her as he yearned to

do, he said, "What's the matter? Did you and Sadie have a disagreement?"

Her pretty mouth pursed. Glancing at the storefronts on their left and the dusty street bustling with wagon traffic on their right, she slowed her pace. "Walter Kerr has discovered your true identity."

His fingers tightened almost imperceptibly on her sleeve. Driving emotion from his face, he kept his gaze on Liam and Lily walking ahead of them. "How?"

"He took your photograph during the war." There was a note of grief in her voice. Whatever image she'd seen of him had troubled her. "He made a habit of writing the names of his subjects on the back of photographs."

"I see."

"Aren't you worried?"

"It's not a positive development." They came to First Street. He waited until a group of cowboys on horseback moved on before guiding her across. "I'll have to speak with him."

Deborah instructed the kids to wait on the bench outside Hagermann's Mercantile. They had no objections to the delay. They weren't looking forward to today's task—issuing appeals for forgiveness to all the affected shop owners.

Deborah pulled Adam out of the flow of foot traffic and against the building.

"What are you planning on telling him?" she asked.

"The same thing I told you."

"The bare minimum, you mean." She arched a brow in challenge, but there was no hiding the hurt in her eyes.

"Deborah, I'd tell you everything if I could."

His prodding conscience mirrored her obvious disbelief. Would he truly reveal *everything*? Because he was certain she wouldn't appreciate the fact that he'd intruded upon her privacy, rifled through her belongings and hidden in her wardrobe cabinet—spying on her when she thought she was alone. Not that he'd had a choice about that last bit.

He could never, ever reveal the fact that he'd suspected her of helping an unscrupulous man take advantage of hardworking citizens and in some cases, attempt to forever silence them.

She'd be heartbroken.

"Your family knows the details, correct?"

He couldn't explain without revealing that this case was special. Personal. "They do."

"You trust them to keep your secrets." Her throat convulsed. "You and I have grown close these past weeks. Why don't you trust me? I wouldn't dream of sharing private information."

A battle waged inside him, his training against his need to prove he cared. He pinched the bridge of his nose and silently begged God for direction.

"I didn't tell Sadie anything," she continued. "Even when she called your character into question, I didn't waver."

"I appreciate that, but—"

A booming voice cut off his words. Mr. Hagermann had exited his shop and approached the bench where Liam and Lily waited. Adam took in the elderly man's posture, his twisted features and fisted hands.

"We may have a problem," he muttered.

Deborah turned her head and covered her mouth with one hand, muffling her exclamation.

Together, they went to investigate. Others had stopped to listen to the man's tirade, as well.

"I don't want the likes of you anywhere near my place of business," he bellowed at the children. "Do you hear me?"

Liam's face was milk-white. "Yes, sir."

Lily clutched her doll to her chest. She looked frail and small and terrified.

Mr. Hagermann waved his finger above the girl's nose. "I didn't hear you, little girl."

She shrunk away. "Y-yes, sir."

Adam's ire flared. "Mr. Hagermann, Miss Frazier and I brought Liam and Lily here to apologize. Might I suggest we take this inside?"

He stiffened to his full height. "Inside? Where they can filch more of my goods?" His hand sliced the air. "No, thank you!"

Deborah bristled. "Are you saying you won't listen to their explanation or offer a chance to make amends?"

"Why should I? If I let them off with a pat on the head, every thief and ragamuffin will view my store as prime pickings."

"They are not hardened thieves, Mr. Hagermann." She spoke through gritted teeth. "They are orphans in need of compassion. They are sorry for what they did and willing to work off what they owe. Did you conveniently forget that portion of the Holy Scriptures?"

Belatedly noticing the gathering onlookers, he flushed a dull red. "Don't place the blame at my door, Miss Frazier. I'm an honest businessman who was taken advantage of."

Adam had had enough. "Have you ever been hungry?"

"Excuse me?"

"It's a simple question. Have you ever been so hungry you couldn't think straight? I'm not talking about skipping a single meal. I'm referring to going days, even weeks, with very little to fill your stomach. The need to eat becomes a constant worry. It edges out everything you've learned about right and wrong."

"Well, I—I—" Mr. Hagermann floundered for a response.

"I have." Adam said. "And I can tell you that it's one of the worst feelings in the world, the constant gnawing in your gut, the weakness that invades your body. It makes a man do desperate things. I wouldn't wish that on my worst enemy, let alone a helpless child."

Deborah's hand folded over his, her palm warm and soft, her fingers slender yet strong.

Some of the bystanders nodded in understanding. Anyone who'd served during the war had likely experienced what he'd just described. A few appeared uncertain, as if they weren't sure whom to support.

One man in a business suit spoke up. "I heard they ran away from their relatives' home. They put themselves in that situation."

"You heard right," Adam told him. "But did you ask yourself what might've spurred them to that decision?"

That silenced the man. Lily started crying, however. Deborah went and sat beside her on the bench.

Mr. Hagermann made a dismissive motion. "I don't know why you'd bother with a pair of runaways. The right place for them is the orphan asylum."

As Deborah held Lily in the haven of her arms, a fierceness entered her eyes. "I'm surprised at you, Mr. Hagermann, a pillar of this town and faithful church member condemning these children without a second thought. You don't know them. You've no idea what they've endured. If you withhold your forgiveness from them, how can you expect God to forgive you?"

The older man glared at her. She didn't flinch. Like a lioness protecting her cubs, she was courageous and fierce. Adam couldn't help but be impressed.

Clapping broke out among the women in the crowd, irking Mr. Hagermann, who stomped into his store and slammed the door behind him.

When the others dispersed, Adam pulled her aside. "I'm proud of you. Legal documents or not, you're their guardian."

"I'd rather have your trust." Her sad smile knocked him back.

There was a chasm between them, put there by his personal vendetta against Zane Ogden. He thought of the newspaperman. Sam had said he only shared his private thoughts with his wife, Marlys. If this were any other case, he would confide in Deborah. But it wasn't. This involved his beloved father. Adam owed it to him to restore his reputation and find the evidence needed to prove Ogden had not only swindled Gilbert Halloway, but murdered him.

"Please, believe me." He seized her hand. "I do trust you."

"Apparently not enough."

Withdrawing, she turned and guided the children farther down the street, increasing the distance between them in more ways than one.

# Chapter Nineteen

"What's all this?" Adam prodded the sack of sugar that Deborah had out, among the other baking supplies on the counter of the boardinghouse. "I thought we agreed to take the kids to Seth's this afternoon."

Deborah scooped another cupful of flour and dumped it into her bowl. "I won't be able to join you, after all. I have to make two dozen miniature shortcakes for a private party tonight."

This event would serve twin purposes—she would earn wages and avoid spending time with Adam and his family. She'd come to the conclusion that being around him was detrimental to her future happiness. The more time in his company, the deeper she fell for him and the more ensnared her heart became. Already the process of disentanglement was causing her pain.

She'd found reasons to avoid being alone with him these past few days. It made her miserable, of course. But it couldn't be helped.

"What party?" he said, obviously disappointed. "Why didn't you mention it sooner? We would've adjusted our plans to include you."

His handsome face begged for her caress, his mouth evoked sweet, sweet memories and the promise of bliss unlike she'd ever known. But his eyes shattered any illusions she might entertain about them as a couple. Deborah hadn't recognized it until recently...the impenetrable guard he'd set in place that kept the world at bay. That he wouldn't lower it for her proved he didn't love her.

Hurt and angry, she charged, "Are you nervous about taking the children yourself?"

His features shuttered closed. "You know I'm not. Why are you shutting me out?" He took a step toward her, his intention to come around to where she stood causing a flare of panic. Lily's arrival saved her.

"Adam said I could ride Cinnamon," she enthused. "Are you going to ride, too?"

Deborah was grateful the little girl hadn't noticed the new tension between the adults. Liam was older and more aware of nuances, but he hadn't questioned either of them.

Pasting on a smile, she gripped the wooden spoon until her fingers protested. "I'm sorry, Lily. I won't be able to come this time. I have an event to prepare for."

Her crestfallen expression further dulled Deborah's spirits. She'd channeled her energy into putting up a brave front for the kids. They had enough to worry about without adding her and Adam's relationship issues to the mix.

"What event is it?" Adam said quietly.

Her pulse leaped. He wasn't going to like her answer.

"Preston's hosting a small gathering. Today is his birthday."

His throat worked. "Lily, would you go outside and wait for me on the porch? I think your brother is already out there."

With a sigh and a nod, she trudged into the hallway. The sound of the door closing echoed through the deserted first floor. Aunt Mae was running errands. Gus and Old Horace were stationed outside Booker & Son's, and she wasn't sure where the other boarders had gone.

"I understand you're upset with me," he said. "But I don't think getting involved with Preston Wells is a wise idea."

"I'm not getting involved with him. This is a business deal, nothing more. If I plan to support Liam and Lily, I have to start saving as much as I can."

"You don't have to shoulder that burden alone," he said, thrusting his fingers through his hair. "I'll gladly pitch in for their needs."

"I appreciate that, Adam. I do. But I have to learn to depend on myself." She dipped her head, and the blossom behind her ear dropped into the bowl. She fished out the wilting flower, rubbing her finger over the velvety petals. "You're not going to be around forever."

His breathing changed rhythm. Before he could ply her with excuses, she said, "Besides, Preston's courting Hildie."

"He may be courting her, but he wants *you*."

"When we spoke before the church service yesterday, he was friendly and upbeat. There was no evidence of his previous forcefulness."

"Some people are skilled actors."

"Are you talking about yourself or Preston?"

He flinched. "I suppose I deserve that." Shaking his head, he said, "I've encountered men like him in my work. I'm not convinced he's given up on his pursuit of you."

She measured out more flour, wishing he'd hurry up and leave. Her desire to accompany them to the White Rock Ranch was difficult to deny. Russell and Anna were supposed to be there. She enjoyed watching Adam interact with his mother and brothers. The Halloway men shared a special bond that trials, time and distance hadn't managed to sever. And he was affectionate with Evelyn, often placing his arm around her shorter frame and hugging her to his side. The woman adored each of her sons, but she seemed to especially thrill in the return of her youngest.

Then there were the children. Tate, Harper and Little John were rambunctious, mischievous and adorable. Violet was still reserved, but she wouldn't be for long if those boys had anything to say about it.

Liam and Lily needed friends like them. Would they still be welcome once Adam left Cowboy Creek? Would she?

"It's one party." Gesturing to the window, she said, "Lily's chomping at the bit to get on that horse. Shouldn't keep her waiting."

"I wish you'd reconsider. My family will be sad to miss out on your company." He paused. "I will, too."

She almost untied her apron. Almost.

"I've spent too long being an outsider to want to do it again with your family."

He looked startled. "Deborah—"

"I have a lot to do in a short amount of time."

Bracing her hands on the counter, she lowered her gaze to the floor.

"I'll leave you to it, then." The whisper of his fading footsteps felt like fists against her heart.

His conversation with Deborah had not gone well. If it had, she'd be here beneath the trees watching Liam and Lily ride in circles and having the time of their lives. Violet was out there, as well, with Seth overseeing the whole production.

Adam kicked at the water barrel, his scowl etched in place.

She'd accused him of being an actor, of all things.

Well, he hadn't been acting when he'd kissed her. Hadn't been acting since pretty much the day they met. Not with her.

This thing with Deborah had shaken his rock-solid view of the Pinkertons and their methods. He'd always told himself that he did what he did for the sake of justice. He'd disregarded the effects of his actions because he was on the right side of the law.

He'd liked, even loved, his work until coming here.

"What's going on with you and the beautiful baker?"

Adam whipped his head up as the fence bowed beneath his brother Seth's sudden weight.

"You're supposed to be supervising the kids."

Seth rubbed at the faded scar above his brow. His back against the fence so that he faced the paddock, he squinted against the bright sun. "Do they look like they're in jeopardy?" He'd chosen the mildest horses for their first ride. "If they moved any slower they'd be standing still." He twisted in Adam's direction. "Are you two quarreling?"

Adam gritted his teeth. "Something like that."

"You've deprived me of the chance to dispense wise advice for quite a while. You can't clam up now."

"I'm accustomed to figuring things out on my own."

"You don't have to anymore. I'm not an expert on women, but I do have more experience than you. I am married."

Adam tugged his Stetson lower to cover his eyes and kicked at the barrel again.

"She's distancing herself from me," he murmured, his heart heavy. "And I can't seem to do anything to change it."

Seth mulled that over. "In her mind, your friendship has been based on a lie."

"I may have a different name and occupation, but I'm still the same man. She says she trusts me. Her actions prove otherwise."

He couldn't believe she'd accepted Preston's invitation. The thought of her in that man's home made his blood run cold. Why couldn't she see he was playing a game with

Hildie and hadn't completely given up hope of having her for himself?

"Maybe she trusts your character but not your feelings for her."

Thanks to her father, Deborah had confidence issues. Being in Cowboy Creek, making friends and finding success with her desserts had helped mend her broken view of herself. In the short weeks he'd known Deborah, Adam had seen a change in her, a shift in her attitude. He hated to think his agenda—or according to his brothers, his *obsession* with Ogden—had impaired her progress. He didn't want her questioning herself again because of anything he'd done.

Seth spoke again. "The problem here is you think like a Pinkerton agent. You haven't lived a normal life since you were eighteen."

He bristled. "I do what most others can't or won't."

"I'm not belittling your profession, little brother." His eyes were serious. "I admire your dedication."

"Then what's your point?"

"You lived the life of a soldier for years, then traded it for the rolling stone existence of a detective. How are you supposed to relate to Deborah's experiences? Understand how this impacts her?"

"I can see it on her face," he burst out, thrusting his hands through his hair. "I hurt her, and I don't know how to fix it."

Seth frowned. "You should tell her about Ogden."

"No."

"You don't still suspect her…"

"No."

Seth released a heavy sigh. "If you care about her as much as I think you do, you should reconsider."

He couldn't tell her. He'd bungled this operation from

the moment he'd stepped into the boardinghouse kitchen and spied her with that ridiculous blindfold.

No, he had to regain his professional footing and refocus on his reasons for coming here in the first place.

Deborah didn't want him around, anyway.

Preston must've been watching for her arrival from the window, because he exited his house before she'd even reached the door.

He met her on the street corner. "Here, let me take those for you."

"They aren't heavy." She'd divided the shortcakes into two square baskets to prevent them from being crushed.

"No, but I'm sure they're awkward to balance." His gaze raked her from head to toe as he took one of the baskets and placed his other hand low on her back. "Come on inside. The party doesn't start for another hour, so you'll have plenty of time to arrange these how you'd like."

His fingers burned into her as he guided her through the yard. Deborah reminded herself he was with Hildie now. He was simply being courteous.

His home was located on a quiet street, far from the hustle and bustle of the main thoroughfare. Built within the last year, the compact design was suited to a bachelor's lifestyle.

"I've cleared this credenza in order to showcase your desserts."

He set his basket on the table and, stepping close, took her remaining one. Was it her imagination, or did his fingers linger over hers? The single window in the space wasn't large enough to dispel the shadows. The sun hadn't yet set, but this side of his house faced away from it, darkening it and lending it an intimate feel that made her uncomfortable.

"Would you mind lighting some candles?"

"Of course. Whatever your wishes, Deborah, I'll do my best to accommodate."

A frisson of unease washed down her back. There was a certain gleam in his eyes that reminded her of the old Preston.

Trying to still her trembling hands, she began to arrange the shortcakes on the oval platters he'd provided. Even if Adam was right, it wasn't as if Preston would act inappropriately. He was expecting guests any minute. Besides, he'd never done anything out of bounds.

He returned with a candelabra and took his time lighting each candle.

"Happy birthday, by the way," she said to fill the silence. "I'm sure Hildie has chosen a memorable gift. She has excellent taste."

Preston was suddenly behind her, so close his hot breath skimmed her exposed neck. Her stomach dropped to her toes.

"Since it's my birthday," he said huskily, "I'd like to ask a favor."

Deborah spun around, shocked at how close he was. Preston was taller and, while on the lean side, certainly stronger than she. And they were alone in his home.

"Wh-what kind of favor?"

Tilting his head, he regarded her with curious awe. He extended a finger and slowly outlined her cheek and jaw. "Are you frightened, Deborah?"

She stiffened her spine. "Are you trying to frighten me?"

"I admire you above any other woman I've ever met. Why would I attempt to make you uncomfortable?"

Her pulse thundered in her ears. She glanced across the room at the only exit. Would he try to prevent her from leaving?

"What about Hildie? I thought she was important to you."

His jaw seized and then relaxed. Taking a step back, he said, "I simply wanted to ask if you'd agree to join us for dinner tonight. As a favor to me, of course, to mark another year of life. Forgive me for getting carried away by your beauty."

Deborah floundered for a response. His sudden retreat caught her off guard. "I don't think so."

Preston's eyes darkened. He opened his mouth to respond, but was cut off by a persistent knocking. "It's too early for any of the guests." Clearly perturbed, he started for the hallway. "Excuse me."

When he was out of sight, she sagged against the credenza and gulped in calming breaths. Deborah hadn't yet finished placing the desserts, but she didn't care. She wanted out of this house as soon as possible.

# Chapter Twenty

She was exiting the room when she encountered Preston and a familiar face.

"Sadie!" she exclaimed, pressing her hand over her racing heart. "I didn't realize you were on the guest list."

"I'm not. I came to assist you." Edging to her side, she grasped her hand. "I'm sorry I wasn't at Aunt Mae's in time to help carry everything over."

Deborah attempted to keep the surprise out of her voice. "Oh, it's all right."

Preston's mouth pinched. "We have everything under control, don't we, Deborah? You're free to return to whatever kept you," he said to Sadie.

Sadie cast him a sugar-sweet grin. "Aunt Mae needs us both to assist with dinner," she said airily. "The sooner we finish here, the sooner we can get back. I'm sure you've heard tale of her temper. Don't want to rile Aunt Mae."

Without waiting for his response, Sadie tugged Deborah to the credenza, chatting about Aunt Mae's menu as if the stifling tension in the room didn't exist. Preston stood like a disapproving sentinel in the doorway, his brows low over hooded eyes. When they'd unloaded the final cake, Sadie snatched up the empty baskets.

"Enjoy your party, Preston."

They were passing him when his hand shot out and seized Deborah's wrist. "Are you certain you can't stay?"

She forced herself to be honest. "Even if I could, I wouldn't."

His nostrils flared with displeasure.

"Good night, Preston."

Wresting free, she urged Sadie toward the front door. It wasn't until they were outside in the fresh air and waning light that she could breathe freely.

"There's something off about that man," Sadie huffed, her pace akin to a startled rabbit. "Judging by the look on your face, I arrived in the nick of time."

Deborah didn't dare look behind her. If he'd followed her outside to watch her leave, she'd never sleep again. "How did you know?"

"That you might be in over your head?" Her eyes cut to her. "Adam sent me."

She couldn't summon anything but gratefulness. He knew people. He'd studied and observed and investigated all sorts. She should've listened to him.

"He's probably in the same place I left him," her friend surmised. "I may not know what he's hiding, but his concern for you is genuine."

Indeed, when they reached the gate, she spotted him through the tree branches. He was pacing the length of the porch in an endless rotation. At the creak of the gate hinges, he strode toward them, his gaze doing a quick inventory. His shoulders relaxed somewhat, but his brows remained drawn together.

To Sadie, he said simply, "Thank you."

"You're welcome." Her gaze bounced between them. "I'll be inside if you need me."

They both understood that it was a subtle warning to Adam. When they were alone, he peered deeply into her eyes.

"What did he do?"

"He didn't actually *do* anything." Except scare and intimidate her.

He obviously didn't believe her. "You're too pale, and you're fiddling with your pin—a sure sign you're either nervous or agitated."

"He didn't lay a hand on me. Well, that's not quite true."

Adam paled.

"He stood too close for comfort, and he caressed my face."

A vein in his temple leaped. "Anything else?"

Biting her lower lip, she shook her head.

A muttered exclamation escaped his lips. "But he would have. If Sadie hadn't showed up."

"I don't know." The deep disquiet she'd felt inside Preston's home lingered. "I can't say for sure. But I'm glad you sent her."

"I would've come myself, but I figured you'd rather have your friend there." The wounded look in his eyes gutted her.

"Don't look at me like that," she whispered. "Because I'll be tempted to seek solace in your arms, and I'll forget why I'm upset with you. Then we'd wind up kissing—"

Adam reached for her arms and tugged her against him. His strength and warmth surrounded her, driving away the last remnants of anxiety.

He buried his face in her neck. "I'll make sure he doesn't bother you again."

Beneath her cheek, his heart pounded at a frantic clip. She sighed. Where was her indignation? Her determination to keep him at bay?

Pulling away, he settled his hands on her shoulders. "I can't share the details of my case with you right now, but that doesn't mean I won't eventually. This is the one I *have* to get right. Can you try to understand?"

Could she accept his explanation? He was the first detective she'd encountered. It stood to reason she might not understand his methods.

"I can try."

Relief flooded his features. "I want you to know I value our friendship. I don't like it when you're upset with me."

Friendship. That's all she could hope for with Adam. One day soon, he'd get his man and then he'd leave. She'd have to make do with memories and occasional letters.

The kids burst through the door and raced to her side, talking over each other about their afternoon at the ranch. She'd yet to see Liam so animated.

"Whoa! Slow down," she chuckled. "I take it you both had a wonderful visit with Seth and his family."

"Tate and I climbed so far up into a tree, we could see the church steeple," Liam boasted.

Deborah intercepted Adam's contrite gaze. "You allowed this?"

"I stayed in the barn with Lily. But as soon as Seth and I discovered the boys, we told them to climb down."

Liam's unrepentant grin stretched from ear to ear. "Tate's going to ask Seth if we can build a platform on the sturdiest limb where we can go to escape the girls."

"Violet doesn't always play with me," Lily protested. "Who else will I play with?"

Adam smoothed her braid behind her shoulder. "Violet's had a rough start. Like you and Liam, she's lost both parents. She was separated from Marigold for a time, and now she's come to Cowboy Creek to discover her aunt is momma to three boys. I think she was expecting to have Marigold's undivided attention like before."

"Oh." Lily frowned.

Deborah reached for her hand. "She could use a friend like you, don't you think?"

She thought on it for a bit. "I'll take my doll next time. We could play house."

Liam grunted his disgust for that idea. Before the siblings could commence arguing, Adam turned them toward the porch.

"I don't know about you two, but my stomach's rumbling something fierce."

Lily's hand shot up. "I'm hungry!"

"When are you not?" Shaking his head, Liam shot up the steps.

"Be nice." Adam's laughter washed over her.

Deborah soaked in his handsome profile. The affection he felt for Liam and Lily was unmistakable. Had he considered how much he was going to miss them once he left? She might not be enough to hold him here, but were they?

Adam Halloway was devoted to his profession and content with his bachelor lifestyle. A runaway bride and pair of needy orphans couldn't compete with the satisfaction of putting criminals behind bars.

Adam didn't waste any time paying Preston Wells a visit. As soon as he'd eaten and thanked Aunt Mae for the meal, he made his way across town to the telegraph operator's humble abode. He didn't care that his arrival was untimely.

Preston, on the other hand, did.

"You'll have to come back another time." His angular body blocked the doorway. Beyond him, guests mingled in a tight living space with fragile cups and saucers in their hands. "As you can see, I'm entertaining at the moment."

Adam kept his hands firmly in his pockets. "This won't take long," he said, not bothering to lower his volume. "I came to issue a warning. Stay away from Deborah."

The chatter petered out. Color surging and waning on his cheeks, Preston affixed a false smile on his face. "I didn't realize Miss Frazier had assigned you as her keeper. She's past the age of requiring a guardian."

The man's smugness picked at Adam's control. Deborah's overwrought state had made this task necessary. Adam wouldn't allow her to be bullied by this or any other man.

He stepped closer. "You brought her into your home and proceeded to make her uncomfortable. You're fortunate nothing happened to warrant more than a vocal reprimand."

"Whatever she told you is a lie."

Adam pulled his hands out of his pockets, not willing to hear one word spoken against Deborah's integrity. But before he could say or do anything, Hildie pushed into the space beside her beau.

"You shouldn't be here, Adam."

Her former friendliness had transformed into cold disdain.

"Neither should you."

Her gasp competed with the sudden swell of crickets.

Preston's face turned the shade of a boiled beet. "That's it. I'm going for the sheriff."

Hildie restrained his arm. "No need, my dear."

"He's ruining my birthday celebration," he whined.

"Adam's simply jealous," she announced. "He had his chance with me and has realized his mistake too late." Looking down her nose at him, she sniffed. "Go back to Deborah and those grubby brats. You're not welcome here."

"No, Hildie, you're the one who's not truly welcome. Ask Preston about his behavior today. Or better yet, ask Deborah." His gaze snared Preston's. "I won't practice the same restraint next time. Remember that."

Spinning on his heel, he stalked into the shadows. Anger fueled his steps. His mind wandered to the future. Who would protect Deborah after he was gone? Who would coax Liam out of the upper reaches of trees? Who'd teach him to hunt and fish and shoot?

Who would fill Adam's shoes?

Deborah was a lovely, desirable woman with a sweet spirit and infectious personality. She wouldn't be alone for long. His chest felt full of rocks at the thought.

He was imagining the unimaginable when movement at the mouth of the alley up ahead jerked him back to the present. The half-moon overhead shed scant light on the two figures locked in heated conversation.

Slowing, Adam used a tree as cover. He couldn't hear their words, but he could tell they were both men. The one facing him moved farther into the light. The badge on his vest glinted.

Sheriff Getman.

Adrenaline pumped through his body. This didn't look like a casual meeting.

Shifting to get a better view, he waited for a glimpse of the other man. Minutes ticked past. Leaves swayed with the occasional breeze, tickling his neck. He batted away a handful of flies. Surveying the street behind him and finding it deserted, he made the decision to get closer.

Crouching low, he crossed to a parked wagon near the livery and hunkered beside a rear wheel. Hopefully no stray dogs would catch his scent and alert the men to his presence.

"Where's your lady friend been?" The sheriff sounded almost afraid to ask the question.

"Handling a personal matter. Why?"

A buzzing sound filled Adam's head. He knew that voice. It hadn't changed in the years since Zane Ogden and another sheriff rode onto Halloway land and delivered the news of their father's disappearance.

"You sure you can count on her?" the sheriff asked.

"She's devoted to me." He snorted. "She'll do anything I ask."

A cat screeched in the distance, and the man angled his head, allowing light to spill over the craggy features. Age had weathered Zane Ogden's visage and grayed his hair at the temples.

The world tilted. Adam put a hand to the hard earth.

His enemy stood within pistol range. It would be so easy to sink a bullet into him. After the damage and destruction Ogden had wrought, his death would be justified.

Sweat trickled beneath Adam's collar. His weapon sat heavy on his hip.

*Do it. Hasn't this been what you've wanted all these years? To end him?*

Squeezing his eyes shut, he petitioned God for a return of reason. He had to control the thirst for revenge pulsing inside.

Another scene taunted him. Another sheriff in league with Ogden, come to inform the Halloway brothers that their father had not only failed them but fled the area like a coward.

The pearl handle of his revolver fit in his palm like an old friend's handshake. The metal slid silently along the leather holster.

Ogden deserved to die. Who else better to deliver justice than one of his victims?

*Justice? Or revenge?*

Seth's and Russell's faces swam in his mind's eye. Adam wrestled with his knowledge of right and wrong. Maybe his brothers were right. Maybe this hunt had become less about exonerating their father and more about settling a score.

Adam let his weapon slide back into place. A verse he'd memorized as a lad cemented his decision. *Dearly beloved, avenge not yourselves, but rather give place unto wrath: for it is written, Vengeance is mine; I will repay, saith the Lord.*

For the first time since embarking on this journey, he accepted that Ogden's fate rested in God's hands. Not Adam's.

The men's voices faded. During his moments of indecision, they'd finished their conversation and were leaving the alley.

He considered arresting Ogden, but without evidence to support Adam's claims, no judge would convict him. Certainly Adam wouldn't have Getman's support.

No, it was smarter to wait until he had enough ammunition to put Ogden away for the rest of his days. He had to find the female. He had to make her talk.

## Chapter Twenty-One

"I need a favor." Adam pushed the paper and pencil across the top of the bookshelf toward his sisters-in-law.

Anna relinquished a stack of books into Marigold's arms and inspected the blank paper before lifting her confused gaze. "What's this?"

Marigold peered over her shoulder at Deborah, who was arranging a seating area in the spacious entrance of what was to be the new library—Will and Tomasina's former home. Since they'd pinned their hopes on Washington, DC, the mayor and his wife had built a more modest home in town and had sold this one at a reduced price to their friend Daniel Gardner. He, in turn, had generously donated the well-appointed, multilevel house to Cowboy Creek.

"If I had to guess, I'd say Adam wants ideas for romantic gestures." Grinning cheekily, Marigold slid the books one by one onto the middle shelf.

"Flowers are always a good start," Anna said, accepting the other woman's explanation as fact. "Unless she's sensitive. Do they make her sneeze?"

Adam shook his head. "This has nothing to do with Deborah."

His gaze drifted to her standing at another shelf, and once again, he let himself admire the way her summery pink cotton dress draped becomingly over her figure. She caught him looking and, gifting him with a smile, continued with her task.

He found himself longing for the carefree camaraderie they used to enjoy. While she'd thawed in his company, she hadn't fully relaxed her guard.

Marigold's snicker brought his head around. Both women regarded him with soft, knowing gazes. Wasn't tough to figure out where their thoughts had led them.

"You're aware of the true reason I'm in town."

The cloud of dreamy hopes hanging over them dissipated.

"Our husbands informed us." Anna's small hand came to rest atop her bulging stomach. "How can we help?"

"I need a list of the women in this town whose names begin with *D* as soon as possible."

Marigold chewed on her lip. "Are there any limitations? Age, for instance?"

"I don't have exact parameters. Let's say no younger than eighteen and no older than sixty."

"I'll start with my students' mothers and expand from there," Marigold said.

"We can work together to avoid overlap," Anna suggested.

"I appreciate it, ladies."

One important aspect of his line of work was utilizing valuable local resources, everyone from lawmen to shopkeepers. He would've asked for the information days ago if he hadn't gotten distracted by personal matters. Before Cowboy Creek, Adam hadn't had to balance a personal and professional life. The handful of married agents he'd been in contact with had made it seem effortless. Not that he'd given it much thought. Any ideas about courtship or marriage had been fleeting, shelved for the foreseeable future.

Now he not only had his mother and brothers and their

families to contend with, he had a former-suspect-turned-friend and a pair of sweet kids depending on him.

He rejoined Will and Daniel on the second floor and helped them reposition a piano in the music room that would house instruments, sheet music and books pertaining to music and the great composers.

Volunteers worked throughout the morning. His stomach was registering the long hours since breakfast when Deborah found him in the kitchen with several others, indulging in coffee and pastries.

"We have a picnic to attend," she reminded him. "The basket's already packed. We simply have to fetch Liam and Lily."

"I'm ready."

Draining the creamy brew, he placed his empty cup in the dish basin and thanked Tomasina, Leah and Grace. The three friends had been directing the volunteers and managing the chaos with aplomb.

Deborah hugged each woman. "I'm sorry we have to leave, but we'd already promised the kids we'd take them fishing."

"The grand opening isn't until the last day of June," Grace Burgess said with a dismissive gesture. "We have another ten days to prepare. I promise there will be more opportunities to pitch in."

"You can count on us," Adam said.

"I'm happy to hear it." Tomasina accompanied them to the main door and waved goodbye.

Deborah cast a final look at the sprawling house. "What a wonderful asset this will be for Cowboy Creek's citizens."

They strolled along the lane toward the street. "Big Bend wasn't large enough to support a lending library, unfortunately. The locals swapped their private collections."

"You do the best with what you have," she said. "St.

Louis has an adequate one, but I rarely used it. We had enough books at the estate to satisfy me."

Eager to learn every detail about her life—not because of a case, but because he wanted to know her as well as he possibly could—Adam peppered her with questions. After initial hesitation, she spoke at length about her upbringing, her mother and the pain of losing her, her home in what sounded like a behemoth display of wealth and her social activities. Not surprisingly, Deborah had been involved in her church and various charitable endeavors.

He was disappointed when their arrival at Aunt Mae's curtailed their conversation. The kids' excitement soon eclipsed that, however. Such a short time ago, Liam would barely speak to anyone besides his sister, and Lily had been cloaked in sadness. They'd been in a poor, desolate state.

Because of Deborah's care, they were cheerful, energetic and on the road to better health. As Liam skipped along and plied him with questions about what type of fish they could hope to catch, Adam liked to think he'd had a part in their improvement, as well.

Glancing over, he caught Deborah's sparkling gaze. They shared a smile, eerily similar to the ones he'd seen Seth and Marigold swap.

Was she thinking what he was thinking? That the siblings made life richer? More unpredictable but also interesting?

"Who's that?" Lily said, pointing to a horse and rider heading their way.

"No idea." Adam strode a few steps ahead of the others. They were only a quarter of a mile from town and the stockyards, but there was no one else around. "You all hang back until after I've had a chance to meet him."

Deborah gathered the kids to her side, her eyes shadowed by more than her straw hat.

When the stranger guided his horse to a stop not far

from where Adam stood, he pulled off his hat and ran his hand over the short, graying strands. "Good day, folks. Out for an afternoon of recreation, I see."

The lazy drawl and muddy eyes sparked recognition in Adam. "Doc? Is that you?"

He leaned forward in the saddle. "Halloway?"

"In the flesh." Grinning, Adam reached up and pumped his hand. "How long has it been? Eighteen months? Last I heard, you'd retired."

"I discovered that sittin' around coolin' my heels wasn't for me." His gaze cut to Deborah, interest sparking to life. "I missed the news of your nuptials. I didn't figure you'd ever relinquish your solitary life."

"There were no nuptials," Adam choked out. "This is my friend, Deborah, our famous local baker. And these are the Quinn siblings." He tugged at his collar. "Doc and I used to work together on occasion."

Liam and Lily mumbled greetings. Deborah welcomed him to town, though her curiosity was plain.

"Adam's one of the best men in the agency," Doc told her. "Devoted. Sharp. A true asset."

The praise meant a lot coming from someone Adam had aspired to emulate. "No one's better than Doc."

"Agency," Deborah stated. "What agency?"

"Only the best in the nation," Doc boasted. "The Pinkerton National Detective Agency."

Adam watched her absorb the news, shock her dominating emotion. He couldn't tell whether she was impressed or appalled.

He turned back to Doc. "Tell me, did Pinkerton himself beg you to return?"

"Nothing like that," he chuckled. Pointing to the fishing pole in Liam's grip, he said, "I won't keep you any longer. I'd like to catch up whenever you're available."

"Where are you staying?"

"The Cattleman."

"I'll meet you for supper tonight, if you're so inclined."

"It's a deal."

After they'd agreed upon a time, he rode away, a puff of dust trailing behind him. Adam couldn't wait to hear what Doc had been up to and what had brought him to Kansas. He might confide in him about Ogden and get his advice.

He turned to find the kids at the stream's edge. Deborah had remained in the same spot, her face a mask of worry.

"What's troubling you?"

"Nothing."

"You sure?"

She shifted her gaze to his and offered a tremulous smile. "What a coincidence that your old colleague showed up here. Is he from this area?"

"Doc? No, he's from Chicago. He always said he'd retire there." Taking the basket from her, he led her to a shaded spot beneath the trees. "I'll find out tonight if he's working out of that office or if he transferred elsewhere."

Deborah spread out the quilt and, sinking onto the faded material opposite him, she began to unpack the containers. "Why do you call him Doc?"

He laughed. "Quite a few of the agents earned nicknames. You'd think with a name like Doc, he'd have medical knowledge, but that's not the case. He's prone to swooning at the sight of blood."

"Oh? What's his actual name?"

He stopped and thought. "I don't remember. Isn't that odd? Everyone always called him Doc."

"Well, I'm as eager as you are to discover exactly what he's doing in Cowboy Creek."

While Adam and Liam waited for the fish to bite, Lily skipped along the bank, her twin braids flopping and her new, snowy white pantaloons flashing from beneath her hem. She hummed a hymn they'd sung in church on Sunday, one that spoke of God's sustaining peace.

Deborah did not feel peaceful. Perched on the quilt, she fretted over her sister's message and this sudden appearance of Adam's colleague. Were the two connected? Could Doc be the agent her father hired to track her down?

The rational part of her brain insisted it was simply a coincidence. Doc resided in Chicago, not St. Louis. Plus, how many women named Deborah could there be in a boomtown like Cowboy Creek? She hadn't changed her name because, in her distressed state, she hadn't thought to make up one when Sadie asked on the train.

At least his arrival had given her insight into Adam's life before Cowboy Creek. The Pinkertons were highly respected for their work. Made sense he'd be part of an organization like that.

Lily plopped down beside her. "You don't like fishing, either?"

"It's not so bad, but I'd rather relax and soak in God's beautiful handiwork while I can. Soon I'll have to return to Aunt Mae's and start on tonight's dessert."

Her eyes lit up. "Can I help?"

"You don't have to ask. You're my official helper now."

Deborah was having such fun passing along her cooking and baking knowledge to her willing pupil.

Lily wrapped her arms around Deborah and snuggled close. "Can we stay at the boardinghouse forever?"

Inhaling the gentle scent clinging to Lily's hair, Deborah rested her arm across her back and sighed. "I was thinking we could find a house to rent one day soon."

Tilting her head, she gazed up in awe. "Truly?"

"Would you like that?"

"Oh, yes! What about Adam? Would he move to the house with us?"

"Oh." Deborah snuck a glance at him, relieved he hadn't

overheard. "Well, Adam and I aren't married. Besides, his job takes him all across the nation."

Her joy squelched, the little girl fiddled with the ribbon around Deborah's waist. "I don't want him to leave."

*Me, either.* "He'll return for frequent visits, I'm sure. His family is here, and you and Liam. He cares about you as much as I do."

"Who will take Liam fishing?" she asked quietly.

"Seth or Russell, perhaps. If not, *I'll* take him." The expression on Lily's face made Deborah burst out laughing. "What? You don't think I'm capable of digging up and baiting worms?"

Lily shrugged, reluctant to say something negative. Deborah started tickling her. Their cackles brought Adam and Liam over.

"What's so funny?" Liam demanded.

Lily lay on the blanket, panting. "It's a secret for the girls."

Adam staved off a stinging, brotherly retort by announcing they'd given up for the day but would return that weekend. He enlisted the kids' help with gathering the rest of their belongings. Deborah folded the quilt, her thoughts on her family back home.

Should she pen a letter to her father and explain everything that had happened since her spontaneous flight? Outline her new plans for a future of her own choosing?

*What should I do, Lord? Continue to hide out like a common criminal or fight for what I want?*

"Halloway." Doc shuffled to his feet and gestured to the seat opposite him in The Cattleman, his mood noticeably grimmer than it had been that afternoon. "Glad you could make it."

He'd chosen a secluded table in the far corner of the swanky hotel restaurant. There were a dozen or so diners scattered throughout the room, a mixture of traveling businessmen and couples he'd seen around town.

Adam made himself comfortable and spread his napkin across his lap. He ordered coffee and braised beef with scalloped potatoes and trimmings, then set about discerning what had occurred to put that worried gleam in Doc's eyes.

"Are the accommodations not to your liking?"

Doc rubbed an endless ring around his coffee mug. "Nothing like that. The bed's nice and soft—I'm getting old enough to require daily naps—and the walls are thicker than most."

"Is it a case you're working on? I'd be happy to provide a listening ear. Truth be told, I've got a wily one myself."

No matter where he went, he was always on alert for another sighting of Ogden. He wouldn't fully relax until the man was in custody.

"As a matter of fact," Doc said, "I could use your insight into my current case."

Adam leaned back against his chair and crossed his arms. "Start from the beginning. I've got as much time as you need."

"The beginning, huh? That would be the day a man named Gerard Frazier darkened my door."

# Chapter Twenty-Two

Time slowed. The name Frazier hit him with the force of a Minié ball.

Doc placed a pristine tintype beside his silverware. Adam picked it up and studied the beautiful, familiar face smiling back at him. Deborah, at probably fifteen or sixteen years of age. Doc had to have known who she was the instant he saw her earlier today, yet he hadn't let on. He was a seasoned detective.

Lips pressing together, Adam returned the tintype.

"She told you, then?" Doc prodded. The agent's gaze missed nothing. "About her reasons for fleeing St. Louis?"

Blanking his face, he balled the napkin in his hand. "She told me. You're here on behalf of her father?"

"Mr. Frazier is worried about his daughter."

Anger sparked inside Adam. "From what she's told me, he's more concerned with maintaining business relations than with Deborah's happiness."

Doc sagged against the chair, a hint of censure in his muddy eyes. "What about his side of the story?"

Adam averted his gaze. Beyond the window framed with heavy draperies, folks hurried about their business. He couldn't stop worrying how Deborah was going to handle being found.

Doc was right to question him. Their training emphasized objectivity. Theirs was the first national detective agency, and Allan Pinkerton had ensured his agents were equipped with the tools and knowledge necessary to solve crimes. How could Adam justify his support for Deborah without revealing he'd allowed things to get personal while conducting an investigation? The fact that it wasn't an official Pinkerton case didn't matter.

"Did you meet the man she was betrothed to?" Adam asked his colleague.

"I did."

His wait for further details proved futile. "And? What's he like?"

"He's irrelevant to this conversation," Doc insisted. "You should be asking about Mr. Frazier and how you can help me reunite him with his daughter."

Their meals arrived, giving Adam a chance to try to cool his ire. Ignoring the enticing aroma wafting from his plate, he sent a hard stare across the table.

"I'm not going to do either of those things. Deborah doesn't want to marry Tobias Latham."

Doc didn't so much as blink. "Who does she wish to marry? You?"

The tips of his ears burned. "I realize the scene you happened upon today might've given you the wrong impression—"

Doc's disbelieving cackle drew the other patrons' attention. "Might have? Son, to anyone with eyes, the four of you looked like a cozy family unit." Leaning forward, he tapped the tintype he had yet to put away. "Admit it. You've gone and fallen for her."

"She's a friend," Adam insisted, the lie bitter on his tongue.

*That kiss went beyond mere friendship, and so did his*

*feelings. He just wasn't sure how to classify what he felt for her.*

After considering him for what felt like a lifetime, Doc tucked into his fried chicken and mashed potatoes. Adam ate without tasting. His thoughts were on Deborah and the kids back at the boardinghouse. She had no idea what was about to befall her.

"You ever hear of an agent named Peter Calhoune?" Doc spoke with his mouth half-full, his head slightly bent, the single globe light on their table glinting in his hair.

"Can't say that I have."

"Peter was the finest agent I've ever worked alongside. He snagged more outlaws than any other man in Pinkerton's employ. According to the rumors, he received the highest wages of any of us." Waving his fork around, he shrugged. "He deserved it, in my opinion."

"Why wouldn't the agency celebrate his success?"

His eyes darkened. "He made a fatal mistake, that's why. Peter caught a case that would prove his undoing. While trying to find a horse rustler who was causing problems for several Texas ranchers, he interviewed family members, neighbors and associates. One of his sources of information was the rustler's younger sister."

Adam guessed where the tale was headed. He ceased eating and set his fork aside. "He developed feelings for her and bungled the case."

"He married her in secret, believing she was on his side. He misjudged her loyalties. Peter paid for that mistake with his life."

"What does this have to do with me?"

"Miss Frazier has impacted your current case, has she not?"

Adam gritted his teeth. If Doc knew the details, he'd rake him over the coals.

"You're an asset to the Pinkertons," he went on. "I don't

want to see another good agent fail like Peter did. Distractions like her can become a weakness you can ill afford."

Deborah wasn't a distraction. In the beginning, maybe. Now he couldn't imagine life without her.

Doc curved forward, his eyes intense. "Help me convince her to return to St. Louis and settle her affairs. Both our problems will be solved."

Adam passed his crumpled napkin over his mouth and, fishing out his wallet, tossed enough coin to cover both meals on the table.

"Deborah is a grown woman capable of making her own decisions. If and when she's ready to speak to her father, she'll do it on her own terms." Standing, he grabbed his Stetson from where it dangled on the chair. "I will inform her of your agenda."

Doc's mouth thinned with displeasure. "Let's hope she doesn't hop on the next train out of here."

"He found me."

Deborah slumped against the side of the post office building, the words of her sister's telegram blurring as tears smarted. The well-known Pinkerton agent sent to find her, Lyle Canton, had sent word to Gerard last evening. Even now, her father was probably riding the rails to Cowboy Creek. According to Lucy, he was determined to fetch her home and continue with the wedding as planned. Deborah's feelings didn't matter. They never had.

Glad she'd sought privacy in the alley, she let the rough wall support her while she tried to regain her composure. As she'd feared, Doc and Lyle Canton were the same man. Her thoughts returned to yesterday afternoon and their one and only encounter. He must've identified her right away. Still, there hadn't been the slightest flicker of recognition in his steady gaze, no flare of victory. He'd acted completely unaffected. How did Pinkertons learn that particular skill?

She sucked in a sharp breath. Doc and Adam were colleagues. Had Doc told Adam his true reason for being here?

A stray cat meowed and rubbed against her legs. Reaching down, Deborah stroked the feline's soft fur. When he realized she didn't plan to feed him, he trotted toward the boardwalk.

She hadn't seen Adam return last evening. Lily had developed an upset stomach, so Deborah had ushered her upstairs earlier than usual. After getting her in bed, she read to her for a while. She'd thought perhaps the reason he didn't stop by their room to say good-night was because he didn't wish to disturb Lily.

This morning, she'd been helping Aunt Mae prepare breakfast when Sadie returned from posting a letter with the news that Deborah had received an urgent telegram.

The thud of heavy footsteps approached from farther down the alley. Suddenly, a rough hand seized her elbow. "I've been searching everywhere for you, Dora. Where have you been?"

The telegram she'd been gripping so tightly, along with a thin stack of bills her sister had mailed, fluttered to the ground. Looming before her was the man she'd encountered twice before—once with the woman who bore a striking resemblance to Deborah and once in front of Hannah's shop. He was the type of man whose very presence turned her body cold with dread.

"Y-you've got the wrong person."

His black bowler hat cast a shadow across the top half of his craggy face. His irate gaze burned into her. "Who are you?"

"I—I'm not the woman you're looking for. I don't know

her." Her arm ached where his clamp-like fingers held her fast.

His upper lip curled. With a disgusted puff of air passing through his fleshy lips, he bent and scooped up the money, all without releasing her.

"Never mind. I'll find her myself." He waved the bills near her nose. "You should be more careful with your money."

Deborah couldn't move. She got the feeling he was taunting her.

"What's going on here?"

Adam's harsh demand was like music to her ears. Angling toward him, she was stunned by the sheer hatred marring his handsome features. His brown gaze had darkened to black murder and was affixed on the stranger before her.

She opened her mouth but didn't get a chance to speak. The stranger shoved her with enough force to send her sprawling to the hard earth. His retreating footsteps filled her ears. She started to get up, fully expecting Adam to rush to her aid. But he sprinted past her without a second glance, his gun drawn.

Confusion mingling with fear, Deborah scrambled to her feet. Should she follow them? Or would that distract Adam? She shivered in the morning heat. He had been almost unrecognizable.

After brushing the dust from her layered skirts and straightening her bonnet, she crossed and retrieved the telegram. She folded the paper and stuck it into her reticule. She was scouring the dirt for the few remaining bills when Adam bounded down the alley.

"You lost him?" she said, her attention switching between the deadly weapon in his hand and his black, black gaze.

Panting, he holstered his gun and shoved the hair off his forehead with an impatient flick. "I did."

"Who is he?" His anger was a palpable thing. It unsettled her. It almost felt as if some of his anger was directed at her, but that was crazy. And that's when it hit her. The thought ricocheted in her head. "Wait, was he the man you've been hired to find?"

Stalking close, he made a point of scrutinizing the money in her hand. "I've got to hand it to you, Deborah. You're a fine actress. The best I've ever encountered."

She took a step in retreat. "Actress? I don't understand your meaning."

His features twisted in derision…directed at her or himself? "Your lies slide out like sweet honey. And your pretense where the kids are concerned? Brilliant."

"What pretense?" Exasperation bubbled up inside her. "Adam, you're talking in riddles. Please, explain yourself."

"The money Ogden gave you." He nodded toward it in her hand. "What exactly did you do for him?"

"I don't like your tone." Now *she* was angry. "I've never heard the name Ogden before. He didn't give me this money. My sister did."

"Oh, yes, the flawless Lucy Frazier. That's a convenient excuse." He snorted, his gaze snagging on something near his boots. He bent and retrieved her reticule. Instead of handing it to her, however, he loosened the ribbon drawstring.

"Adam!"

Ignoring her outrage, he sifted through the contents and removed her handkerchief. He examined the embroidered square. His shoulders slumped.

"It was you at the Gainses' ranch, wasn't it?" When he lifted his gaze to hers, the sorrow and accusation and betrayal knocked her back another step. "Sam and I discovered this out at the destroyed windmill." He held up the handkerchief, embroidered with purple flowers. "He was keeping it at his office for the time being, since he doesn't trust the sheriff. But guess what? It was stolen a couple of nights ago." He swallowed hard. "How could you hurt an innocent man, Deborah? You've heard Gains probably won't walk again. He's fortunate to be alive. If he had died, you'd be charged as an accomplice to murder."

*"Murder?"*

"Zane Ogden doesn't have a compassionate bone in his body. How could you associate with a blackguard like him?" he said hotly.

Deborah could hardly breathe as the meaning behind his words penetrated. This Ogden fellow was a terrible person who'd committed horrific acts, and Adam thought she was in league with him. Her heart throbbed. Physical pain arrowed through her chest. It felt like someone was severing it in two with a blazing hot blade.

Snatching her reticule from his grasp, she turned to leave. His hands found her shoulders and spun her to him. He looked to be in agony.

"Help me capture him," he implored. "You'll serve a lesser sentence. I'll hire Russell to defend you—"

"Let me go!" Shoving his chest, she scrambled out of reach. "I don't need you or your brother's help because I've done *nothing* wrong. I thought you were the one person in this world who actually understood me. I thought you cared—" Her voice broke.

Adam scrubbed his hands down his face. "I do care, Deborah. Too much."

"It's my turn not to believe you."

Spinning on her heel, she picked up her skirts and bolted for the boardwalk, desperate to find a private spot where she could release the grief mounting inside. The man she loved thought her a soulless criminal.

"Deborah, wait!"

She quickened her pace. If he caught up to her, would he haul her to jail?

Intent on crossing the street, she miscalculated the distance between her and the approaching creak of wagon wheels and jangle of horses' harnesses. She stepped into the direct path of a two-horse team. Too late to duck out of the way, she braced herself for impact.

## Chapter Twenty-Three

Adam reached Deborah with mere seconds to spare. Clamping onto her arm, he jerked her back against him. The wagon driver cast them a baleful glare as his conveyance clamored past. The spinning wheels were so close, it was a wonder her bell-shaped skirts weren't caught in the spokes.

For a moment, neither moved nor spoke. Then she lurched away from him.

"Let me go!"

With onlookers nearby, he had no choice but to free her. He ground his teeth. "We have more to discuss—"

"I have nothing of import to say to you." Her brilliant eyes had dulled with misery. Her pallor alarmed him. Even her lips were white. "You've already made up your mind about me."

She backed away from him, one arm aloft as if to ward him off.

A cowboy intervened, putting his body between Deborah and Adam. "Is there a problem here, ma'am?"

"N-no, thank you." With one final glance, she hurried past Zimmerman's Lumber and Longhorn Feed & Grain.

The cowboy shot Adam a warning glance before joining a friend on the opposite street corner. They appeared to be discussing him, but he paid them no heed. Adam watched Deborah melt into the crowd, his blood still hot with the aftermath of her treachery. He was angry and hurt and wrecked. Yes, she'd helped his enemy. Worse than that, she'd betrayed the bond they'd built, broken his trust and destroyed any chance they'd had to be together. He wanted to shake her. He wanted to lock her in a cell until she explained how she'd arrived at this low point. He wanted this to be a cruel illusion, a nightmare from which he'd soon wake.

The condemning handkerchief stuffed in his pocket, he returned to the alley and retraced the path Ogden had taken. He roamed the streets of Cowboy Creek for hours in a circuitous path, his mind replaying the shocking scene of Deborah and Ogden standing inches apart. The money Ogden had handed her was even more incriminatory than the handkerchief. It was an obvious exchange—his money for her cooperation.

He'd been played for a fool. Peter's sad tale remained fresh in his mind. If Doc or any of his fellow agents found out, Adam would never hear the end of it. His reputation would be shot, and his career possibly ruined. Not that that mattered when he'd lost the only woman he'd ever cared about, a woman he'd started to consider his best friend.

His stomach roiled. He might possibly lose his breakfast.

Focusing on breathing in through his nose and out through his mouth, he managed to avoid that humiliation. Still, he felt as if a fever ravaged his body.

"Why, Deborah?" he murmured aloud, earning a suspicious glance from the businessman passing him.

Her reaction to his charge bothered him. There hadn't been a hint of guilt. Not one. She'd been adamant about her innocence.

He walked until the soles of his feet ached. Spying a

couple of sawed-off logs arranged in a semicircle beneath an old, gnarled tree in a vacant lot, he took refuge from the heat.

"What am I supposed to do, God?" he moaned, resting his elbows on his thighs and burying his face in his hands.

His gut insisted she was telling the truth. But how to refute what he'd seen?

He shouldn't be wasting time. He should be scouring the prairie, checking every house, barn and stable for Ogden. Adam couldn't be certain that the other man had recognized him. He couldn't anticipate whether he'd hunker down or skip town.

At this point, he didn't care.

He groaned aloud. That he was more concerned about Deborah proved he'd made a mess of everything. He'd overestimated his professional competence.

Since the day he met her, he hadn't done what he was supposed to do. He'd lost his way, his pride and his heart.

Deborah had a blinding headache caused by holding tears at bay. Afraid to return to the boardinghouse for fear of another confrontation with Adam, she'd sent word to Aunt Mae to watch the kids until that evening. The proprietress wouldn't mind. While she probably wouldn't admit it aloud, it was obvious their company pleased her.

Thoughts of Liam and Lily brought another wave of sorrow. Would Adam convince Russell to block her petition for guardianship?

"Deborah?"

The man himself hailed her from his law office entrance, jarring her to a sudden halt.

"Watch out, lady," someone grumbled from behind.

"Excuse me." Shuffling out of the flow of foot traffic, she reluctantly greeted Russell, searching for signs his brother had paid him a visit. Apparently not, considering the lack of condemnation in his eyes.

"You don't look well." He stepped closer. "Would you like to come inside and sit for a while?"

Her legs were tired and her body fatigued, but there'd be no respite for her battered spirits, especially with Adam's brother.

"I don't think that's wise," she murmured. Still, she didn't move to leave.

His face a mask of concern, he touched her sleeve. "Please, come inside. I've got a jar of ginger tea on my desk. You're welcome to it."

Deborah nodded, thinking more about her parched throat and throbbing feet than anything else. She would sit and rest and regather her wits, then she'd thank him and—

What would she do? Return to the boardinghouse and perhaps find Adam and the sheriff waiting for her?

Inside the office, Russell motioned her to the supple leather seats grouped beside the large window. While he retrieved the tea, she situated herself on a chair with a view of the street. She scrutinized each person, half hoping, half dreading one of them would be the man who'd evoked such fury in Adam.

Russell held out an elegant crystal glass three-quarters full of amber liquid. "Would you like me to fetch Adam?"

"No," she burst out. "I have no wish to see him."

His brows drawing together, he lowered himself to the seat opposite and propped his elbows on the armrests. "Did you and he quarrel?"

"You haven't seen him today?" she countered. "I thought this would be one of his first stops."

"I've been busy with clients and paperwork."

Deborah sipped the spice-laced tea. "Who's Ogden?"

Russell's knuckles went white. "Someone dangerous. Did Adam tell you about him?"

"He told me nothing," she said bitterly.

"I'm afraid I'm at a loss, Deborah. What exactly occurred?"

Gripping the glass in both hands, she stared into the remaining liquid and relayed that morning's events, as well as her hasty flight from St. Louis and the reason for her sister's telegram and letter.

Russell, who'd been silent throughout, handed her a crisp, white handkerchief.

She lifted her gaze to his, stunned to see sympathy and understanding. "You believe me?"

"I do."

Fresh tears threatened. "Why doesn't he?"

"In order to answer that, I'll have to start at the beginning." Standing, he poured himself a glass of tea, his gaze far-off. "Did Adam tell you we had a ranch in Missouri?"

"In Big Bend?"

He nodded. "We weren't wealthy by any means, but we led a comfortable life. We worked hard, went to church every Sunday, helped our neighbors, exasperated our ma with our frequent spats." A sentimental smile curved his lips, then faded away. "As you probably know, ranchers are dependent upon the weather. In the year 1860, we faced a drought. A long one that strained our resources for both beast and man. When Zane Ogden arrived in Big Bend with full pockets and grand promises, many of our neighbors accepted his offers of assistance. Our father, Gilbert Halloway, had serious reservations about the money Ogden was lending the ranchers. His warnings went unheeded. The ranchers agreed to loans with ruinous interest payments and stiff penalties. When they couldn't pay, one by one, our friends lost everything."

"How awful," she murmured.

His eyes sad, he returned to his seat and gulped down his drink. "Seth, Adam and I were grateful Pa hadn't taken out a loan. Our ranch was our home, our legacy. We couldn't imagine having it ripped away. Then one night, he decided to go to speak with Ogden. I'm not sure what he hoped to accomplish." He shrugged. "Maybe persuade him to be lenient. We won't ever know, because Pa never returned."

Deborah covered her mouth with her hand. She was beginning to form a terrible understanding of why Adam had looked at Ogden the way he had.

"Ogden and the sheriff arrived on our doorstep later that same night with a loan document, ostensibly signed by Pa and witnessed by the sheriff. They claimed he skipped town because he was too humiliated to face us and the townspeople."

"Do you think it was a forgery?"

He clamped his lips together, turmoil in his eyes. "I don't know what I believe anymore. I used to think Pa took out the loan but hid it from us. The drought impacted us, just as it did everyone else."

"And Adam?"

"Adam thought our father incapable of mistakes. He rejected Ogden's account and accused the sheriff of lying. He and Seth argued about our options. When Seth decided to sell off some of our property in order to satisfy the loan, Adam couldn't stomach it. He joined the army and never looked back."

Adam was as passionate about his work and dedicated to the idea of justice for victims. "That's why he joined the Pinkertons."

"His life mission is to restore our father's good name and to discover the truth of what happened to him that night. Seth says he's obsessed with this mission of his. Deborah, you shouldn't take his accusations to heart."

She shot to her feet and stalked to the window. "You weren't there. It was terrible, Russell."

He took up position nearby. "I won't make excuses for him. What I will say is that he's obviously developed deep feelings for you. Otherwise, he wouldn't have reacted the way he did."

Deborah wished she could believe that.

"He's a good agent. A good man," Russ said. "He'll eventually come to his senses and realize his error. Then he'd better make a grand apology."

The doorknob twisted, and a gush of tepid air stirred the curtains as the door swung inward. Deborah's heart climbed into her throat as Adam's countenance registered before her.

"Deborah," he rasped. "I'm glad you're here. We need to talk."

"About what? Your plans to have me thrown in jail?"

The corners of his mouth turned down. He closed the door behind him and sent a beseeching glance at his brother, which Russell promptly ignored.

"I've told him the truth," she said hotly. "If you want answers, talk to him."

Feeling as if she were close to collapsing, she moved to leave. Russell remained where he was, but Adam blocked her path, his hands pressed together as if in prayer.

"I'm sorry for the way I handled things in the alley. I should've given you a chance to defend yourself." Regret churned in his eyes.

"You're saying you didn't mean the horrible things you accused me of?"

He opened his mouth to speak, but no sound came out. He grimaced. His hesitation was all the answer she needed.

Shoving past him, she prayed she could escape without bursting into tears. Her fingers closed over the knob.

"Deborah, I'd like to understand," he implored. "I know in my heart you wouldn't willingly agree to help a man like Ogden, nor would you harm anyone. If he coerced or threatened you or even deceived you into helping him, there's no reason to be embarrassed or ashamed. Swindlers often take advantage of bright, good-hearted people—"

A sob escaped her lips without warning. Her back to the room, she yanked open the door and hurried outside.

"Wait!"

Russell's firm command carried through to the board-walk. "Let her go, Adam."

Deborah didn't look back to see if he complied. All she could think about was escape.

# *Chapter Twenty-Four*

"**Y**ou know nothing about women, little brother."

Adam waffled in the doorway. Should he go after her and demand she talk to him, and possibly receive a black eye for his efforts? Or do as Russell suggested and give her time to sort through everything?

He swiveled around. Russ was perched on his desk, his arms folded over his suit vest, his eyes full of recrimination.

"You can hardly be blamed, I suppose." Russell sighed, his head cocked to one side. "The battlefield imparted skills of survival and cunning. Certainly it did nothing to nurture the finer feelings of compassion. Roaming the nation in search of thieves and murderers compounded the problem."

"What problem?"

"You don't know the slightest thing about how to treat a lady."

"That may be true, but it has nothing to do with the fact that I caught money exchanging hands between our family's greatest enemy and Deborah."

"You're accustomed to searching for the worst in people. You've grown cynical."

Adam sank his hands into his pockets. His brother was claiming he'd jumped to conclusions. Had he?

Russell pushed off the desk. "You care about her. I know you do."

"I can't deny it. I let my personal feelings interfere with a case."

"Exactly. That's why you misread what was happening in that alley."

As the hours since then had ticked off, he'd prayed he was wrong. That's why he'd sought her out, to get her side of the story—something he should've done as soon as he lost sight of Ogden.

"What do *you* think happened?" Adam asked his brother.

"If you'd bothered to read the telegram in her reticule while you were digging through the contents, you would've seen the sender was her sister, Lucy. You could've checked the time stamp. There was also a letter from her sent days ago. In it, Lucy explains she sent money in case the agent their father hired managed to locate her and she needed to leave town."

"She showed all this to you?"

Nodding, Russ checked his pocket watch. "I forgot I promised to accompany Anna to a meeting at Will and Tomasina's. I have to go."

"I'll walk with you."

Russell motioned him through the door and, locking it behind him, started toward their home. "I don't have anything more to tell you."

They dodged a man rolling a barrel to his wagon. "She didn't mention the handkerchief?"

"Oh, yes. She challenged you to visit the ladies' section in any mercantile across the state of Kansas. Apparently that particular design is a common one."

"How would I know that? The last time I shopped for

a woman was the Christmas of 1860. Nine years ago," he retorted, his annoyance focused inward. "I purchased a brooch for ma."

Russell uttered a knowing *humph*. But the sound spoke volumes. He accused Adam of making a colossal error in judging Deborah's action.

"It was a natural mistake."

"It was an erroneous assumption that drove a wedge between you and the woman you would wed if given a chance." Russell rounded the corner of First Street and suddenly stopped. He raised his arm to chest level, which Adam subsequently bumped into.

"What are you doing?" he demanded. "Hang on, are you implying I love her?"

"Not implying. Stating." He inclined his head. "Do you see that woman over there? The one peering into the furniture store?"

"What woman?"

"The one who, from this distance, could pass for Deborah."

Adam studied the profile of the woman Russ pointed out. The hair was the same rich hue and thickness as Deborah's. Her skin was on the fair side, too.

"It's possible Ogden approached Deborah thinking she was *this* woman," Russell said.

Details clicked into place. "This could be the same one who was spotted in Centerville, the one who wrote the note." He realized his grave error with dawning horror. "I have to learn her name."

His boot met the dirt street. Russ seized his arm. "Ogden might've recognized you this morning. If so, he would've warned her. Let me try."

Adam struggled with the burning need for answers. Finally, he jerked his thumb toward Drovers Place. "I'll wait there."

He found an unobtrusive spot in the cowboy hotel to observe Russell as he strolled across the street as if he had nowhere pressing to be. When he reached the woman, he stopped and introduced himself. A pleasant expression plastered on his face, he handed her a card and chatted for a few minutes. Adam couldn't see her face full-on from his vantage point, but she seemed receptive.

By the time Russell bid her good day and slowly made his way to the hotel, Adam was about to climb out of his skin. "Well?"

He looked grim. "Her name is Dora Edison. Her parents own Longhorn Feed and Grain."

"Dora," he repeated, feeling numb. "Her name wasn't on the list Marigold and Anna provided."

"They did warn you it wouldn't be exhaustive. They can't be expected to know every single woman in town."

"No, of course not." He shook his head. "How could I not entertain the possibility there might be someone who could pass for Deborah?" So much for considering problems from all angles the way he'd been taught. "I let my obsession blind me to reason." His mood blackened. "I accused an innocent woman. Deborah was never involved in this."

"I'm glad you finally puzzled it out," Russ said drily.

He scraped his hand down his face. "I have to see her. Ask—no, get down on my knees and beg—for her forgiveness."

"Let's hope your apology skills are brilliant enough to earn you a second chance." He gripped Adam's shoulder and nodded across the street. "But first, why don't we follow Dora? She just might lead us to our man."

The children had drifted off to sleep when a soft knock interrupted Deborah's frustrated effort to forget her troubles with a borrowed book. It was half-past ten, too late to be anyone else except Adam. Checking to see that her hairpins were in place, she pinched her cheeks and scowled at her hollow-eyed reflection. Why should she care what she looked like? It wouldn't alter his view of her.

Cracking the door open, she wedged into the scant inches. "I'm not ready to discuss anything."

Adam's bloodshot gaze seemed to drink her in. A shadow of a beard graced his drawn features, and his tousled appearance added to the fatigue cloaking him. "I'm not here to pressure you."

Confronted with his obvious distress, her susceptible heart threatened to forget all that had transpired. She had to act fast.

"Then you have no reason to stick around." She started to close the door, but he used his boot to block it.

"Hold on." His warm, callused fingers closed over hers where she gripped the wood. "Please, give me five minutes of your time. That's all I'm asking."

The heat from his touch filled her with wondrous yearning. It was comforting and familiar, like a treasured friend, yet thrilling, too, like a massive display of fireworks. Would he ever sit beside her in church again and secretly hold her hand? Would he tug her close and kiss her again? Or did this spell the end of the special bond they'd shared?

Emotion welled up, threatening to pull her under. She jerked her hand from beneath his. "Five minutes."

Regret dancing over his features, he lowered his arm to his side. "I came to Cowboy Creek armed with information that I was convinced would lead me to Zane Ogden. Russ said he told you everything. I had reason to believe he was being assisted by a woman matching your description and a note signed by someone with a name starting with *D*."

"So you naturally assumed it was me."

"Russ and I happened upon her today. She's a local. Her name is Dora Edison."

Deborah sagged against the door frame. It was the woman Hannah had told her about. "You found her? The person actually helping Ogden. Are you positive she's the one? Or are you guessing, like you did about me?"

He winced. "There's no question Dora is the one I've been searching for. Russ and I followed her outside town, to one of the outlying ranches recently vacated by its owner. After hours of waiting, we caught sight of them together. Ogden must've given up his room at The Lariat. This place offers him more privacy." His jaw hardened. "Ogden escorted her to her horse and, after a romantic goodbye, sent her on her way."

"They're involved?" Deborah shuddered. How any woman could place her trust in a man like him confounded the mind.

"There's something else." The sconce light flickered over his hair, glinting in the strands. "It's about your father."

"What about him?"

"You remember the man I introduced you to? Doc?"

"I already know why he's here."

"You do?" His brows crashed down. "I was planning to tell you at breakfast—"

"But I wasn't there. I'd gone to the post office for my sister's telegram. Turned out I had a letter from her, as well, with money for a train ticket out of town. Mr. Canton didn't have to pay me a visit. Lucy broke the news."

Before she could guess what he was about to do, Adam cupped her cheek. His eyes burned with the need to make amends. "Deborah, please forgive me. I never should've accused you of those things," he said in a rush. "In the beginning, I didn't know you like I do now. Those frequent, mysterious strolls in the dark, the food hidden in your apron pockets... I had to follow you. But it wasn't

Ogden you were feeding, it was a pair of needy orphans. You can't imagine my relief."

"You followed me?" She pushed his hand away. "The night you ambushed us with a gun. You thought it was Ogden in that tent, didn't you?"

"I hoped it wasn't. Prayed it wasn't." His gaze flicked beyond her to the room. Squaring his shoulders, he said, "Before I discovered you helping Liam and Lily, I snuck into your room to search for answers."

The blood drained from her face. "You went through my things?"

He looked ashen. "It's my job. I've done it a hundred times before, but it never bothered me until…" He trailed off, his gaze lowering to the floor.

Deborah couldn't believe her ears. Adam had invaded her privacy. She felt very close to fainting.

"I want you to find another place to stay."

"Deborah, I know it doesn't seem like it, but I care about you. I'd made up my mind that you were innocent until Doc started spouting warnings about objectivity and distractions. And then I saw Ogden giving you the money, and I lost my ability to reason. But I've regained my perspective, and if you'd be willing to forgive me, I'd do anything to try to make it up to you—"

She couldn't look at him. If she looked at him, she'd cave.

"If you don't leave the boardinghouse by tomorrow evening, the children and I will."

He fell silent.

"I mean it, Adam. We'll find somewhere else to board. I don't want to be anywhere near you."

"I understand." His voice thick, he stepped back. "I'll honor your wishes."

"Thank you."

Deborah closed the door and, sinking to the floor, buried her head in her hands and wept.

"Did you hear the news? Seth Halloway discovered gold on his property! Loads of it."

"They're saying there's enough to fill a dozen barrels with the stuff."

"A dozen? I heard it was more like two dozen."

The bakery's atmosphere buzzed with excitement. At a nearby table, cousins Minnie and Millie openly discussed the news with their new husbands, brothers Freddie and Billy Simms.

"Is it true?" Liam asked, his eyes round. "Are Seth and Marigold rich?"

Lily bounced in her seat. "I want to see gold. Can we go there after we eat?"

Deborah stifled their enthusiasm. "I have no idea whether or not it's true. Besides, it's none of our business."

She glanced around at the bakery's early-morning patrons—mostly bachelors who didn't have the luxury of a wife to cook for them. The thrill of discovery sparkled in their gazes. The speculation, envy and greed she witnessed in some of them troubled her. Seth Halloway was an astute, private man. She doubted he would share such information with anyone outside the family.

Deborah found it hard to chew the dry cinnamon bun. Aunt Mae's breakfast would've been far more satisfying, but she still wasn't ready to interact with the other boarders. They were all curious why Adam had abruptly moved out.

Liam pinched off a corner of his raisin loaf and lifted it up for inspection. "How come we've been eating here every morning?"

When Deborah hesitated, he added hastily, "I mean, we're grateful, but..."

"I don't like this place," Lily declared, her small nose wrinkling. "I miss Aunt Mae's eggs and ham. And I miss Adam."

Deborah smoothed the napkin in her lap. Leaning forward, she lowered her voice. "I'm not a fan, either. We'll eat breakfast at the boardinghouse tomorrow morning."

If the others pumped her for answers, so be it. Besides, she couldn't bring herself to continue paying for food unfit to feed a dog. The other bakery would've been a better choice, but it was located near the cowboys' quarters and more popular with single men who wouldn't think twice about interrupting her breakfast to issue dinner invitations.

Both children sighed in relief.

"As for Adam," she said, "I told you he's been busy with work, remember?"

"He's coming back, right?" Lily's face looked pinched.

Reaching out, she smoothed one of the girl's braids behind her shoulder. "He hasn't left Cowboy Creek."

"What does he do, exactly?" Liam said.

Deborah racked her brain for a suitable response. "It's complicated. I'll let Adam explain it to you." She pointed to their plates. "Finish up. We have chores awaiting us."

An argument arose between one of the patrons and the owner, Mr. Lowell. The patron was demanding his money back after discovering mold on his cinnamon bun. But instead of accommodating the man, Mr. Lowell refused.

Someone jabbed a finger in Deborah's direction. "You should take baking lessons from her."

Heads swiveled her direction. Liam and Lily grew still, while Deborah squirmed in her seat.

"I tasted her pastries once," another man piped up. "Melted in my mouth. I'd pay double for food like that."

Deborah couldn't enjoy the praise with so much male attention focused on her. They seemed to expect a response.

What was she supposed to say when the proprietor's wares were being demeaned?

Mr. Lowell glowered, his jowly cheeks flushing. "This ain't her bakery, Lewis. It's mine. If you ain't happy, get out."

Tossing the plate with the moldy bun on the table, Lewis grumbled beneath his breath and lumbered outside, the door slamming behind him. A hushed silence blanketed the room. Deborah sensed Mr. Lowell's anger shifting toward her.

She ushered the children outside, leaving their food unfinished.

"I'm still hungry," Lily said in a small voice.

"There's always leftovers at Aunt Mae's. We'll get you something there."

Already unsettled, Deborah couldn't hide her surprise when they reached the yard and found Anna waiting on the porch swing.

Russ's wife stood awkwardly to her feet, her hand flitting to her bulging middle. "Good morning," she greeted with a self-conscious smile. "I hope you don't mind the unannounced visit."

Deborah joined her on the porch. "No, of course not."

Sending the children inside, she offered Anna something to drink.

She laughed softly. "I drank three cups of hot tea with my omelet and fried potatoes. I can't manage anything else at the moment. Another hour or two, however, and I'll be ready for a snack. I didn't anticipate how hungry I'd be."

Deborah settled in a lone wicker chair opposite the swing and waited for Anna to resume her seat. The notion of having a child with the man she loved was foreign yet wondrous. She wouldn't have that luxury. Any dreams of being with Adam, of being a family with him and the children, had evaporated with his accusations.

Clasping her hands tightly together, she said, "For what's it worth, you are the picture of health."

Anna blushed. "That's kind of you. But I didn't come here to discuss my impending motherhood." Her forehead wrinkled. "I came to ask how you're faring."

"Me?"

"My husband told me what transpired with Adam."

Flustered, she adjusted the bloom nestled above her ear. "Do you know about my arranged marriage and the groom I left in St. Louis?"

"I won't speak of it to anyone," Anna reassured her. Compassion shone in her expressive eyes. "I'm sorry you were put in that position. My sister, Charlotte, was promised to Russell at one time. She was in love with someone else, however, and stayed true to her heart. If she hadn't, I wouldn't've wound up with him."

"I had no idea."

"What I'm trying to say is that I commiserate with your situation."

"Thank you."

"Adam must also be relieved you followed your heart."

"Why would you say that?"

"He cares for you. He's miserable over what he's done."

"You've seen him?"

"He's been staying with us." At Deborah's sharp inhale, she lifted a hand. "Not that he's there often. He drops in at odd hours, and not for very long. I don't know where or when he's sleeping."

Concern blossomed inside Deborah. Was he getting enough to eat? Was he being careful? The man she'd encountered briefly in the alley, the Halloway family's greatest enemy, struck her as being ruthless.

No matter how hurt, no matter how brokenhearted, she didn't want any harm to befall Adam.

"Are they close to capturing Ogden?"

"I don't know. Russ has been going into the office every day as usual, to keep up appearances, and afterward he disappears. He returns in the wee hours of the night, exhausted and reluctant to share details. He's trying to protect me, I know, but I'm worried."

"I will continue to pray for their safety."

"Once this is resolved, will you give Adam a chance to redeem himself?"

"I honestly can't say what will happen between us. His lack of faith has devastated me." She drew in a shaky breath. "I'm also beginning to think I need to go home and sort things with my father before I can move forward."

Anna frowned. "I thought you wanted to make Cowboy Creek your permanent home."

"I do."

When she'd fled St. Louis, she'd been thinking only about herself. With the distance of time, she was starting to comprehend how her actions had made others feel, including her father, Tobias and their many guests. She'd been selfish and cowardly, and that didn't sit well with her.

"What of Liam and Lily?"

"I will take them with me, as long as my petition for guardianship is granted."

"What if your father's stance remains unchanged?"

Deborah opened her mouth to speak, but an unfamiliar voice supplied the answer.

"It hasn't."

Standing, she glared at the gentleman ambling across the yard.

"I know why you're here," she sputtered, "and I can promise you won't get what you came for."

# Chapter Twenty-Five

The Pinkerton agent stopped a polite distance away and, tugging at his hat brim, bid them both a good afternoon.

"I was hoping we could have a rational conversation, Miss Frazier."

Anna moved close and laid a hand on Deborah's arm. "Do you know this man?"

"We haven't been formally introduced," she said, trying to exude calm when a storm of anxiety raged inside. "This is Lyle Canton, the man my father hired to retrieve me."

His muddy gaze reflected amusement. "You make it sound like you're a child or a favored pet."

"My father affords his pets greater freedom than he does his daughter."

His brows hit his hairline. "It's my understanding you went along with the wedding plans, Miss Frazier. You attended an engagement celebration, assisted in the choosing of church decorations and made no protest in the days before the ceremony. That sounds like a willing bride-to-be, wouldn't you agree?"

Anna exuded disapproval. "Deborah, would you like for me to summon Aunt Mae?"

"That's not necessary." Crossing her arms, she said,

"I've been expecting Agent Canton's visit." Dreading the meeting, truth be told, but she was ready to be done with it.

His gaze bounced between them. "I'm sorry to keep you waiting. Your *friend*, Adam, has intentionally kept me preoccupied."

"Doing what?"

He wagged his finger. "I'm here to discuss your case, not Adam's."

"I am not a case."

Gesturing to the house, he said, "Am I to be invited inside?"

"This won't be a lengthy discussion. I have decided to return to St. Louis."

Lips parting, he took a step forward. "I'm happy to hear that. We can go to the depot together. Your father sent enough money to cover the ticket cost, of course. How long will it take you to pack?"

"You misunderstand. I'm not going today, and I'm certainly not going with you."

He lifted a hand. "Miss Frazier—"

"Canton!" Russell's harried hale reached them from the street. Astride a black horse, he waved his hand high above his head to get their attention. He dismounted and pushed through the gate. He wasn't his typical unflappable self. His suit jacket wasn't in evidence, and both his vest and shirt were wrinkled. A shiny leather gun belt encircled his waist, weighted by a revolver, which was out of character for the lawyer.

The agent twisted toward him, impatience flashing. "You can tell your brother I'm through playing games. He can't keep me from speaking with Miss Frazier indefinitely."

"This isn't a game," he retorted, his gaze hard. "Adam's in trouble. He's minutes away from meeting with Ogden. I couldn't dissuade him."

Deborah's heart climbed into her chest. "He's facing him alone?"

Russell's glance encompassed her and his wife. "The rumors about gold on Seth's land were a ruse to lure Ogden out of hiding. Adam ran out of patience, so he arranged a meeting by posing as a hotel employee with evidence of Ogden's part in the local mishaps and he's demanding payment for his silence." He turned to the Pinkerton agent. "I need you there not only to aid in his capture, but as a witness. I'm family, so I don't count."

Agent Canton nodded his acquiescence. "We'll have to continue this discussion at a later time, Miss Frazier."

She descended the steps. "I'm coming with you."

Russell's head reared back. "You can't. Adam would kill me."

"He's right. This is ugly business," Canton stated. "You'd only prove a distraction, just as you've done since the moment Adam met you."

The men weren't giving her an option. Russell hugged Anna before hurrying to his horse. Canton reached his and, without a glance back, nudged the animal into motion.

Deborah followed them into the street, desperate to reach Adam but with no way of doing so. By the time she borrowed a horse, they'd be long gone, and she had no way of knowing where they were headed.

Anna approached and put her arm around her. "He's going to be fine."

"I hope you're right."

Because if he wasn't, she'd never get to a chance to tell him she forgave him.

He'd been waiting his whole adult life for this moment.

Clad in the official uniform of The Lariat—black with maroon and gold accents—Adam rode into the agreed upon field, his Stetson sitting lower than usual on his brow.

Dusk blanketed the prairie in a yellow haze. Soon the sun would disappear beneath the distant horizon.

His palms were clammy, his stomach leaden.

*I've made a lot of mistakes, Lord. I haven't always done things Your way, and I'm sorry about that. Please forgive me. Please end this with Ogden. Put a stop to his reign of corruption. Give us the answers we've longed for.*

Thundering hooves signaled the approach of more than one rider. Sliding out of the saddle, he withdrew his weapon and guided his horse beneath the cover of a nearby tree. Ogden had agreed to come alone. They both had.

Trusting Ogden to adhere to their terms had been a risk. He surely wouldn't have brought Dora with him, but he might've brought the other Maroni "brother."

Adrenaline arrowing through his veins, Adam couldn't get a good grip on the gun handle. His usual composure had deserted him. If he lost this chance, he might not ever get another.

He watched the three men from behind the cover of green leaves. The moment he recognized them, he left the safety of his hiding place and charged toward them.

"What are you doing here?" he barked.

The trio managed to keep their mounts from trampling him.

Glaring, Russell pulled back hard on the reins. "Are you trying to get yourself killed?"

"I told you I was coming alone." He pointed at Seth. "Why did you involve him?"

"This is a family matter," Seth said calmly, patting his horse's heaving flank. "It involves all of us."

"I'm here to provide an objective witness account," Doc drawled.

Scanning the surrounding fields, Adam checked his pocket watch. "Ogden will be here in ten minutes. You three have to find a place to hide."

Fortunately, he'd chosen a spot near the river with plenty of trees and underbrush. Doc immediately went to do just that. He should've guessed his older brothers wouldn't do his bidding.

Dismounting, Russell and Seth regarded him with matching hangdog expressions.

"Don't make any sudden moves," Russ advised.

"But be ready in case he does," Seth tacked on.

"I've trained for this moment," he told them, inwardly relieved they'd shown up despite his express wishes otherwise. "And I've prayed all I know to pray."

Seth nodded in approval. "We've got the womenfolk praying, as well."

Thoughts of Deborah threatened to carve up his remaining veneer of calm. She was desperately unhappy with him. It wasn't likely she'd bother to pray for him, even if she had been aware of what was about to take place.

*God, please soften her heart. I'm not asking for a life with her. I know that's out of the question now. But I'd like to have her forgiveness.*

His brothers retreated into the lengthening shadows between the trees. Adam got a better hold on his weapon and braced himself for the coming confrontation. The minutes crawled past. He paced a line in the grass, trampling the tender stalks and sending insects scurrying. He checked the hour a dozen times until, at long last, he heard the distinct sound of a rider.

Zane Ogden entered the clearing without a hint of reserve. He was either arrogant or stupid, and history had proven he was clever.

Remaining in the saddle, he thumbed his hat up and took Adam's measure.

"You were in the alley," he stated. "Why'd you come after me? I didn't lay a finger on the woman."

Adam swallowed, his throat parched as if it were high

noon. Ogden hadn't connected him with Big Bend. Eighteen at the time, Adam hadn't had much interaction with the man posing as a wealthy, kindhearted entrepreneur.

"I've been after you for four years."

Confusion—not wariness—flickered over his features. He assumed a cocky smile. "You don't work for the hotel, do you?"

"No."

"That's too bad." His hand went for his saddlebag. Adam raised his weapon.

"No need to get antsy. I'm only going to retrieve the money you asked for."

Ogden slowly lifted a bulging sack and tossed it to the ground near Adam's feet.

"Count it. It's all there. Plenty of coin to leave behind whatever petty life you lead for a more lucrative one."

"Pinkertons don't accept bribes." He watched with satisfaction as Ogden shifted in the saddle. One didn't toss out the respected name without a reaction. "That's right. I'm in the employ of the Pinkerton National Detective Agency. But this isn't official business. It's personal."

His lips thinned. "Who are you?"

Removing his hat, he said, "You don't recognize me? Adam Halloway's the name. I'm the youngest son of Gilbert Halloway."

Finally, there was a flicker of unease in the other man's eyes. "Ah, you do remember our ranch in Big Bend, Missouri. You remember murdering my father and forging his signature on a loan document, don't you?" He cocked the revolver and lowered the hammer, the click loud in the hushed evening. "My family has gone without answers for nearly a decade. I'm not leaving until I get them."

Ogden shrugged. "Not much to tell. I remember your father. He was a thorn in my side, warning the others and trying to sway them against me. I would've gotten rid of him sooner, but I was too busy emptying ranchers' pockets."

Anger whipped through Adam like a grass fire. It took all of his self-control not to shoot him square in the heart. "What happened that night? When he challenged you?"

"Why does it matter?" he drawled, not an ounce of remorse in his tone. "Won't bring him back from the grave."

His father didn't have a grave. Didn't have a proper burial.

Adam's hand trembled. *Tell me.*

"I put a bullet in his chest. The good sheriff helped me dispose of the body. When I had the brilliant idea to implicate Halloway in a loan, he agreed to assist with that, too."

The confession didn't take away his anger, didn't wipe out his grief or make him feel better. But it did confirm what they'd assumed happened to their father.

"Doc," he called over his shoulder, "I hope you wrote all that down."

Ogden didn't react when Doc materialized from the trees. Something wasn't right. He should be reaching for his weapon. Trying to escape.

The haze had thickened to near-night. Ogden squinted into the darkness around them.

Adam waved Doc forward. "Ogden, meet my colleague, Agent Canton. He'll be joining me as we escort you to your temporary home—the nearest jail."

"You've already met my colleague," Ogden retorted, nodding to a spot behind them.

Adam turned in time to see Seth and Russ approaching with their hands above their heads. The man who'd forced them from their hiding place was none other than Cowboy Creek's sheriff.

Adam's temper threatened to boil over. He had a knack for discovering weak-minded men to whom justice held no meaning.

"Where's your other accomplice? Your supposed brother?"

"That was a ruse. I pretended to be two men. It's not that difficult to alter your appearance these days." Ogden's eagle gaze sharpened. "Some people change as they age. Take you, for instance. I wouldn't have pegged you as Gilbert Halloway's youngest." Grinning ruthlessly, he nodded at Seth. "He's another story. He's your brother, is he not?"

"I'm the one who decided to ignore Adam's convictions and satisfy your loan requirements," Seth growled, lowering and fisting his hands. "You will pay for your crimes, Ogden. God will see to that."

The sheriff poked his gun in his back. "Hands above your head."

Russell spoke up. "I'm part of the family, too. Remember me?"

Ogden eyed him, then chuckled. "All three Halloway boys in one place. I couldn't have asked for a better opportunity."

Adam sent a sideways glance at Doc. They had to think of a way to outmaneuver these two. He'd lost his father to this man's greed. He wasn't about to lose anyone else.

## Chapter Twenty-Six

"What is it about Zane Ogden that appeals to you?"

The rope binding Deborah's wrists together chafed her tender skin. Forced to walk through fields with very low lamp flame to light the way, she'd stumbled twice, falling to her knees and ripping her dress. She was attempting to stave off panic by trying to understand her captor's motivation.

"Shut up." Dora's fingers dug into her upper arm. "You wouldn't understand."

"You don't know me," she managed. "You might be surprised."

"I know enough. After our chance run-in, I tracked you to Aunt Mae's. You're like the other women in our town. You lack imagination. You do what's expected, like choosing a staid man who couldn't possibly make you happy."

Deborah would've laughed if the other woman hadn't been wielding a gun. If she'd done what was expected of her, she wouldn't be in this situation. She'd be trapped in a loveless marriage. She wouldn't have fallen in love with Adam.

Anxiety rose up to choke her. Thoughts of him at the mercy of Ogden had plagued her long after Russell and

Agent Canton had ridden out of town. Where was he now? Did they reach him in time? Was he all right?

"Did Ogden know you were watching me?" A shudder of revulsion wiggled down her spine. The notion that she'd been observed unawares made her feel vulnerable and exposed.

"Zane doesn't waste his energy on matters that don't impact him personally. He wasn't intrigued by our similarities like I was."

"I'm nothing like you," Deborah retorted. "Not on the inside where it counts."

Dora responded by forcing her to go faster. Lights flickered in the distance, but she couldn't determine the source.

What exactly awaited her was a mystery. Deborah had been weeding the garden alone in a desperate attempt to divert her thoughts when Dora had accosted her, waving the gun in her face and threatening to harm Liam and Lily if she didn't go quietly.

"There's no harm in telling me where we're going," she tried again. "Do you need my help leaving town?"

An unladylike snort rent the night. "I can manage that on my own, thank you. You'd be surprised what being the daughter of prominent citizens can achieve."

"That's right. Your parents own Longhorn Feed and Grain." She needed more information if she was going to try to survive. "A successful business, I've heard. You must reap the benefits of their good standing, not to mention the material rewards."

They left the knee-high grass for the dirt-hardened road. "My parents do earn a healthy profit, but they're tight-fisted. Zane is different. He's generous with his wealth."

Deborah couldn't comprehend such skewed priorities. "Are you and he planning a future beyond Cowboy Creek?"

Her captor's breathing hitched. "We'll be together no matter where we go. You're my guarantee."

"Me?"

As they approached a copse of aged trees, the lights became more distinct. Was Ogden waiting for them? Was Adam?

"Your beau and another man followed me to Zane's. I didn't realize it until too late. H-he wasn't pleased. I promised I'd fix the problem, and I did. I trailed Mr. Draper and saw him procuring the hotel uniform. When Zane got the note luring him to this meeting, we knew it was a ruse."

Deborah's insides flushed with fear. That meant they were prepared. Adam had walked into a trap.

*Lord Jesus, please protect him. Please let good triumph evil.*

If anything happened to him, she'd have only their last conversation to cling to. She'd have the ugly memory of her unwillingness to accept his sincere remorse. She'd remember turning him away. The anguish churning in his eyes would haunt her for the rest of her days.

*Please, God, give us another chance.*

The one bright spot in this situation was that Deborah wasn't anywhere around. She was safe, and so were the kids. Adam regretted getting her entangled in his mess, but he couldn't regret the time they'd spent together or the special moments they'd shared.

"What do you want to do with them?" Sheriff Getman jiggled his gun, aiming first at Russell and then Seth.

Ogden remained astride his horse, one arm resting atop his thigh, the barrel of his gun pointing to the ground. His gaze was trained on Adam and Doc, who were nearest him.

"The Halloway name is already sullied. I say we concoct a tale that blackens it beyond repair." He tapped his chin. "What sordid affair should we say caused brothers to turn on each other in cold-blooded murder?"

Adam caught Seth's eye. Did he understand they didn't have much time? That they needed to act without delay?

The sheriff shrugged. "You don't pay me to devise schemes. We do have to be circumspect if we're to do away with all three."

"No one knows of Adam's connection to the other two. We could use that to our advantage."

"Russell's a respected lawyer and is favored to take the mayor's place."

"I don't care if he's a preacher," Ogden shot back. "Everyone's got their hidden sins."

"Seth's got a ranch you'd be interested in," the sheriff mused. "Not to mention a pretty wife."

"Any kids?"

"A passel."

"Widows with kids make easy marks," he said suggestively.

A murderous sound emanated from deep in Seth's throat. Adam glanced over his shoulder and made eye contact with Russ. He couldn't mouth instructions or gesture. Instead, he tried to communicate with his eyes.

Russ hunched over and put his hand to his forehead. "I don't feel right." He stumbled to the side. "I'm going to pass out."

The sheriff faltered for a split second. It was all the time they needed.

Without warning, Russ whirled and slammed his shoulder into the sheriff's gut. Seth leaped into the fray.

Doc sprinted toward the left side of Ogden's horse, while Adam targeted the right. He was grabbing for Ogden when a shot rang out.

Doc crumpled to the ground. Free of that threat, Ogden turned his full attention to Adam, who managed to seize a fistful of his adversary's jacket and yank him half out of the saddle. In the process, Ogden's gun handle connected with Adam's cheek. Jagged spikes of pain radiated through his skull. Stars filled his vision.

He blocked a second blow with his arm, then hooked onto Ogden's collar and hauled him to the ground. The horse reared, powerful front legs pawing the air. Adam's world titled. Battling dizziness and nausea, he scuttled out of the way.

*Focus, Halloway.* He sucked in air and willed the weakness away.

Tackling his enemy, he used his knees to pin his chest to the ground. He unsheathed his weapon and jammed it beneath his chin. "Put your gun down!" he barked.

Ogden glared up at Adam with the heat of a thousand suns. Sweat poured off him. Panting, he slowly dropped the gun in the grass.

Digging the point deeper into Ogden's throat, Adam said, "You're going to spend the rest of your life in jail for what you've done."

"I'd rather hang," he spat.

"That can be arranged."

"Stop!"

The female scream took a moment to register. Adam glanced to where he'd last seen his brothers. They'd overtaken the sheriff and were binding his hands and feet, but at the high-pitched scream both men now wore dumbstruck expressions. Adam whipped his head toward the small rise leading to the road.

And his heart almost ceased beating.

"Deborah." He shook his head as if to clear it, the motion sending fresh waves of pain along his jaw. "What are you doing here?" He narrowed his gaze at the woman latched on to her. "What is she doing here?"

Wearing a sneer, Dora Edison shoved Deborah to her

knees and aimed the gun at her head. "I'm here to make a trade. Zane for your ladylove."

Adam scrambled off Ogden but kept his gun trained on him.

Deborah's eyes were huge, the topaz irises almost obscured by her pupils. She looked tired and rumpled, her hair hanging down and her dress ripped in places, but she didn't appear harmed. He studied her expression and read its silent message. She begged him not to do it. Of course she'd think of him before her own safety. She understood how important capturing Ogden was to him and, despite his failures, she still cared. What she didn't yet know, what he hadn't taken the time to tell her, was that nothing else on this earth compared to her. If he didn't have Deborah, his life would mean nothing.

He looked at Dora. Yes, there were similarities between the two, but Dora's tainted spirit made her ugly. Nothing but goodness radiated from Deborah.

"What are you gonna do, Halloway?" Ogden demanded, arrogant to the very end.

He looked at Dora. "You release her, and I'll give him to you."

"Adam, no." Deborah's fingers curled into balls. The sight of the rope digging into her wrists made him want to claw Dora's eyes out.

Dora silenced her with a yank of the rope. "Zane comes with me and my friend here. We'll leave a note at the hideout telling you where you can find her."

And take the chance they'd hurt her? "I don't accept those terms."

A surprised laugh escaped Dora. "You don't have a choice."

"Don't I?" he retorted. "My goal has always been to make Ogden face justice. Whether that comes from a prison sentence or a death sentence makes no difference to me."

Her nostrils flared. Her fingers flexed on the gun pointed at Deborah. "Nor do I care if she lives or dies. But you do."

When she used the sole of her boot to push Deborah flat on the ground and stretched out her weapon arm, Adam didn't think. He sprinted toward them, his only goal to protect the woman he loved.

Deborah yelled his name. Scuffling sounded behind him. Grunts of exertion. Struggle. But everything faded around the edges of his vision, narrowing only to the two women a short distance away.

He had to reach her.

Had to save her.

The shot resounded through the fields. It stopped him in his tracks, jerking him the opposite way. He felt himself falling, the ground rushing up to meet him. Wetness on his chest registered first. Then explosive pain that made him want to howl.

He didn't have the energy to speak. The sound escaping his lips sounded like a kitten's mewling.

Adam blinked up at the stars sprinkled across the navy sky, hating the weakness sweeping through his body, stealing his thoughts and words until there was only black shadows.

## Chapter Twenty-Seven

$\sim$

Adam was going to die.

He was going to die, and there was nothing she could do to prevent it. His motionless body broke something inside her.

Sorrow engulfed her. Rage joined it.

Never in her life had she felt this out of control.

A cry building in her chest, Deborah levered herself off the ground and reached for Dora's throat even though the rope around her wrists put her at a disadvantage. Her decision to fight back caught the other woman by surprise. She floundered to stay upright as Deborah clawed and shoved and pummeled her.

Dora stumbled to the ground, her gun sliding from her hold. She put her hands up to protect her face. Still, Deborah didn't stop her assault.

Strong arms encircled her waist from behind, firmly pulling her away.

"Let me go!"

"It's okay. It's me, Russ." Holding fast to Deborah, he used his boot to kick Dora's weapon out of her reach. "You're going to be okay. Ogden's restrained."

"She shot Adam," Deborah sobbed, struggling to free herself.

"That's why we need to deal with her. So we can get him to the doctor." The emotional strain in his voice finally pierced the storm engulfing her.

She went limp. "Is he…"

"I don't know."

Releasing her, he cut Deborah's rope. He hauled Dora up and marched her over to where Ogden and the sheriff lay trussed in the grass. Doc had managed to sit up and was holding a wadded-up bandanna to his thigh.

Deborah forced her feet to take her to Adam's side. Seth ripped his shirt open to view the wound. The amount of blood was astonishing. Unable to stand, she fell to her knees and latched on to his hand, willing him to make it. Disjointed prayers filtered through her mind.

Seth's face set in stone, he removed his handkerchief and pressed it to the bullet site.

"Deborah, I need you to keep pressure on this while I fetch my horse."

She stared at Adam's still features, all the things she should've said bombarding her. Would he open those beautiful brown eyes again? Would he smile that charming smile for her?

"Deborah."

Seth's sharp voice cut through her shock.

"Yes, of course." Shuffling closer, she nudged his hands aside and placed her own atop the soaked fabric. "He's going to make it, isn't he?"

There was a burst of raw anguish in his eyes. "I've just got him back." His jaw hardened. "I'm not prepared to lose him now."

Shoving to his feet, he jogged away, leaving Deborah alone with Adam.

Keeping her hands in place, she bent and brushed a kiss on his brow. "I can't lose you, either, you know. You have to fight. You have people who love you." Tears dripped from her chin onto his cheek, where a mottled bruise had blossomed. "I love you," she whispered.

Seth returned short minutes later and, with Russell's help, got Adam on the horse. Seth climbed on behind him. Russell urged Deborah to use his horse. She would accompany Adam to town while Russ and Agent Canton escorted the others to jail. Canton's injury was superficial and could wait for medical attention.

Grateful to be allowed to remain with Adam, she gave Russ a quick hug. The ride to town was too slow for her liking, but she understood Seth wouldn't want to jostle Adam and cause more damage.

Her nerves were strained to breaking by the time they got him into Dr. Mason's office. If Marlys was intimidated by the task before her, she didn't show it. When Deborah would've gone into the examination room with them, Seth stopped her with his hands on her shoulders.

"I know you'd rather be here with my brother, but I need a favor. My mother needs to be informed of what's happened. Marigold, too. Would you mind?"

Deborah's gaze shot past the open doorway. All she could see were Adam's boots where he lay on a table.

Her eyes filled with fresh tears. "Seth, I—"

"This will take some time." Marlys swept past carrying a box of supplies. "He won't know you're gone." She paused in the doorway. "And I'll need to tend to your wrists when you return."

Deborah slowly nodded, even though everything inside her resisted. "I'll do it."

"Thank you," he rasped, already turning to join the others.

"Seth?"

He gripped the doorjamb and raised his brows.

"If he wakes, tell him…" She sucked in wobbly breath. There were so many things she needed to say. "Tell him I'm sorry, too."

\* \* \*

"Why hasn't she come, Russ?"

Adam threw off the thin blanket and rearranged the pillows propping him up for the umpteenth time. The stitches in his chest pulled at tender skin. He hid a grimace. Any sign of discomfort, and Russ would try to force more foul-tasting medicine down his throat. He'd had enough of the hovering. While he appreciated his brother and sister-in-law's hospitality—the bedroom was bright and spacious, with a window overlooking a flower garden—the walls were starting to close in. Their home was too still, too quiet. It wasn't the boardinghouse.

Fresh confusion further soured his mood. Deborah's continued absence was not a good sign, despite his family's reassurances.

Sighing, Russ snapped closed the heavy law tome he'd been reading and slid it onto the bedside table. "I've told you a dozen times, she was there during the procedure to remove the bullet and the long days afterward. She remained at your bedside while you battled fever and infection. We had to make her go home every evening to eat with the kids and get some rest. She's been beside herself with worry."

"Then why haven't I seen her?" he growled. "I've been here five days. I'm telling you, Russ, if she doesn't come soon, I will go to her, even if I have to walk down Eden Street wearing these ridiculous pajamas."

"You wouldn't make it past the front door, and you know it," Russ responded with infuriating calmness. "She claims she doesn't want to hinder your recovery in any way."

"What's that supposed to mean?"

*Not* seeing her was causing him immense frustration. The last thing he remembered was that terrible Dora woman preparing to shoot her. He had to see for himself that she was all right.

"You'll have to ask her that."

"How can I when she refuses to visit me?"

"You look flushed." Russ stood and picked up the empty water pitcher. "I'll get you more water."

"I don't *want* water." He tossed a pillow at his brother's retreating figure. It landed on the polished floor with a sigh and slid into the hallway. "I want out of here!"

He wanted his strength to return. He wanted not to be at the mercy of his weakened body. Sinking against the pillows, he closed his eyes, pinched the bridge of his nose and asked the Lord for forgiveness. He was grateful, so very grateful no one had lost their life. Deborah and his brothers were fine. Doc was on the mend. Ogden and his cohorts were locked away awaiting trial.

He simply wasn't accustomed to sitting around and stewing over his problems.

"Adam, you have visitors."

He opened his eyes to see Anna ushering Liam and Lily into the room. "There are a couple of kids impatient to see you."

His heart beat faster. Did this mean Deborah was somewhere in the house?

Noticing their uncertainty, he extended his hand. "I won't bite, I promise."

Anna laughed. "He only snarls and growls."

"I haven't been a model patient," he told the children. "But now that you're here, I have no reason to be grumpy. I've missed you both something terrible."

Anna slipped out of the room. To visit with Deborah? Someone had to have brought the children.

Lily approached his bedside, her solemn gaze taking inventory. "We wanted to come sooner," she whispered, "but Deborah said you needed peace and quiet."

"I've had enough of that, I promise."

"Oh. So I don't have to whisper?"

He ruffled her hair. "No whispering required."

Liam propped his arms along the footboard; his worry was plain. "I've never known anyone to get shot and live to tell about it. Does it hurt?"

"Not so much now. I've had excellent care."

Lily clambered onto the bed. "We prayed for you every night. Sometimes I heard Deborah crying into her pillow."

Adam's chest squeezed.

"Lily," Liam chided. "That's private."

"She doesn't smile anymore. And she doesn't make desserts anymore, either. Aunt Mae only shakes her head and sighs."

"Will you stop thinking about your stomach? She's been worried about him."

Ignoring her brother, she ran her fingers along Adam's scruffy beard, apparently fascinated by the prickles. "I think it's because he's leaving us."

"Where did you hear that?" Adam said.

"Deborah said you've finished the work keeping you here."

Curving his arm around her, he said, "I'm not leaving."

He wasn't sure what his future held, but he'd decided to stay in Cowboy Creek.

He looked them both in the eye. "I'd like to continue to be a part of your lives, if that's okay with you."

Relief brightened Liam's features. "Yes, sir!"

Lily hugged him tight. "I want you to be my papa."

His heart melting, he patted her back and tried to think of what to say. He couldn't tell her the truth, that he would be honored to fill that position, because then he'd have to answer questions about Deborah.

Someone cleared their throat. "May I come in?"

Anticipation surged through him. Lily jumped off the

bed and skipped to the doorway to where Deborah waited, her hands knotted at her waist. Adam drank in the sight of her, achingly beautiful in an elegant creation of sea-shell pink, her dark hair cascading in soft curls around her shoulders. She reached for the rolling pin brooch on her bodice and clung to it, her knuckles going white.

His frustration melted. "Hello, Deborah."

"Hello, Adam."

Lily tugged on her sleeve. "He doesn't want peace and quiet."

Deborah smiled tremulously down at the girl. "He doesn't?"

"And he's not leaving Cowboy Creek."

"Is that right?" Deborah slowly lifted her gaze to his. "I—I'm glad."

"That means we can go fishing anytime we want!" Liam exclaimed.

"And play with Violet's kittens and ride Seth's horses," Lily added.

Deborah tore her gaze away from Adam and tried to silence the children. "Well, I—"

"Liam. Lily." Just then Anna returned with a plate of cookies, interrupting Deborah. "Why don't you two join Russ and me in the dining room for a treat?"

The kids readily agreed with the plan. As they ran from the bedroom, the resulting silence resonated with anxiety.

She shifted from one foot to another. "I don't have to stay. I can come back another time o-or not at all, if that's what you wish."

"It's not," Adam said huskily.

Everything he wanted to say, everything he'd practiced, froze on his tongue. He was afraid of spooking her. He wasn't in the position to chase after her if he did.

She let go of the brooch and took a couple of steps toward the bed. Her eyes studied the bandage peeking from the neckline of his pajama shirt.

"How are you feeling? Has Marlys been monitoring your progress?" Her lips turned down. "I hope there's no sign of the infection returning. Are you eating enough—"

His own question stopped her. "How am I feeling? I'm feeling neglected, that's what. Are you still angry with me? Is that why you've stayed away?"

"What? No!" Her eyes widened, and she closed the distance between them. "I'm the reason you're in that bed. You almost died saving me. When I think of you lying in that field, unconscious and bleeding—" Her lips starting trembling.

He found her hand and threaded his fingers through hers, reassured when she clung to him. "By God's grace, I survived."

"You endured agonizing pain from the gunshot wound. Then the fever sucked you into its grip. I can't help thinking if I hadn't been so stubborn that night you came to my room, if I'd accepted your apology instead of hardening my heart, things might've unfolded differently."

Adam leaned forward and, ignoring the discomfort the sudden movement evoked, cupped her waist and pulled her down to sit on the edge of the mattress.

"No, sweetheart. You wouldn't have even been involved if it weren't for me. If I hadn't been blinded by my need for revenge, I wouldn't have made so many mistakes with you." He squeezed her hand. "Can you ever forgive me?"

Her eyes brimmed with tears. "Oh, Adam." Looping her arm around his neck, she buried her face in his shoulder and wept. "I don't know what I would do without you."

Overcome with emotion, he nestled her tight against his good side and rested his whiskered cheek against her silken hair. "I'm relieved to hear you say that. I thought you'd never speak to me again. I feared you despised me."

Deborah abruptly sat up. "Never." Her cheeks were damp, her mouth glistening. Cradling his cheek, she gazed at him with unbridled affection. "Sometimes you infuriate me, but nothing could stop me from loving you."

Happiness filled the holes in his heart created by unresolved bitterness. Capturing his enemy hadn't restored him. It had been this woman's healing love. Her love renewed the hope he'd thought had died with his father.

*A man's heart plans his way, but the Lord directs his steps.* The Proverbs verse struck him as perfect for his journey. He'd come to Kansas seeking revenge. The Lord had given him love, instead.

Adam framed her face and brought his mouth close to hers, veering off at the last second to nuzzle her cheek. "I infuriate you, huh?"

Her lids drifted closed, her breathing sped up. "Yes, when you sample my pastries without asking—"

He kissed her temple.

"A-and when you rifle through my personal belongings—"

He kissed her nose.

"You, ah—" Licking her lips, she shivered. "When you're determined to be the hero and risk your life, frightening me to within an inch of mine…"

He ceased his assault. "Deborah?"

Her lids fluttered open, revealing twin pools of brilliantly dazed topaz. "Hmm?"

"I love you."

She caught her breath, then smiled so sweetly he couldn't delay a second longer. He slanted his mouth over hers, surrendering to the love flowing between them, showing her without words how much she meant to him.

# Chapter Twenty-Eight

Deborah couldn't take her eyes off Adam. He'd insisted on attending the library's grand opening, despite not having fully regained his strength. Wearing a formal black suit that enhanced his dark good looks, he'd found a comfortable seat in one corner of the main room and was surrounded by well-wishers. With Zane Ogden in custody, the truth about Adam's identity and profession was no longer a secret.

"You're glowing, you know."

Smiling, she turned to her friend Sadie. "I'm happy."

"You sound surprised," Sadie said, sipping her lemonade.

"Before I met Adam, I didn't think I deserved to be."

Sadie frowned. "That's your father's doing."

"Partly. I did allow him to shape my view of myself." She thought of the letter she'd penned and wondered how he'd react. "I might not have gone about things the right way, but I'll forever be grateful for that abandoned train ticket."

She sensed Adam's gaze on her, and her eyes were drawn to his. His slow smile sent giddiness zinging through her. He'd shaved that morning for the first time since getting shot, and she recalled testing the smoothness of his lean jaws and then reveling in his kiss. Aware they'd almost lost something precious, neither had wanted to be apart. They'd spent the last few days together ensconced in Russ and Anna's parlor. Thankfully, the other couple hadn't seemed to mind the intrusion.

Sadie nudged her. "Would you two stop it already?" she said good-naturedly.

Deborah's cheeks heated. "You have no room to complain, considering I've caught you and Walter doing the same thing."

Sadie's attention went to the prominent photograph Walter had unveiled once the official library dedication had been completed. A simple style not typical for him, it featured an up-close view of a pair of rings—one a solid band and the other topped with a stunning jewel.

"I hoped and prayed he'd propose," Sadie said on a sigh. "But I never imagined it would be in such a fanciful manner."

Deborah linked arms with her. "I'm thrilled for you, Sadie. The two of you are perfectly suited."

"Has Adam spoken of marriage?"

"Not yet." They'd discussed everything under the sun except what the future might hold for them as a couple. "I have unresolved matters back home. I posted a letter to my father yesterday, but I'm not sure that will be enough. Before Agent Canton left, he promised to speak with my father." She sighed. "I will probably need to make the journey and speak to him face-to-face."

"Well, Adam adores you and the kids. There's no question he wants the three of you in his life. Any word on the guardianship?"

"Not yet." Deborah was starting to wonder what was taking so long. Russell had been vague. When she questioned Adam, he'd told her the process was sometimes slow.

She had decided to rejoin Adam when Preston blocked

her path. She hadn't seen him arrive. Despite the crowd, Preston evoked a fluttery feeling of foreboding. His gaze cut through her, a subtle, strange mixture of anger and yearning in the depths.

"Deborah, you're looking well."

Beside her, Sadie rolled her eyes. "Have you forgotten Adam's warning?"

"I'm not threatening her," he sniffed.

"You're bothering her," she retorted. "Where's your constant companion?"

He arched an imperious brow. "Are you referring to my fiancée?"

"You and Hildie plan to marry?" Deborah couldn't help feeling sorry for Hildie. No doubt she'd been so eager to wed, she'd rushed into the first relationship that presented itself.

Preston nodded. "We're moving back to my hometown, to be closer to my parents."

"When do you leave?" Sadie piped up, not bothering to mask her eagerness.

"That's what I'd like to know."

At the sound of the deep voice, Preston turned, scowling at Adam. "Deborah is in no danger, Halloway. I was merely paying her a compliment."

A muscle ticked at Adam's temple. Beneath his tan, he looked pale. Concern immediately flared within Deborah. Adam was determined to rush his recovery for no reason that she could figure.

Going to his side, she threaded her fingers through his. "Congratulations are in order, Adam. Preston and Hildie are engaged and will be moving to…" She aimed the unspoken question at Preston, whose enigmatic gaze lingered on their hands.

"Illinois."

Hildie rushed over, a possessive light in her eyes.

"You've heard the happy news, I see. We were planning on making an announcement until Walter stole our thunder."

"You shouldn't let our engagement stop you." Sadie waggled her fingers at the milling guests. "I'm sure everyone will be delighted. You will probably find many folks happy to help you pack."

Hildie's features became pinched. She urged Preston to join her in fetching a drink. When they left, Sadie decided it was time to find Walter.

Once they were alone, Adam sent Deborah a smile somewhat dimmer than usual. He seemed nervous as opposed to upset.

"He wasn't bothering me," she said to reassure him. "There's nothing to be concerned about. With you and your brothers around, he won't try anything."

Squeezing her hand, he drawled, "I'm not worried. I heard in great detail how you defended yourself against Dora. You're stronger than you look." He winked. "But I'll still be glad when he's gone."

Instinctively, she went up on tiptoe and kissed his cheek. Then, remembering their audience, she felt heat surging onto her face.

"I apologize. I somehow always lose sight of decorum. I'm grateful my father isn't around to scold me."

He rubbed his jaw. "About that…"

A commotion at the front entrance of the library caused a break in the hum of conversation. "Where's my daughter?" a voice boomed. "Deborah Frazier. Is she here?"

Deborah's stomach dropped to her toes. "Adam—"

"Sweetheart, I have to tell you something."

The crowd parted like a sea to allow the blustering stranger through the parlor. A kaleidoscope of emotions swirled through her. She hadn't realized she'd missed him until her father stood before her. They might share a difficult relationship, but she loved him.

"Deborah Elaine Frazier!" He puffed out his chest and set his jaw. The bulldog posture used to intimidate her. Oddly, it didn't have the same effect this time. "How dare you refuse to return with the man I hired to bring you home! You've devastated your sister, and this continued snubbing of Tobias is unacceptable."

She felt the weight of everyone's stares. "Father, please—"

"And you." He jabbed his finger toward Adam. "I assume you're Adam Halloway?"

Adam nodded solemnly. "I am."

"You have the audacity to ask me for my daughter's hand when she's engaged to my dearest friend?"

A collective gasp went up, Deborah's included. Adam angled toward her, earnest appeal in his brown eyes. "I wrote to your father and asked for his blessing. I had no idea he'd answer me in person."

"You didn't say anything."

"I've been trying to think of a way to broach the subject," he said sheepishly. "I wanted my proposal to be memorable."

"She's not likely to forget this," someone nearby commented.

Gerard thumped his foot. "Deborah is already pledged to another."

"You're making a scene, Father," she said.

Gerard glanced about him and shrugged. "I believe I'm due one."

Deborah's jaw slacked. What happened to decorum above all else?

"Deborah didn't show for the wedding," Adam pointed out. "Your dearest friend should've gotten the message by now. She's not interested."

"Father, I wrote to Tobias apologizing for the way I left things. I explained that I'm in love with someone else."

She sucked in a breath. "I wrote to you, as well, but you wouldn't have received it before you left. I'm sorry I disappointed you. I agreed to the match solely to please you."

"You humiliated me and tarnished our good name. Do you have any idea how this debacle has affected my business relationships?"

"Business isn't everything, Father," she admonished.

His skin flushed red. "Don't pretend you haven't enjoyed the fruits of my labor."

"Since leaving St. Louis, I've rented a single room in a modest boardinghouse. I've done without most of my belongings and lived on a fraction of my former allowance. You know what I've discovered? My surroundings don't dictate my happiness." At his disconcerted look, she said, "I remember when Mother was still alive. Your family mattered then. Your daughters weren't mere trophies to be paraded about and bartered to the men of your choosing."

He paled. Grief surged in his eyes. "Leave your mother out of this."

"Lucy and I are all you have left of her. I urge you to examine your heart. Do you truly wish to continue in this shallow vein? Or do you wish to pursue meaningful relationships with us?"

Gerard's lips trembled.

Deborah dared to place her hand on his arm. "I'd like to begin anew, Father."

His gaze swept the room and, seeming to recover his need for decorum, straightened to his full height. "This is a private matter, Deborah. When you've come to your senses, you can find me at The Cattleman."

He marched through the parting crowd without a single look back.

Adam's hand settled on her shoulder. "Give him time. He'll come to his senses."

She reached up and squeezed his hand, grateful for his

support. "He's not used to me standing up to him. I don't think I've ever been candid about my feelings."

"I'm proud of you," he murmured. "It couldn't have been easy."

His compassion and understanding bolstered her spirits. How blessed she was to have met and fallen in love with this man!

"Are you gonna marry Halloway or not?" someone said.

Laughter trickled through the crowd.

Adam moved close and tenderly smoothed a stray curl from her forehead. His smile made her knees weak, the look in his eyes made her feel like she was the only woman around for miles. Going down on one knee, he took her hands in his and gazed up at her with naked hope.

"I hadn't planned on an audience, but I don't have any secrets left. Deborah, you've taught me the meaning of love and trust, courage and self-sacrifice." His thumbs grazed endless paths over her knuckles, and there was a telltale tremor in his voice. "You make me want to be a better man. I want to spend the rest of my life with you. What's your answer? Will you have me?"

"Yes." She nodded, her smile splitting her face. "Yes. The sooner, the better."

With a shout of joy, he got to his feet and hugged her around the waist. "I love you so much," he murmured above the cheering and clapping. "I can't wait to start our lives together."

She held him tightly, overwhelmed with gratitude. "I thought we already had."

Then, no longer caring who was watching or what they thought, she pulled him to her for a kiss to seal the deal.

# Epilogue

*Three months later*

"What if I disappoint her?" Adam ran a finger beneath his suit collar.

"Trust me, you will." Russ dusted the lint from Adam's sleeves. "You'll make too many mistakes to count."

"You're not helping."

The chairs set up on the lawn were beginning to fill. The three town founders had arrived with their wives and children. Will, Daniel and Noah's friendship had given birth to this town. How proud they must be to see it flourishing. Will's campaign was gaining steam, and Russ was looking forward to being mayor. Adam was confident his brother would do a splendid job.

The reverend chatted beneath a wooden arbor profuse with vibrant autumn flowers. Adam examined the house that, from this day forward, would be his and Deborah's home. She was inside with Sadie and his sisters-in-law, preparing for their nuptials.

He'd waited impatiently for this day to arrive. Now that it was nearly time to make Deborah his wife, he was confronted with his failings.

"I don't know the first thing about being a husband."

He yearned to be a good partner to her. "I know even less about being a father."

His gaze searched out Liam, who stood chatting with Tate, his new best friend. The boy no longer resembled the one Adam had surprised in that tent. Liam was confident and happy. He was also starting to enjoy being a carefree boy and lessen his overprotective stance regarding Lily. He trusted Adam and Deborah to care for them both.

Seth grinned. "Stop fretting, little brother. You learn as you go. That's what I did." He nodded toward the wide porch, to where Marigold was emerging with Anna. "I'm still learning."

Adam's anticipation ratcheted up. Any minute now, Deborah would step through that door. He couldn't wait to see her.

Stepping up beside the brothers, Evelyn smoothed Adam's hair, her eyes shining with pride. "You love each other. That's what counts."

Deborah emerged at last, resplendent in a beaded white gown and trailing veil. Her hair was caught up in a mass of curls, thin, shiny ribbons wound through it. A sparkling topaz necklace adorned her neck, the perfect match for her eyes. She was beautiful, inside and out. And she was his.

His mouth went dry. What had he done to deserve her? *Thank you, Lord, for this gift.*

A bright smile curved her mouth as she surveyed their property and the wedding-related decorations. Tables had been set up beneath the trees, some boasting gifts and others platters of food. A tall cake she'd baked herself anchored the far end.

Lily shot out of the house, dancing around Deborah and the others, her joy unmistakable. She clutched her original doll, Sally, which Adam had located at Daniel Gardner's. They'd found the doll and were happy to release it to the rightful owner.

He chuckled, his anxiety evaporating. The Lord had blessed him with a fresh start, an amazing woman and children he hoped one day he could call his own. God would guide and strengthen him.

"I'm so grateful," Evelyn said, the tears already starting. "My three sons in one place, with families of their own. This is a new chapter in the Halloway saga, and it's going to be better than the last. Your pa would be so proud."

Adam bent and kissed her cheek. He wished his pa could be here on this special day, but he found comfort in the fact that his reputation had been restored and his name cleared. He looked at his brothers. "It's good to be around family again." He gestured to the acres of prime land he'd purchased from one of the ranchers who Ogden had driven off. The rancher had already settled elsewhere and was happy to sell. "And to be working the land again."

He'd resigned his position with the Pinkertons and had no regrets. He'd had enough solitude and danger to last a lifetime.

"Now, if you'll excuse me, my bride awaits."

Adam crossed the yard to her side, took her hand and brushed a kiss on her knuckles. "You are flawless, sweetheart."

Deborah blushed a becoming pink. "I had help." She caressed his cheek. "You have never looked more handsome. Maybe because you're about to officially belong to me."

"I would dearly like to kiss you."

She grinned. "Why don't you? Who cares what anyone thinks?"

"Your father's in attendance." While Gerard hadn't yet given Deborah his blessing, his continued presence in Cowboy Creek and attendance today pointed to the possibility of a reconciliation.

"This is my wedding." She lifted her chin. "If I want to kiss the groom before the vows, I can."

Deborah's gown made whispering sounds as she inched closer and, rising on her tiptoes, planted a lingering kiss on him that made his blood heat.

His sisters-in-law spoiled the moment.

"It's time to start the ceremony," Marigold admonished. "You can tend to that later."

Deborah remained unapologetic as they proceeded to the arbor. His bride exuded radiant confidence in herself and in his love for her. Gazing into her misty golden eyes, he pledged his devotion and commitment. They sealed their vows with another kiss that curled his toes.

Not long after Reverend Taggart made the official announcement and the guests meandered toward the food tables, Russell pulled them aside, an official-looking envelope in his hand.

"What's this?" Adam said, his arm anchored around Deborah's waist.

"A wedding present." He held it out. "Open it."

Deborah opened the letter and gasped. She turned tear-filled eyes to Adam. "It's adoption papers."

Adam scanned the words. "Liam and Lily are officially Halloways."

They took turns hugging Russell. When he'd rejoined Anna, Adam pulled Deborah into his arms and smiled down at her.

"Can you believe it?"

"If you'd asked me when I boarded that train if my life would turn out this way, I would've said no." Joy sparkled in her eyes. "I have everything I've ever wanted."

"A bakery of your very own."

After consulting Deborah, Adam had approached Mr. Lowell and offered him a generous amount for the bakery. The man had accepted reality—that he wasn't qualified— and taken him up on it. She'd been cleaning and painting for days, and soon she'd host a grand opening. He had no doubt she'd be a success.

She looped her arms around his neck. "The bakery is wonderful, but I could do without it. What I couldn't do without is you, my dearest love. And the kids."

He settled his hands on her waist. "I love you, Deborah. I'm fortunate that you chose me."

"We chose each other."

Their kiss spoke of dreams fulfilled and hope for the future. When he reluctantly eased away, he gestured to their guests. "I'm looking forward to being alone with my bride. For now, how about we find Liam and Lily and give them the good news?"

She laughed. "I can tell you where we'll find Lily."

"Drooling over the cake?"

That's exactly where they found her. They urged Liam to join them. Their news was met with squeals and tears and lots of leaping for joy.

They were a true family unit with a permanent home. God had brought them together, and Adam had faith He'd lead them into the future.

\* \* \* \* \*

*Don't miss a single installment of*
RETURN TO COWBOY CREEK:

*THE RANCHER INHERITS A FAMILY*
*by Cheryl St.John*
*HIS SUBSTITUTE MAIL-ORDER BRIDE*
*by Sherri Shackelford*
*ROMANCING THE RUNAWAY BRIDE*
*by Karen Kirst*

*Find more great reads at www.LoveInspired.com*

Dear Reader,

Thank you for taking the time to read my book. I hope you enjoyed returning to Cowboy Creek and our heroines and heroes—familiar and new—as much as I did. Adam and Deborah's love story was such fun to explore. Some fictitious couples give me more trouble than others. Not so the detective and the runaway bride! These two took an almost instant liking to each other, so I was glad to have all those secrets keeping them apart until the very end. They also have a lot of personal issues to work through. Toss in a pair of adorable orphans, and I had my work cut out for me.

Writing this book has been a bittersweet experience. It will be my last for the Love Inspired Historical line, which is unfortunately closing this month. I feel blessed to have been able to work with the wonderful Love Inspired editors and complete this, my seventeenth book. While I will miss writing about the past, I'm fortunate that I will be switching to the Love Inspired Suspense line. You can find more information on my website, *www.karenkirst.com*. I'm also active on Facebook and Twitter @KarenKirst.

If you missed the first two books in this Return to Cowboy Creek continuity, check out Cheryl St. John's book, *The Rancher Inherits a Family*, and Sherri Shackelford's *His Substitute Mail-Order Bride*.

Many blessings,
*Karen Kirst*

We hope you enjoyed this story from
**Love Inspired® Historical**.

Love Inspired® Historical is coming to
an end but be sure to discover more
inspirational stories to warm your heart
from **Love Inspired®** and
**Love Inspired® Suspense**!

Love Inspired stories show that
faith, forgiveness and hope have the power
to lift spirits and change lives—always.

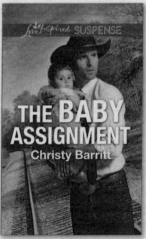

Look for six new romances every month
from **Love Inspired®** and
**Love Inspired® Suspense**!

# Get 4 FREE REWARDS!

## We'll send you 2 FREE Books plus 2 FREE Mystery Gifts.

**Love Inspired®** books feature contemporary inspirational romances with Christian characters facing the challenges of life and love.

FREE
Value Over
**$20**

## SPECIAL EXCERPT FROM

*Love Inspired®*

*Her family's future in the balance, can Clara Fisher find a way to save her home?*

*Read on for a sneak preview of*
*HIS NEW AMISH FAMILY by* **Patricia Davids**,
*the next book in* **THE AMISH BACHELORS** *miniseries,*
*available in July 2018 from Love Inspired.*

Paul Bowman leaned forward in his seat to get a good look at the farm as they drove up. Both the barn and the house were painted white and appeared in good condition. He made a quick mental appraisal of the equipment he saw, then jotted down numbers in a small notebook he kept in his pocket.

"What is she doing here?" The anger in his client Ralph's voice shocked Paul.

He followed Ralph's line of sight and spied an Amish woman sitting on a suitcase on the front porch of the house. She wore a simple pale blue dress with an apron of matching material and a black cape thrown back over her shoulders. Her wide-brimmed black traveling bonnet hid her hair. She looked hot, dusty and tired. She held a girl of about three or four on her lap. The child clung tightly to her mother. A boy a few years older leaned against the door behind her holding a large calico cat.

"Who is she?" Paul asked.

"That is my annoying cousin, Clara Fisher." Ralph opened his car door and got out. Paul did the same.

The woman glared at both men. "Why are there padlocks on the doors, Ralph? Eli never locked his home."

"They are there to keep unwanted visitors out. What are you doing here?" Ralph demanded.

"I live here. May I have the keys, please? My children and I are weary."

Ralph's eyebrows snapped together in a fierce frown. "What do you mean you live here?"

"What part did you fail to understand, Ralph? I… live…here," she said slowly.

Ralph's face darkened with anger. Paul had to turn away to keep from laughing.

She might look small, but she was clearly a woman to be reckoned with. She reminded him of an angry mama cat all fluffed up and spitting-mad. He rubbed a hand across his mouth to hide a grin. His movement caught her attention, and she pinned her deep blue gaze on him. "Who are you?"

He stopped smiling. "My name is Paul Bowman. I'm an auctioneer. Mr. Hobson has hired me to get this property ready for sale."

*Don't miss*
*HIS NEW AMISH FAMILY by Patricia Davids,*
*available July 2018 wherever*
*Love Inspired® books and ebooks are sold.*

www.LoveInspired.com

Looking for inspiration in tales
of hope, faith and heartfelt romance?

Check out **Love Inspired**® and
**Love Inspired**® **Suspense** books!

**New books available every month!**

**CONNECT WITH US AT:**

Harlequin.com/Community

Facebook.com/HarlequinBooks

Twitter.com/HarlequinBooks

Instagram.com/HarlequinBooks

Pinterest.com/HarlequinBooks

ReaderService.com

## Inspirational Romance to Warm Your Heart and Soul

---

Join our social communities to connect with other readers who share your love!

Sign up for the Love Inspired newsletter at **www.LoveInspired.com** to be the first to find out about upcoming titles, special promotions and exclusive content.

---

**CONNECT WITH US AT:**

Harlequin.com/Community

 Facebook.com/LoveInspiredBooks

 Twitter.com/LoveInspiredBks

LISOCIAL2017